Date Due

APR			
AUG 2 8 00			
NOV 06 02			
JUL 12 06			

LARGE
PRINT
EDITION

RANDOM
HOUSE

ALSO AVAILABLE
IN RANDOM HOUSE LARGE PRINT
Golf Dreams

John Updike

BECH
AT BAY

A QUASI-NOVEL

Published by Random House Large Print
in association with Alfred A. Knopf, Inc.
New York 1998

The Czech at the end of "Bech in Czech" is taken from the translation of "Bech Panics" by Antonin Přidal in *Milenci a manželé* (Prague: Odeon, 1984).

The poem by Seng Ts'an (third Ch'an patriarch in China, circa 600 A.D.) quoted in "Bech Noir" is found in *The Teachings of the Compassionate Buddha,* edited by E.A. Burtt (New York: Mentor Books, New American Library, 1955).

Library of Congress Cataloging-in-Publication Data

Updike, John.
Bech at bay : a quasi-novel / John Updike.
p.   cm.
ISBN 0-375-70417-5
1. Jewish men—United States—Fiction. 2. Novelists, American—Fiction.   I. Title.
[PS3571.P4B43   1998]
813' .54—dc21   98-26252
                                                          CIP

Random House Web Address: http://www.randomhouse.com/
Printed in the United States of America
FIRST LARGE PRINT EDITION

This Large Print Book carries the
Seal of Approval of N.A.V.H.

To the youngest people I know:

SAWYER MICHAEL UPDIKE
ADÈLE CATLIN BERNHARD
HELEN RUGGLES BERNHARD
SENECA DUNN FREYLEUE
ANNA BERNHARD

*Something of the unreal is necessary
to fecundate the real.*

—WALLACE STEVENS,
  Preface to William Carlos Williams'
  Collected Poems 1921–1931 (1934)

Contents

BECH IN CZECH   1

BECH PRESIDES   42

BECH PLEADS GUILTY   140

BECH NOIR   182

BECH AND THE BOUNTY
OF SWEDEN   253

Bech in Czech

THE AMERICAN AMBASSADOR'S RESIDENCE in Prague has been called the last palace built in Europe. It was built in the early 1930s by a rich Jewish banker, Otto Petschek, whose family, within a decade of its construction, had to flee Hitler. The Americans had acquired the building and its grounds after the war, before Czechoslovakia went quite so Communist. The whole building gently curves—that is, it was built along the length of an arc, and a walk down its long corridors produces a shifting perspective wherein paintings, silk panels, marble-topped hall tables, great metalicized oaken doors all slowly come into view, much as islands appear above the horizon to a ship at sea and then slowly sink behind it, beyond the majestic, roiling, pale-turquoise wake.

Henry Bech, the semi-obscure American author, who had turned sixty-three in this year of 1986, felt majestic and becalmed in the great Residence, where, at one end, he had been given a suite for the week of his cultural visit to this restive outpost of the Soviet empire. As a Jew himself, he was conscious of the former owners, those vanished plutocrats, no doubt very elegant and multilingual, who with such pathetic trust, amid the tremors of the Diaspora's Middle-European golden age (not to be confused with the golden age in Saracen Spain, or the good times under the Polish princes), had built their palace on the edge of an abyss. For a Jew, to move through post-war Europe is to move through hordes of ghosts, vast animated crowds that, since 1945, are not there, not there at all—up in smoke. The feathery touch of the mysteriously absent is felt on all sides. In the center of old Prague the clock of the Jewish Town Hall—which, with the adjacent synagogues, Hitler intended to preserve as the relic of an exterminated race—still runs backwards, to the amusement of tourists from both sides of the Iron Curtain. The cemetery there, with its four centuries of dead crowded into mounds by the pressures of the ghetto, and the tombstones jumbled together like giant cards in a deck being shuffled, moved Bech less than the newer Jewish cemetery on the outskirts of town, where the Ambassador felt that the visiting author should see Kafka's grave.

The Ambassador was an exceptionally short and peppy man with sandy thin hair raked across a freckled skull; he was an Akron industrialist and a Republican fund-raiser who had believed in Reagan when most bigwig insiders still laughed at the notion of a movie actor in the White House. For his loyalty and prescience the Ambassador had been rewarded with this post, and there was an additional logic to it, for he was Czech by ancestry; his grandparents had come to Pittsburgh from the coalfields of Moravia, and the language had been spoken in his childhood home. "They love it when I talk," he told Bech with his disarming urchin grin. "I sound so damn old-fashioned. It would be as if in English somebody talked like the King James Bible." Bech fancied he saw flit across the Ambassador's square face the worry that Jews didn't have much to do with the King James Bible. The little man quickly added, for absolute clarity, "I guess I sound quaint as hell."

Bech *had* noticed that the Czechs tended to smile when the Ambassador talked to them in their language. It was all the more noticeable because Czechs, once a wry and humorous race, found rather little to smile about. The Ambassador made Bech smile, too. Having spent most of his life in the narrow precincts of the Manhattan intelligentsia, a site saturated in poisonous envy and reflexive intolerance and basic impotence, he was charmed by the breezy and carefree ways of an authentic power-broker, this cheerful representative of the triumphant right wing. In entrepreneurial style, the Ambassador was a quick study, quick to pounce and quick to move on. He must have skimmed a fact sheet concerning his cultural guest, and it was on the basis of this information that he took Bech—freshly landed that morning, jet throb still ringing in his ears—to Kafka's grave. "It's the kind of thing that'll appeal to you." He was right.

The official limousine, with its morosely silent and sleepy-eyed chauffeur, wheeled along steep cobblestoned streets, past the old parapets and trolley tracks of Prague, and came, in what had once been outskirts, to a long ornate iron fence. The tall gate was locked and chained. The Ambassador rattled at the chains and called, but there was no answer. "Try the flag, honey," said the Ambassador's wife, a leggy blonde considerably younger than he.

Bech, who had travelled in Africa and Latin America and seen the Stars and Stripes attract rocks and spittle, winced as the Ambassador plucked the little American flag from the limousine's front fender and began to wave it through the gate, shouting incomprehensibly. He noticed Bech's wince and said in quick aside, "Relax. They love us here. They love our flag." And indeed, two young men wearing plaster-splattered overalls shyly emerged, at the patriotic commotion, from within a cement-block shed. The Ambassador talked to them in Czech. Smiling at his accent, they came forward a few steps and spoke words that meant the cemetery was closed. The flag was given a few more flutters, but the boys continued, bemusedly, to shake their heads and pronounce the soft word *ne*. The Ambassador, with a playful and shameless aggressiveness that Bech had to admire even as he blushed for it, wielded a new inspiration; in his next spate of words Bech heard his own name, distinct in the rippling, Stygian flow of the opaque language.

The politely denying smiles on the faces of the young men gave way to open-eyed interest. They looked away from the Ambassador to the American author on the other side of the bars.

"*Travel Light,*" the taller one said in halting English, naming Bech's first novel.

"*Big Idea,*" said the other, trying to name his last.

"*Think Big,*" Bech corrected, his blush deepening; he wouldn't have guessed he had left in him so much spare blood as was making his cheeks burn, his palms tingle. This was absolutely, he vowed, his last appearance as a cultural icon.

"Ahhhh!" the two boys uttered in unison, enraptured by the authentic correction, out of the author's mouth. With cries of jubilation from both sides, the locks and chains were undone and the three Americans were welcomed to the Strašnice cemetery.

It was an eerie, well-kept place. Impressive and stolid black tombstones stood amid tall trees, plane and ash and evergreen, and flourishing ivy. The vistas seemed endless, lit by the filtered sunlight of the woods, and silent with the held breath of many hundreds of ended lives. Most of the inhabitants had been shrewd enough to die before 1939, in their beds or in hospitals, one by one, before the Germans arrived and death became a mass production.

The visitors' party walked along straight weeded paths between grand marble slabs lettered in gold with predominantly Germanic names, the same names—Strauss, Steiner, Loeb, Goldberg—whose live ranks still march through the New York City telephone directories. The Ambassador and the two young workmen led the way, conversing in Czech—rather loudly, Bech thought. To judge from the Ambassador's expansive gestures, he could be extolling the merits of the free-enterprise system or diagramming the perfidy of Gorbachev's latest arms-reduction proposal.

"I find this very embarrassing," Bech told the Ambassador's wife, who walked beside him in silence along the lightly crunching path.

"I used to too," she said, in her pleasantly scratchy Midwestern voice. "But, then, after a couple of years with Dick, nothing embarrasses me; he's just very outgoing. Very frontal. It's his way, and people here respond to it. It's how they think Americans ought to act. Free."

"These young men—mightn't they lose their jobs for letting us in?"

She shrugged and gave a nervous little toss of her long blond hair. It was an affecting, lustreless shade, as if it had been washed too often. Her lips were dry and thoughtful, with flaking lipstick. "Maybe they don't even have jobs. This is a strange system." Her eyes were that translucent blue that Bech thought uncanny, having seen it, through his youth, mostly in toy polar bears and mannequins on display in Fifth Avenue Christmas windows.

"How well," Bech said, looking around at the elegant and silent black stones, "these people all thought of themselves."

"There was a lot of money here," the Ambassador's wife said. "People forget that about Bohemia. Before the Communists put an end to all that."

"After the Germans put an end to all *this,*" Bech said, gesturing toward the Jewish population at rest around them. There were, curiously, a few death dates, in fresh gold, later than 1945—Jews who had escaped the Holocaust, he supposed, and then asked to be brought back here to be buried, beneath the tall straight planes with their mottled trunks, and the shiny green ivy spread everywhere like a tousled bedspread. Lots, records, permits—these things persisted.

"Here he is, your pal," the Ambassador loudly announced. Bech had seen photographs of this tombstone—a white stone, relatively modest in size, wider at the top than at the bottom, and bearing three names, and inscriptions in Hebrew that Bech could not read. The three names were those of Dr. Franz Kafka; his father, Hermann; and his mother, Julie. In his last, disease-wracked year, Kafka had escaped his parents and lived with Dora Dymant in Berlin, but then had been returned here, and now lay next to his overpowering father forever. A smaller marker at the foot bore the names of his three sisters—Elli, Valli, Ottla—who had vanished into concentration camps. It all struck Bech as dumbfoundingly blunt and enigmatic, banal and moving. Such blankness, such stony and peaceable reification, waits for us at the bottom of things. No more insomnia for poor hypersensitive Dr. Franz.

Bech thought he should try a few words with their young hosts, who had shown some knowledge of English. "Very great Czech," he said, pointing to the grave.

The broader-shouldered young man, who had wielded the key that let them in, smiled and said, "Not Czech. *Žid. Jude.*"

It was a simple clarification, nothing unpleasant. "Like me," Bech said.

"You"—the other boy, more willowy, with plaster even in his hair, pointed straight at him—"wonderful!"

The other, his eyes merry at the thought of talking to an internationally famous writer, made a sound, "R-r-r-r-rum, *rrroom,*" which Bech recognized as an allusion to the famous rubber-faced motorcyclists of *Travel Light,* with its backseat rapes and its desolate roadside cafés on their vast gravel parking lots—Bech's homage, as a young Manhattanite, to the imaginary territory beyond the Hudson. "Very *americký, amerikanisch,*" the young man said.

"*Un peu,*" Bech said and shrugged, out of courtesy abandoning English, as his conversational companions had abandoned Czech.

"And *Big Thinking,*" the shorter boy said, emboldened by all this pidgin language to go for an extended utterance, "we love very much. It makes much to laugh: TV, skyscrapes." He laughed, for absolute clarity.

"Skyscrapers," Bech couldn't help correcting.

"I loved Olive in that novel," the Ambassador's wife said huskily at his side.

This, Bech felt, was a very sexy remark: Olive and the entire television crew, under the lights; Olive and her lesbian lover Thelma, in the West Side apartment as the tawny sun from New Jersey entered horizontally, like bars of music. . . .

"Kafka more *Schmerz,*" his Czech fan was going on, as if the buried writer, with his dark suit and quizzical smile, were standing right there beside the still-erect one, for comparison. "You more *Herz.* More—" He broke down into Czech, turning to face the Ambassador.

"More primitive energy," the Ambassador translated. "More raw love of life."

Bech in fact had felt quite tired of life ever since completing his last—his final, as he thought of it—and surprisingly successful novel, whose publication coincided with the collapse of his one and only marriage. That was why, he supposed, you travelled to places like this: to encounter fictional selves, the refreshing false ideas of you that strangers hold in their minds.

In Czechoslovakia he felt desperately unworthy; the unlucky country seemed to see in him an emblem of hope. Not only had his first and last novels been translated here (*Lekhá cesta, Velká myšlenka*) but a selection of essays and short fiction culled from *When the Saints* (*Když svatí*). All three volumes carried opposite the title page the same photo of the author, one taken when he was thirty, before his face had bulked to catch up to his nose and before his wiry hair had turned gray; his hair sat on his head then like a tall turban pulled low on his forehead. The rigors of Socialist photogravure made this faded image look as if it came not from the 1950s but from the time before World War I, when Proust was posing in a wing collar and Kafka in a bowler hat. Bech had ample opportunity to examine the photo, for endless lines formed when, at a Prague bookstore and then a few days later at the American Embassy, book-signing sessions were scheduled, and these Czech versions of his books were presented to him over and over again, open to the title page. His presence here had squeezed these tattered volumes—all out of print, since Communist editions are not replenished—up from the private libraries of Prague. Flattered, flustered, Bech tried to focus for a moment on each face, each pair of hands, as it materialized before him, and to inscribe the difficult names, spelled letter by letter. There were many young people, clear-eyed and shy, with a simple smooth glow of youth rather rarely seen in New York. To these fresh-faced innocents, he supposed, he was an American celebrity—not, of course, a rock star, smashing guitars and sobbing out his guts as the violet and magenta strobes pulsed and the stadium hissed and waved like a huge jellyfish, but with a touch of that same diabolic glamour. Or perhaps they were students, American-lit majors, and he something copied from a textbook, and his signature a passing mark. But there were older citizens, too—plump women with shopping bags, and men with pale faces and a pinched, pedantic air. Clerks? Professors? And a few persons virtually infirm, ancient enough to remember the regime of Tomáš Masaryk, hobbled forward with a kindly, faltering expression like that of a childhood sweetheart whom we cannot at first quite recognize. Most of the people said at least "Thank you"; many pressed a number of correctly shaped, highly complimentary English sentences upon him.

Bech said *"Děkuji"* and *"Prosím"* at random and grew more and more embarrassed. Across the street, Embassy underlings gleefully whispered into his ear, Czech policemen were photographing the line; so all these people were putting themselves at some risk—were putting a blot on their records by seeking the autograph of an American author. Why? His books were petty and self-indulgent, it seemed to Bech as he repeatedly signed them, like so many checks that would bounce. In third-world countries, he had often been asked what he conceived to be the purpose of the writer, and he had had to find ways around the honest answer, which was that the purpose of the writer is to amuse himself, to indulge himself, to get his books into print with as little editorial smudging as he can, to slide through his society with minimal friction. This annoying question did not arise in a Communist country. Its citizens understood well the heroism of self-indulgence, the political grandeur of irresponsibility. They were voting, in their long lines, for a way out, just as Bech, forty years before, stuck on Manhattan like archy the cockroach, had composed, as a way out, his *hommages* to an imaginary America.

The Ambassador and his minions arranged for Bech to attend a party of unofficial writers. "Oh, those sexy female dissidents," the Ambassador's wife softly exclaimed, as if Bech were deserting her. But she came along. The party, and the apartment, somewhere off in the unscenic suburbs that visitors to historic Prague never see, and that Bech saw only that one night, by the veering, stabbing, uncertain headlights of the Ambassador's private little Ford Fiesta, were reminiscent of the Fifties, when Eisenhower presided over a tense global truce and the supreme value of the private life was unquestioned. Bookshelves to the ceiling, jazz murmuring off in a corner, glossy-haired children

passing hors d'oeuvres, a shortage of furniture that
left people sprawled across beds or hunkered down
two to a hassock. The hostess wore a peasant
blouse and skirt and had her hair done up in a single thick pigtail; the bald host wore a kind of
dashiki or wedding shirt over blue jeans. Bech felt
taken back to the days of relative innocence in
America, when the young were asking only for a
little more freedom, a bit more sex and debour-
geoisation, a whiff of pot and a folk concert in a
borrowed meadow. These people, however, were
not young; they had grown middle-aged in protest,
in dissidence, and moved through their level of
limbo with a practiced weariness. Bech could see
only a little way into the structure of it all. When
husbands could not publish, wives worked and
paid the bills; his hostess, for instance, was a doc-
tor, an anesthesiologist, and in the daytime must
coil her long amber pigtail into an antiseptic cap.
And their children, some of them, were young
adults, who had studied in Michigan or Iowa or
Toronto and talked with easy American accents, as
if their student tourism were as natural as that of
young Frenchmen or Japanese. There was, beyond
this little party flickering like a candle in the dark
suburbs of Prague, a vast dim world of exile,
Czechs in Paris or London or the New World who
had left yet somehow now and then returned, to
visit a grandmother or to make a motion picture,
and émigré presses whose products circulated
underground; the Russians could not quite seal off

this old heart of Europe as tightly as they could, say, Latvia or Kazakhstan.

The wish to be part of Europe: the frustration of this modest desire formed the peculiarly intense Czech agony. To have a few glass skyscrapers among the old cathedrals and castles, to have businessmen come and go on express trains without passing through pompous ranks of barbed wire, to have a currency that wasn't a sham your own shop owners refused, to be able to buy fresh Sicilian oranges in the market, to hang a few neon signs in the dismal Prague arcades, to enrich the downtown with a little pornography and traffic congestion, to enjoy the harmless luxury of an anti-nuclear protest movement and a nihilist avant-garde—this was surely not too much to ask after centuries of being sat on by the Hapsburgs. But it was denied: having survived Hitler and the anti-Hussites, the Czechs and the Slovaks had become ensnared in the Byzantine clutches of Moscow. Two dates notched the history of dissidence: 1968, the year of "Prague Spring" (referred to so often, so hurriedly, that it became one word: "Pragspring") and of the subsequent Russian invasion; and 1977, when Charter 77 was promulgated, with the result that many of its signatories went into exile or to jail.

Jail! One of the guests at the party had spent nearly ten years in prison. He was dapper, like the café habitués in George Grosz drawings, with a scarred, small face and shining black eyes. He spoke so softly Bech could hardly hear him, though he bent his ear close. The man's hands twisted under Bech's eyes, as if in the throes of torture. Bech noticed that the fingers were in fact bent, broken. How would he, the American author asked himself, stand up to having his fingernails pulled? He could think of nothing he had ever written that he would not eagerly recant.

Another guest at the party, wearing tinted aviator glasses and a drooping, nibbled mustache, explained to Bech that the Western media always wanted to interview dissidents and he had become, since released from his two years in prison, the one whom the avid newsmen turned to when needing a statement. He had sacrificed not only his safety but his privacy to this endless giving of interviews, which left him no time for his own work. Perhaps, he said with a sigh, if and when he was returned to jail, he could again resume his poetry. His eyes behind the lavender lenses looked rubbed and tired.

What kind of poetry did he write, Bech asked.

"Of the passing small feelings," was the considered answer. "Like Seifert. To the authorities, these little human feelings are dangerous like an earthquake; but he became too big, too big and old and sick, to touch. Even the Nobel could not hurt him."

And meanwhile food was passed around, the jazz was turned up, and in the apartment's other room the Ambassador and his wife were stretched out on the floor, leaning against a bookcase, her long legs gleaming, in a hubbub of laughter and

Czech. To Bech, within his cluster of persecuted writers, the sight of her American legs seemed a glint of reality, something from far outside yet unaccountably proceeding, as birds continue to sing outside barred windows and ivy grows on old graves. The Ambassador had his coat off, his tie loosened, a glass in his hand. His quick eyes noticed the other American peering at his wife's legs and he shouted out, in noisy English, "Show Bech a book! Let's show our famous American author some *samizdat*!"

Everyone was sweating now, from the wine and pooled body heat, and there was a hilarity somehow centered on Bech's worried, embarrassed presence. He feared the party would become careless and riotous, and the government police surely posted outside the building would come bursting in. A thin young woman with frizzy black hair—a sexy dissident—stood close to Bech and showed him a book. "We type," she explained, "six copies maximum; otherwise the bottom ones too blurred. Xeroxing not possible here but for official purposes. Typewriters they can't yet control. Then bound, sometimes with drawings. This one has drawings. See?" Her loose blouse exposed, as she leaned against Bech to share the book with him, a swath of her shoulders and a scoop of her bosom, lightly sweating. Her glazed skin was a seductive tint, a matte greenish-gray.

Bech asked her, "But who binds them so nicely? Isn't that illegal?"

"Yes," was her answer. "But there are brave men." Her reproachful, inky eyes rolled toward him, as she placed the book in his hands.

The page size was less than that of American typewriter paper; small sheets of onionskin thickness, and an elite typewriter, had been used, and a blue carbon paper. The binding was maroon leather, with silver letters individually punched. The book that resulted was unexpectedly beautiful, its limp pages of blue blurred text falling open easily, with an occasional engraving, of Picassoesque nudes, marking a fresh chapter. It felt lighter, placed in Bech's hands, than he had expected from the thickness of it. Only the right-hand pages held words; the left-hand held mirrored ghosts of words, the other side showing through. He had been returned to some archetypal sense of what a book was: it was an elemental sheaf, bound together by love and daring, to be passed with excitement from hand to hand. Bech had expected the pathos, the implied pecking of furtive typewriters, but not the defiant beauty of the end result. "How many such books exist?"

"Of each, six at least. More asks more typing. Each book has many readers."

"It's like a medieval manuscript," Bech said.

"We are not monks," said the young woman solemnly. "We do not enjoy to suffer."

In the Ford Fiesta, the Ambassador's wife teased him, saying to her husband, "I think our celebrated author was rather taken with Ila."

The Ambassador said nothing, merely pointed at the ceiling of the car.

Bech, not understanding the gesture, repeated, "Ila?" Ila, Elli, Kafka's sister. "Is she Jewish?" The bushy hair, the sallow matte skin, the tension in her slender shoulders, the way she forced meaning through her broken English.

The Ambassador's wife laughed, with her scratchy light-hearted voice. "Close," she said. "She's a gypsy."

"A gypsy," Bech said, as if he and she were playing a game, batting words back and forth in the car's interior. He was sitting in the back seat, and the Ambassador's wife in the front. Feeble Socialist streetlight intermittently shone through her straw-pale hair, which had been fluffed up by the fun of the dissident party. "They have those here?" he asked.

"They have those here of course," she said, her tone almost one of rebuke. "The French word for gypsy is '*bohémien.*' Many are assimilated, like your new lady friend. Hitler killed quite a few, but not all."

Hitler. To come to Europe is somehow to pay him a visit. He was becoming a myth, like the Golem. Bech had been shown the Old-New Synagogue, where the cabalist and alchemist Rabbi Loew had read from the Talmud and concocted a Golem whose giant clay remains still wait in the synagogue attic to be revived. And the Pinkas Synagogue, its walls covered with the names of seventy-seven thousand concentration-camp victims. And the nearby hall filled with the drawings Jewish children drew while interned at the camp at Terezín, houses and cows and flowers such as children draw everywhere, holding their crayons tight, seizing the world with stubby beginner's fingers. Communists can always say in their own defense that at least they're not Hitler. And that *is* something.

In alternation with the light on the filaments of the American woman's hair, a vague black dread penetrated Bech's stomach, a sudden feeling he used to get, when six or seven, of being in the wrong place, a disastrously wrong place, even though he was only three blocks from home, hurrying along upper Broadway in a bedlam of indifferent strangers. "Those poor guys," he abruptly said. "The one with the slicked-down hair had been ten years in jail, and I glanced at a couple of his stories he showed me. They're like Saki, harmless arch little things. Why would they put him in jail for wanting to write those? I was looking at him, trying to put myself in his shoes, and he kept giving me this sweet smile and modest little shrug. You know the one I mean—old-fashioned suit and vest, one of those names full of zizzes—"

The Ambassador cleared his throat very noisily and pointed again at the low ceiling of the little car. Bech understood at last. The car was bugged. They spoke hardly a word all the rest of the way back to the Residence, through the gabled and steepled profile of midnight Prague. There was never, it seemed to Bech, any moon. Did the moon shine only on capitalism?

At the Residence, in the morning, it was nice to awake to the sound of birds and of gardeners working. One crew was raking up the winter leaves; another crew was getting the tennis court ready for the summer. Bech's bathroom lay many steps from his bed, through the sunny parqueted living room of his suite, with its gently curved walls. Mammoth brass fixtures, the latest thing in 1930, gushed water over Art Deco shower tiles or into porcelain basins big enough to contain a fish pond. Otto Petschek had bought only the best. Breakfast appeared at a long table in a dining room next door, where timid women fetched Bech what he had checked off on a printed form the night before. *"Prosím,"* they said, as Italians say *"Prego."*

"Děkuji," he would say, when he could think of the word, which he found an exceptionally difficult one. *Jakui* is how the Ambassador's wife pronounced it, very rapidly. She was never at breakfast; Bech always ate alone, though sometimes other place settings hinted at other guests. There were others: a suave plump Alsatian photographer, with a slim male assistant, was photographing the place, room by room, for *Architectural Digest,* and some old friends from Akron had come by on the way to Vienna, and the Ambassador's wispy

daughter by a former marriage was taking school vacation from her Swiss *lycée*. But in the mornings all this cast of characters was invisible, and Bech in lordly solitude took his post-breakfast stroll in the garden, along the oval path whose near end was nestled, like an egg in a cup, into the curve of the palace and its graceful flagstone patio, past the raking gardeners and the empty swimming pool, around to where three men in gray workclothes were rolling and patting flat the red clay of the tennis court, just the other side of the pruned and banked rose garden, from which the warming weather had coaxed a scent of moist humus. He never met another stroller. Nor did he ever see a face—a princess, gazing out—at any of the many windows of the Residence.

It seemed that this was his proper home, that all men were naturally entitled to live in luxury no less, amid parquet and marquetry, marble hall tables and gilded picture frames, with a young wife whose fair hair would flash and chiffon-veiled breasts gleam when, in an instant, she appeared at a window, to call him in. As on a giant curved movie screen the Residence projected the idea of domestic bliss. What a monster I am, he thought—sixty-three and still covetous, still a king in my mind. Europe and not America, he further thought, is the land of dreams, of fairy-tale palaces and clocks that run backwards. Hitler had kissed the princess and made her bad dreams come true. But, then, there have been many holocausts. Bech had been shown

the window of Hradčany Castle from which the
Defenestration of Prague had occurred; though the
emissaries defenestrated had landed unharmed on a
pile of manure, the incident had nevertheless com-
menced the Thirty Years' War, which had deci-
mated Central Europe. Bech had seen the statue of
Jan Žižka, the one-eyed Hussite general who had
piously slaughtered the forces of the Pope and
Holy Roman Emperor for five years, and the statue
in the baroque Church of St. Nicholas that shows a
tall pope gracefully, beatifically crushing with the
butt of his staff the throat of a pointy-eared infidel.
For centuries, conquest and appropriation piled up
their palaces and chapels on the crooked climbing
streets of Prague. The accumulation remained
undisturbed, though the Nazis, ever faithful to their
cleansing mission, tried to blow things up as they
departed. The mulch of history, on these moist
mornings when Bech had the oval park to himself,
was deeply peaceful. The dead and wronged in
their multitudes are mercifully quiet.

A young citizen of Prague had thrust himself
upon the cultural officers of the Embassy and was
conceded an appointment to meet Bech. He
bravely came to the Embassy, past the U.S. Marine
guards and the posters of the dismantled Statue of
Liberty, and had lunch with Bech in the cafeteria.
He was so nervous he couldn't eat. His name was
unpronounceable,   something   like   Syzygy—
Vítěslav Syzygy. He was tall and dignified, however, and less young than Bech had expected, with

a dusting of gray in his sideburns and that pedantic strict expression Bech had come to know as characteristically Czech. He could have worn a pince-nez on his high-bridged narrow nose. His English was impeccable but halting, like a well-made but poorly maintained machine. "This is very strange for me," he began, "physically to meet you. It was twenty years ago, just before Pragspring, that I read your *Travel Light*. For me it was a revelation that language could function in such a manner. It is not too much to say that it transformed the path of my life."

Bech wanted to say to him, "Stop sweating. Stop trembling." Instead he dipped his spoon into the cafeteria *bramborovka* and listened. Syzygy, officially silenced as translator and critic since his involvement nearly two decades ago in "Pragspring," had spent these past years laboring upon an impossibly good, dizzyingly faithful yet inventive translation into Czech of a Bech masterwork, *Brother Pig*, not yet favored by a version into his language. *Bratr vepř* was at last completed to his satisfaction. Never, in his severely, precisely stated opinion, has there been such a translation—not even Pasternak's of Shakespeare, not Baudelaire's of Poe, constituted such scrupulous and loving *hommage*. The difficulty . . .

"Ah," Bech said, wiping his lips and, still hungry, wondering if it would be gross etiquette to dip his spoon into Syzygy's untouched bowl of milky, spicy *bramborovka*, "so there is a difficulty."

"As you say," Syzygy said. Bech now knew the code: the lowered voice, the eyes darting toward the ubiquitous hidden bugs—as great an investment of intramural wiring here as of burglar alarms in the United States. "Perhaps you remember, in the middle chapter, with the amusing title 'Paradoxes and Paroxysms,' how the characters Lucy and Marvin in the midst of the mutual seduction of Genevieve make passing allusions to the then-new head of the Soviet state, a certain Mr. —" Syzygy's eyes, the gentle dull color of the non-inked side of carbon paper, slid back and forth helplessly.

"Begins with 'K,'" Bech helped him out.

"'X,' in Russian orthography," Syzygy politely corrected, hawking. "A gutteral sound. But exactly so. Our friends, how can I say—?"

"I know who your friends are."

"Our friends would never permit such an impudent passage to appear in an official publication, even though the statesman in question himself died in not such good official odor. Yet I cannot bring myself to delete even a word of a text that has become to me, so to speak, sacred. I am not religious but now I know how certain simple souls regard the Bible."

Bech waved his hand magnanimously. "Oh, take it out. I forget why I popped it in. Probably because Khrushchev struck me as porcine and fitted the theme. Anything for the theme, that's the way we American writers do it. You understand the word, 'porcine'?"

Syzygy stiffened. "But of course."

Bech tried to love this man, who loved him, or at least loved a version of him that he had constructed. "You take anything out or put anything in that will make it easier for you," he said. But this was bad, since it implied (correctly) that how Bech read in Czech couldn't matter to him less. He asked, apologetically, "But if you are in, as we say, not such good odor yourself with our friends, how do you expect to get your translation published?"

"I *am* published!" Syzygy said. "Often, but under fictitious names. Even the present regime needs translations. You see," he said, sensing Bech's wish to peer into the structure of it all, "there are layers." His voice grew more quiet, more precise. "There is inside and outside, and some just this side of outside have friends just on the inside, and so on. Also, it is not as if—" His very white hands again made, above his untouched soup, that curt helpless gesture.

"As if the present system of government was all your idea," Bech concluded for him, by "your" meaning "Czechoslovakia's."

The Ambassador, as they walked along cobblestones one night to a restaurant, felt free outdoors to express his opinion on this very subject. "Up until '68," he said in his rapid and confident entrepreneurial way, seeing the realities at a glance, "it was interesting to be an intellectual here, because to a degree they had done it to themselves: most of them, and the students, were for Gottwald when he took over for the Communists in *for*ty-eight. They were still thinking of *thir*ty-eight, when the Germans were the problem. But after *six*ty-eight and the tanks, they became an occupied country once more, as they were under the Hapsburgs, with no responsibility for their own fate. It became just a matter of power, of big countries versus little ones, and there's nothing intellectually interesting about that, now is there, professor?"

Addressed thus ironically, Bech hesitated, trying to picture the situation. In his limited experience—and isn't all American experience intrinsically limited, by something thin in our sunny air?—power was boring, except when you yourself needed it. It was not boring to beat Hitler, but it had become boring to outsmart, or be outsmarted by, the Russians. Reagan was no doubt President because he was the last American who, imbued with the black-and-white morality of the movies, still found it exciting.

"I mean," the Ambassador said impatiently, "I'm no intellectual, so tell me if I'm way off base."

Bech guessed the little man simply wanted flattery, a human enough need. Bech sopped it up all day in Czechoslovakia while the Ambassador was dealing with the calculated insults of European diplomacy. "You're right on, Mr. Ambassador, as usual. Without guilt, there is no literature."

The Ambassador's wife was walking behind, with the wife of the Akron couple and the fashionable photographer's young assistant; their heels on the cobbles were like gunfire. The wife from Akron, named Annie, was also blonde, scratchy-voiced, and sexy with that leggy flip shiksa sexiness which for Bech was the glowing center of his American patriotism. *For purple mountain majesties* raced through his mind when the two women laughed, displaying their healthy gums, their even teeth, *for amber waves of grain.*

He was happy—so happy tears crept into his eyes, aided by the humid wind of this Prague spring—to be going out to a restaurant without having to sign books or talk to students about Whitman and Melville, the palefaces and red men, the black-humor movement, imperial fiction, and now the marvellous minimalists, the first wave of writers raised entirely within the global village, away from the malign influences of Gutenbergian literacy. Idolized Bech loved, at the end of a long day impersonating himself, being just folks: the shuffle around the table as he and his fellow Americans pragmatically tried to seat themselves, the inane and melodious gabble, the two American women sinking their white teeth into vodka fizzes, the headwaiter and the Ambassador enjoying their special, murmurous relationship. The husband from Akron, like the Ambassador a stocky businessman, sat nodding off, zombified by jet lag. They had flown from Cleveland to New York, New York to London, London to Frankfurt, rented a Mercedes, driven through the night, and been held six hours at the Czech border because among their papers had been discovered a letter from their hostess that included a sketchy map of downtown Prague. Communists hate maps. Why is that? Why do they so instinctively loathe anything that makes for clarity and would help orient the human individual? Bech wondered if there had ever before been regimes so systematically committed to perpetuating ignorance. Then he thought of another set: the Christian kingdoms of medieval Europe.

The Ambassador announced, "My friend Karel here"—the headwaiter—"informs me that several busloads of Germans have made reservations tonight and suggests we might want to move to the back room." To Bech he explained, "This is the only country in Europe both West Germans and East Germans have easy access to. They get together in these restaurants and drink pilsner and sing."

"Sing?"

"Oh boy, do they sing. They crack the rafters."

"How do the Czechs like that?"

"They hate it," the square-faced man said with his urchin smile.

The restaurant was in a vast wine cellar once attached to somebody's castle. They woke up the dozing Akron husband and moved to a far recess, a plastered vault where only the Ambassador could stand upright without bumping his head. Whereas Mr. Akron kept falling asleep, his wife was full of energy; she and the Ambassador's wife had sat up till dawn catching up on Ohio gossip, and then she had spent the day seeing all the available museums, including those devoted to Smetana and Dvořák and the one, not usually visited by Americans, that displayed the diabolical items of espionage confiscated at the border. Now, exhilarated by being out of Akron, Annie still maintained high animation, goading the Ambassador's wife into a frenzy of girlish glee. They had gone to the same summer camp and private school, come out at the same country-club cotillion, and dropped out the same year of Oberlin to marry their respective Republican husbands. Bech felt it a failing in himself, one further inroad of death, that he found there being *two* of them, these perfect Midwestern beauties, somehow dampening to his desire: it halved rather than doubled it. The thought of being in bed with four such cornflower-blue eyes, a quartet of such long scissoring legs, a pair of such grainy triangular tongues, and two such vivacious, game, fun-loving hearts quailed his spirit, like the thought of submitting to the gleaming apparatus in Kafka's story about the penal colony. Annie, on her second vodka fizz, was being very funny about the confiscated devices displayed in the border museum— radio transmitters disguised as candy bars, poison-dart fountain pens, *Playboy*s from the era when pubic hair was still being airbrushed out—

but gradually her lips moved without sound emerg-
ing, for the Germans had begun to sing. Though
they were out of sight in another part of the subterranean restaurant, their combined voices were
strong enough to make the brickwork vibrate as the
little low nook cupped the resonating sound. Bech
shouted in the Ambassador's ear, "What are they
singing about?"

"Der Deutschland!" the answer came back.
"Mountains! Drinking!"

When the united German chorus began to
thump their beer mugs on the tables, and then
thump the tables on the floor, circular vibrations
appeared in Bech's mug of pilsner. The noise was
not exactly menacing, Bech decided; it was simply
unconsciously, helplessly large. The Germans in
Europe were like a fat man who seats himself, with
a happy sigh, in the middle of an already crowded
sofa. The Czech waiters darted back and forth,
wagging their heads and rolling their eyes in silent
protest, and a gypsy band, having made a few stabs
at roving the tables, retreated to a dark corner with
glasses of brandy. Gypsies: Bech looked among
them for the curly head, the skinny sallow shoulders of his dissident friend, who had talked so mov-
ingly about books, but saw only mustachioed dark
men, looking brandy-soaked and defeated.

Next day—there seemed to be endless such
days, when Bech awakened at his end of the pala-

tial arc, shuffled in his bare feet across the parquet, through a room in which fresh flowers had always been placed, to the brassy, rumbling bathroom, and then breakfasted in enchanted solitude, like a changeling being fed nectar by invisible fairies, and took his proprietorial stroll along the oval path, bestowing terse nods of approval upon the workmen—he had an appointment to meet some literary officials, the board of the publishing house that dealt with foreign translations. Out of loyalty to the dissidents he had met earlier in his visit, he expected to be scornful of these apparatchiks, who would no doubt be old, with hairy ears and broad Soviet neckties. But in truth they were a young group, younger by a generation than the weary dissidents. The boy who seemed to be chairman of the board had been to UCLA and spoke with an oddly super-American accent, like that of a British actor playing O'Neill, and his associates, mostly female, stared at Bech with brighter eyes and smiles more avidly amused than any that had greeted him among the dissidents—to whom he had been, perhaps, as curious in his insignificant freedom as they to him in their accustomed state of danger and melancholy indignation. These young agents of the establishment, contrariwise, were experts in foreign literature and knew him and his context well. They boasted to him of American writers they had translated and published—Bellow, Kerouac, Styron, Vidal—and showed him glossy copies, with trendy covers.

"Burroughs, too, and John Barth," a young woman proudly told him; she had a mischievous and long-toothed smile and might, it seemed to Bech, have gypsy blood. "We like very much the experiment, the experimental. William Gaddis, Joan Didion, the abrupt harsh texture. In English can you say that? 'Abrupt texture?'"

"Sure," said Bech. "In English, almost anything goes." It embarrassed him that for these young Czechs American writing, its square dance of lame old names, should appear such a lively gavotte, prancing carefree into the future.

"Pray tell us," another, pudgier, flaxen-haired young woman said, "of whom we should be especially conscious among the newer wave."

"I'm not sure there is a new wave," Bech admitted. "Just more and more backwash. The younger writers I meet look pretty old to me. You know about the minimalists?"

"And how," the chairman of the board said. "Abish, Beattie, Carver—we're doin' 'em all."

"Well," Bech sighed, "you're way ahead of me. Newer wave than that, you'll have to dig right down into the fiction workshops. There are thousands of them, all across the country; it's the easiest way to get through college."

"*Less Than Zero*," the blonde pronounced, "was evidently composed in one such class of instruction."

The chairman laughed. "Like, really. He does a fantastic job on that sick scene."

"Good title," Bech admitted. "After the minimalists, what can there be but blank paper? It'll be a relief, won't it?"

The long-toothed woman laughed, sexily. "You talk the cynic, as Mortimer Zenith in *Velká myšlenka.* Perhaps, we think here, this novel, with its ironical title *Think Big,* departs your accustomed method. Is your first attempt at post-literary literature, the literature of exhaustion."

"It seemed that bad to you?" Bech asked.

"That *good,* man," interposed the chairman of the board.

"Whereas *Travel Light* was your experiment in the Beatnik school," pursued the mischievous dark woman, "and *Brother Pig* your magic realism."

"Speaking of *Brother Pig*—"

"Is ready to print!" she interrupted gaily. "We have fixed the pub date—that is the expression?— for this autumn that is coming."

Bech continued, "I've met a man, a translator—"

The next interruption came from a slightly older man, nearly bald and so thin-skinned as to appear transluscent, at the far end of the table. Bech had not hitherto noticed him. "We know and value the work," he smoothly said, "of your friend Comrade Syzygy."

Bech took this to mean that they were using Syzygy's labor-of-love translation, and the Pragspring lambs were lying down with the Husák lions, and the levels of this mysterious fractured society were melding and healing beneath his own beneficent influence. With so pleasant a sensation warming Bech's veins, he was emboldened to say, "There's one novel of mine you never mention here. Yet it's my longest and you could say my most ambitious—*The Chosen.*"

The members of the board glanced at one another. *"Vyvolení,"* the sexy long-toothed girl, dropping her smile, explained to the nearly bald, thin-skinned man.

In the face of their collective silence, Bech blushed and said, "Maybe it's a terrible book. A lot of American critics thought so."

"Oh, no, sir," the little blonde said, her own color rising. "Henry Bech does not produce terrible books. It is more a matter—" She could not finish.

The dark one spoke, her smile restored but the sparkle banished from her eyes by a careful dullness. "It is that we are feeling *Vyvolení* is for the general Czech reader too—"

"Too special," the chairman of the board supplied, quite pleased at having found the exact shade of prevarication within the English language.

"Too Jewish," Bech translated.

In chorus, somewhat like the Germans singing, the board reassured him that nothing could be too Jewish, that modern Czechoslovakia paid no attention to such things, that the strain of Jewish-American literary expression was greatly cherished in all progressive countries. Nevertheless, and though the meeting ended with fervent and affectionate handshakes all around, Bech felt he had blundered into that same emptiness he had felt when standing in the crammed Old Jewish Cemetery, near the clock that ran backwards. He knew now why he felt so fond of the Ambassador and his wife, so safe in the Residence, and so subtly reluctant to leave. He was frightened of Europe. The historical fullness of Prague, layer on layer, castles and bridges and that large vaulted hall with splintered floorboards where jousts and knightly elections used to be held; museums holding halls of icons and cases of bluish Bohemian glass and painted panoramas of the saga of the all-enduring Slavs; tilted streets of flaking plasterwork masked by acres of scaffolding; that clock in Old Town Square where with a barely audible whirring a puppet skeleton tolls the hour and the twelve apostles and that ultimate bogeyman Jesus Christ twitchily appear in two little windows above and, one by one, bestow baleful wooden stares upon the assembled tourists; the incredible visual pâtisserie of baroque church interiors, mock-marble pillars of paint-veined gesso melting upward into trompe-l'oeil ceilings bubbling with cherubs, everything gilded and tipped and twisted and skewed to titillate the eye, huge wedding-cake interiors meant to stun Hussite peasants back into the bosom of Catholicism—all this overstuffed Christian past afflicted Bech like a void, a chasm that he could float across in the dew-fresh mornings as he walked the otherwise untrod oval path but which, over the course of each day, like pain inflicted under anaesthesia, worked terror upon his subconscious. The United States has its rough spots—if the muggers don't get your wallet, the nursing homes will—but it's still a country that never had a pogrom.

More fervently than he was a Jew, Bech was a writer, a literary man, and in this dimension, too, he felt cause for unease. He was a creature of the third person, a character. A character suffers from the fear that he will become boring to the author, who will simply let him drop, without so much as a terminal illness or a dramatic tumble down the Reichenbach Falls in the arms of Professor Moriarty. For some years now, Bech had felt his author wanting to set him aside, to get him off the desk forever. Rather frantically hoping still to amuse, Bech had developed a new set of tricks, somewhat out of character—he had married, he had written a best-seller. Nevertheless, and especially as his sixties settled around him, as heavily as an astronaut's suit, he felt boredom from above dragging at him; he was—as H. G. Wells put it in a grotesquely cheerful acknowledgment of his own mortality that the boy Bech had read back when everything in print impressed him—an experiment whose chemicals were about to be washed down the drain. The bowls in his palace bathroom had voracious drains, gulping black holes with wide brass rims, like greedy bottomless bull's-eyes. *Ne, ne!*

Around him in Czechoslovakia things kept happening. Little Akron Annie returned from a shopping expedition in the countryside with an old-fashioned sled, of bright-yellow wood, with the fronts of the runners curved up like a ram's horns. Her children back in Ohio would love it. The photographer and his assistant had a fearful spat in French and German, and the boy disappeared for a night and came creeping back to the Residence with a black eye. The Ambassador, taking his wispy daughter with him, had to drive to Vienna for a conference with all the American ambassadors of Central Europe for a briefing on our official stance in case Kurt Waldheim, a former assistant killer of Jews, was elected President of Austria. There was, in his unavoidable absence, a reception at the Residence; Bech gave a talk, long scheduled and advertised, on "American Optimism as Evinced in the Works of Melville, Bierce, and Nathanael West," and the Ambassador's wife introduced him.

"To live a week with Henry Bech," she began, "is to fall in love with him."

Really? he thought. Why tell me now?

She went on quite brightly, leaning her scratchy voice into the mike and tripping into spurts of Czech that drew oohs and ahs from the attentive audience; but to Bech, as he sat beside her watching her elegant high-heeled legs nervously kick in the shadow behind the lectern, came the heavy, dreary thought that she was doing her job, that being attractive and vivacious and irrepressibly American was one of the chores of being an American ambassador's wife. He stood blearily erect in the warm wash of applause that followed her gracious introduction. The audience, lit by chandeliers here in the palace ballroom, was all white faces and shirtfronts. He recognized, in a row, the young board of the publishing house for translations, and most of the crowd had a well-groomed, establishment air. Communists, opportunists, quislings.

But afterwards it was the dissidents, in checked shirts and slouchy thrift-shop dresses, who came up to him like favored children. The scarred man, his shiny black eyes mounted upon the curve of his face like insect eyes, shook Bech's hand, clinging, and said, apropos of the speech, "You are naughty. There is no optimism."

"Oh, but there is, there is!" Bech protested. "Underneath the pessimism."

The gypsy was there, too, in another loose blouse, with her hair freshly kinked, so her sallow triangular face was nested as in a wide pillow, and only half-circles of her great gold earrings showed. "I like you," she said, "when you talk about books."

"And I you," he answered. "That was *such* a lovely book you showed me the other night. The delicate thin paper, the hand-done binding. It nearly made me cry."

"It makes many to cry," she said, much as she had solemnly said, "We are not monks. We do not enjoy to suffer."

And a blond dissident, with plump lips and round cheeks, who looked much like the blonde at the publishing house except that she was older, and wiser, with little creased comet's tails of wisdom trailing from the corners of her eyes, explained, "Václav sends the regrets he could not come hear your excellent talk. He must be giving at this same hour an interview, to very sympathetic West German newspaperman."

Syzygy, dark-suited and sweating as profusely as a voodoo priest possessed by his deity, could not bear to look at Bech. "Not since the premiere of *Don Giovanni* has there been such a performance in Prague," he began but, unable out of sheer wonder to continue, shudderingly closed his eyes behind the phantom pince-nez.

At last Bech was alone in his room, feeling bloated by the white wine and extravagant compliments. This was his last night in the last palace built in Europe. Tomorrow, Brno, and then the free world. The moon was out, drenching in silver, like the back of a mirror, the great oval park—its pale path, its bushes with their shadows like heaps of ash, the rectilinear unused tennis courts, as ominous as a De Chirico. Where had the moon been all week? Behind the castle. Behind Hradčany. Bech moved back from the window and got into his king-size bed. From afar he heard doors slam, and a woman's voice cry out in ecstasy: the Ambassador returning to his bride, having settled Waldheim's hash. Bech read a little in Hašek's *Good Soldier Schweik,* but even this very tedious national classic did not soothe him or allay his creeping terror.

He lay in bed sleepless, beset by panic. *Jako by byl nemocen, zjistil, že může ležet jen v jedné poloze, na zádech. Obrátit se na druhý bok znamenalo nachýlit se nad okraj propasti, převrátit se na břicho znamenalo riskovat, že utone ve vodách věčného zapomnění, jež bublaly ve tmě zahřívané jeho tělem.* A single late last trolley car squealed somewhere off in the labyrinth of Prague. The female cry greeting the Ambassador had long died down. But the city, even under its blanket of political oppression, faintly rustled, beyond the heavily guarded walls, with footsteps and small explosions of combustion, as a fire supposedly extinguished continues to crackle and settle. *Zkoušel se na tyto zvuky soustředit, vymačkat z nich pouhou silou pozornosti balzám jejich nepopiratelnosti, nevinnost, která byla hlavním rysem jejich prosté existence, nezávisle na jejich dalších vlastnostech. Všechny věci mají tutéž existenci, dělí se o tytéž atomy, přeskupují se: tráva v hnůj, maso v červy. Temnota za touto myšlenkou jako sklo, z něhož se stírá námraza. Zkoušel si příjemně oživit svůj vecěrní triumf, předčítání odměněné tak vřelým potleskem.* He thought of the gypsy, Ila, Ila with her breasts loose in her loose blouse, who had come to his lecture and reception, braving the inscrutable Kafkaesque authorities, and tried to imagine her undressed and in a posture of sexual reception; his creator, however, was too bored with him to grant his aging body an erection and by this primordial method release his terror, there in the

Ambassador's great guest bed, its clean sheets smelling faintly of damp plaster.

Becha to neuspalo. Jeho panika, jako bolest, která sílí, když se jí obíráme, když jí rozněcujeme úpornou pozorností, se bez hojivého potlesku jitřila; nicméně, jako rána, zkusmo definovaná protiinfekčním a odmítavým vzepřením těla, začala nabírit jistou podobu. His panic felt pasty and stiff and revealed a certain shape. That shape was the fear that, once he left his end of the gentle arc of the Ambassador's Residence, he would—up in smoke—cease to exist.

Bech Presides

HENRY BECH had reached that advanced stage of authorship when his writing consisted mostly, it seemed, of contributions to Festschrifts—slim volumes of tributes, often accompanied by old photographs and an uneasy banquet at the Century Club or Lutèce or Michael's Pub, in honor of this or that ancient companion in literature's heady battles. These battles, even for their most enthusiastic veterans, took the form of a swift advance achieved in the dawn dimness of youthful ignorance, the planting of a bright brave flag in some momentary salient of the avant-garde's wavering front line, and then a sluggish retreat back through the mud of a clinging fame, sporadically lit by flares of academic exegesis. Such an honorable retreat could go on virtually forever, thanks to modern medicine, which keeps reputations breathing right through brain death.

Dear Mr. Bech:
    As you doubtless are aware, Isaiah Thornbush will turn seventy in 1991. We of the Aesop

Press, casting about for a suitable commemoration of this significant milestone, came up with the idea of a Festschrift volume, in a boxed limited edition, with marbleized endpapers and a striped linen headband, to be made available only to his inner circle of friends and disciples. Our enthusiasm for this project is matched and heartily seconded by our parent firm, Grigson-Kawabata Corporation Ltd., and by Mr. Thornbush's longtime literary agent Larry "Ace" Laser, and by those of his seven children whom we have been able to trace and contact. Two of his three ex-wives have even agreed to write brief memoirs and to "vet" the text overall for accuracy!

We very much hope you will supply a contribution. Almost anything will do—a reminiscence, a poem, a photograph in which the two of you appear, a shared perception as to where Isaiah Thornbush's sterling example has been most helpful in your own artistic or personal development. Your considerable stylistic debt to him has been often remarked by critics and, though you did not mention him by name, was plainly hinted at in one of your wonderful autobiographical essays. (Exactly which one escaped all of us here at Aesop, though we spent hours this morning racking our brains!)

But anything, Mr. Bech, even the most informal sort of salute, will be gratefully received—the more "unbuttoned" the better, up to a point of course. Contributors will be invited to a festive occasion at the Thornbush Manhattan residence, hosted by his lovely wife Pamela, this fall, and we know you wouldn't want to be a missing face there. We eagerly await hearing from you.

Sincerely yours,
Martina O'Reilly
Associate Editor
Trade Division, Aesop Press

Like an irritatingly detailed fleck in the vitreous humor, Izzy Thornbush's all-too-familiar face floated in Bech's inner eye as he read: the lewdly bald head with its thrusting wings of white gossamer, the bulbous little nose decorated by a sprinkle of blackheaded pores, the wide fleshy mouth that ambitious dental work of recent years had pushed forward into an eerie simulacrum of George Washington's invincible half-grimace. He was two years older than Bech, and ever since the late Forties the two had been espying each other around Manhattan, two would-be lions in too populous a Serengeti. In his younger days Izzy had sported a Harpoesque mop of curly strawberry-blond hair; always he was brain-vain. He tried to write books with his head—heavy, creaking historical allegories, with Aristotle and William of Occam and Queen Nefertiti as historical characters, debating in a fictional auditorium surrealistically furnished with modern appliances. It all

seemed rather lumbering to Bech—giant watch-
works hacked out of wood—and quite lacking in
what he, stylistically, prized: the fuzzy texture of
daily life, that gray felt compacted of a thousand
fibers, that elusive drabness containing countless
minute scintillae. Bech's own tremulous, curvaceous early prose, kept supple by a reverent and
perhaps cowardly close attentiveness to the subjective present tense, was at the opposite aesthetic
pole from Thornbush's dense and angular blocks of
intellectual history; yet both appeared in the short-
lived literary journal *Displeasure* (1947–1953),
and they could not help meeting at those Village
cocktail parties and Long Island cookouts with
which the post-war intelligentsia hoped to restore,
after the austerities of the duration, the bootlegged
gemütlichkeit of the Twenties.

America's imperium, having strangled two
snakes, was still a burly infant in those years. As
the Forties shed their honest khaki for the peacock
synthetics of Fifties populuxe, Bech and Thornbush oozed upward into eminence—Bech's break-
through being the Kerowacky novel *Travel Light*
(1955), and Izzy's his bawdy thousand-page saga,
in mock-Chaucerian English, on the vicissitudes
of philosophical realism in the Middle Ages, culminating in its destruction by the centripetal
forces of nominalism and the bubonic plague
(*Occam's Razor,* 1954). The analogies to McCarthy-
ism, atomic fallout, and gray-suited conformity
scarcely needed to be underlined, but the reviews

underlined them nevertheless, and perhaps political awareness went to Izzy's head, which was
stocked with not just highbrow erudition but low
mercantile cunning.

During the succeeding decades the two writers
met at handsomely financed cultural symposiums
in Aspen and Geneva, on quasi-ambassadorial forays to Communist countries, at sickeningly sweet
prize-bestowing ceremonies, and, as the Sixties
took hold, in the midst of protest marches and ral-
lies. Izzy blossomed, in bell-bottoms and love
beads, while his hair simultaneously thinned and
lengthened, into a guru of the young. His double-
column travesty of the Bible, *The LB-Bull,* setting
forth with gory detail and unmistakable analogic
resonance the anti-Mexican atrocities of the
nineteenth-century war that followed upon the
American annexation of Texas, all in a twangy
slang that plainly aped the accents of the current
President, became a sacred text to college youth, an
impressively erudite encouragement to indignation
and revelry. For Bech, the Sixties were a somewhat
recessive time; a lungful of the mildest marijuana
made him sick, and draft evasion disgusted him,
whether a war was "good" or not. This veteran of
the Bulge and the Rhine crossing found it hard to
cheer the American flag's being burned. His magnum opus of domestic, frankly Jewish (at last) fiction, published in late November 1963, was buried
under the decade's unravelling consensus. His ironical title, *The Chosen,* turned out to be ill-chosen,

since Chaim Potok wrote a thumping best-seller with the same title, used unironically, in 1967, and within a few years the novel's sauciest, most Freudian bits were made to seem tame by the more furious revelations of Philip Roth and Erica Jong.

In the Seventies, however, it was Izzy's star that dimmed. His massive *Nixoniad,* written in intricately "rhymed" couplets of prose chapters, came out, even with a rushed printer, six months after its subject, apotheosized as a stumble-tongued Lord of Misrule, had resigned and dragged his shame into the shadows of San Clemente. Nixon-bashing had gone out of fashion, and students, in an economy hungover from its own binge, were more concerned about getting jobs than with exploring the pleasures of an archly erudite anti-establishment romp weighing in at half a million words. When, as the decade ended, Bech startled himself and the world by outflanking a writer's block and publishing a commercially successful novel for television-heads called *Think Big,* Thornbush's sour grapes spilled over into print, in a *Commentary* review ("Le Penseur en Petit") whose acid content was left undiluted by his alligator tears of professed prior admiration.

Not that Bech had ever liked Izzy's stuff. In fact, at bottom, he didn't like any of his contemporaries' work. It would have been unnatural to: they were all on the same sinking raft, competing for dwindling review space and demographic attention. Those that didn't appear, like John Irving and

John Fowles, garrulously, Dickensianly reactionary
in method seemed, like John Hawkes and John
Barth, smugly, hermetically experimental. O'Hara,
Hersey, Cheever, Updike—suburbanites all living
safe while art's inner city disintegrated. And that
was just the Johns. Bech would not have minded if
all other writers vanished, leaving him alone on a
desert planet with a billion English-language readers. Being thus unique was not a prospect that
daunted him, as he sat warming his cold inspira-
tions, like a chicken brooding glass eggs, in the
lonely loft, off lower Broadway, to which he had
moved when his suburban marriage to his longtime
mistress's sister had been finally dissolved. Solip-
sism was the writerly condition; why not make
it statistical? Certainly the evaporation of Izzy
Thornbush was a pleasing fancy. Those protruding
eyes and hair-wings; those oversize, over-white
capped teeth; that protruding intellect, like the out-
thrust boneless body of a poisoned mollusc whose
shell has fatally relaxed—*pffft*! Bech's disrespect
had intensified when, in the flat wake of the miscal-
culated *Nixoniad,* Thornbush, whose three previous wives had been muscular, humorous, informal
women of Jewish ancestry and bohemian tastes,
had bolstered his ego by capturing the hand of a
shiksa heiress—apple-cheeked, culturally ambitious Pamela Towers, whose father, the infamous
Zeke Towers, a New Jersey cement mixer, had
made good on his family name by becoming, as
vertical plate-glass replaced stepped-back brick in

the skyline, one of Manhattan's real-estate magnates. In the luxury of Park Avenue, Palm Beach, and East Hampton residences Izzy, the former artificer, maker of mazy verbal Pyramids, need build no more; a magnificently kept man, he need oversee only the elaborate buttressing of his crumbling reputation. Nevertheless:

Dear Ms. O'Reilly:

The voice of praise, rising in my throat to do justice to my dear old friend Isaiah Thornbush, is roughened by the salty abrasions of affection and nostalgia. How different the map of post-war American fiction would be without the sprawling, pennanted castles of his massive, scholastically rigorous opuses—intellectual *opera* indeed! "Here be dragons" was the formula with which the old cartographers would mark a space fearsomely unknown, and my own fear is that, in this age of the pre-masticated sound-bite and the King-sized gross-out, the vaulted food court where Thornbush's delicacies are served is too little patronized—the demands that they, pickled in history's brine and spiced with cosmology's hot stardust, would make upon the McDonaldized palate of the reader, to whom, were he or she ideal, every linguistic nuance and canonical allusion would be mentally available, have become, literally (how else?), unthinkable. Not that my delicious old friend Izzy ever betrays by any slackening of his dizzying pace the slightest suspicion of being cast by fate in the role of a wizard whose tricks are beyond his audience's comprehension, or, like those of a magician on doctored film, too easily accounted for. *Au,* as the well-worn phrase runs, *contraire*: he continues to bustle—there is no other word—hither and yon on errands of literary enterprise, judging, speaking, instructing, introducing, afterwording, suffering himself to be impanelled and honored to the point where we shyer, less galvanic of his colleagues vicariously sag under the weight of his medals and well-weighed kudos. Soldier on, comrade, though the plain where ignorant armies clash is more darkling than ever; sail on, Izzy, and remind all those who glimpse your bellying spinnaker upon the horizon that there was once such a thing as Literature!

Ms. Reilly, the above is for publication and oral recitation—what follows is for your eyes and no doubt dainty ears only. You may not think it unbuttoned enough. If you deign to use it, don't, I repeat DO NOT, change my punctuation or break up the continuous rhapsodic exhalation of my paragraph. By the way, Aesop is good to undertake this; the commercial houses are conspicuously sitting on their hands in the case of serious writers like Thornbush. I understand his last romp through the stacks (Middle Kingdom, pre–Marco Polo, right?)

saw seven publishers before the eighth, who printed it only with extensive cuts and elimination of all passages not in Roman typeface and the English language. Also by the way, how did a maiden called Martina meet a man called O'Reilly? Or are you the product of a tempestuous mating between a Communist expat and an IRA gunrunner?

Your nosy pal,
Henry Bech

The Festschrift party was held in the Thornbush penthouse, the fifteenth and sixteenth floors of a chaff-colored brick building on Park in the Sixties. Sharp-edged minimalist statuary was dangerously scattered about on veneered French antiques. Moonlighting young actresses and actors in all-black unisex outfits passed, with the eerie schooled grace and white-faced expressionlessness of mimes, slippery hors d'oeuvres besprinkled with scallion snips. High on the two-story wall of the duplex, above a circular spiralling glass stairway, a huge Tibetan banner, a *thang-ka,* suspended above the heads of the living a tree, a *tshog shing,* of rigid, chalk-colored, but basically approachable deities. In the vast living room that yet was too small for this gabbling assemblage, cigarette smoke, that murderous ghost of the past, was briefly thick again. Bech saw around him dozens of half-forgotten faces, faces of editors and agents and publicists and publishers who had moved on

(fired and rehired, sold out to a German conglom-
erate, compelled to scribble news briefs for a Stam-
ford cable station) yet remained eerily visible
within the gabby industrial backwater of New York
publishing. And there were painters—hawk-nosed,
necktieless, hairy, gay—because Izzy was among
his other accomplishments a reviewer for *ARTnews*
and an expert on Persian miniatures, Quaker
furniture, misericords, and so on. And there were
composers—smooth, barrel-chested party animals
in double-breasted suits, their social skills brought
to a high polish by lives of fine-tuning students and
buttering up patrons—because Izzy was himself an
accomplished amateur violinist who, had not his
big brain dragged him away from his finger exer-
cises, might have had a concert career and who, it
was said, contributed not just the words but the
melody line of several crowd-pleasing songs in the
musical comedy, *Occam!,* based upon his first
novel, as well as several of the numbers in the
bawdy review, *Nefertiti Below the Neck,* loosely
derived from his second. And there were history
professors Izzy had befriended in the course of his
researches, including the famously tall one and the
famously short one, who insisted on huddling *tête-
à-tête,* like the letter "f" ligatured to the letter "i,"
and, finally, there were writers—in a single glance
Bech spotted Lucy Ebright with her shining owl
eyes and swanlike neck, and Seth Zimmerman with
his self-infatuated giggle, and Vernon Klegg in his

alcoholic daze. But it was Pamela Thornbush, Lady Festschrift herself, who came up to Bech, her rosy cheeks echoed by the freckled pink breasts more than half exposed by the velvet plunge of her plum-colored Prada. She had another woman in tow, a firm-bodied young woman dressed in mousy gray, with the dull skin and militant, faintly angry bearing that Bech associated with the beauties of Eastern Europe, those formerly Communist hussies whose attractions were at the service of the Stasi, the ÁVÓ, the KGB. "Dear Henry," Pamela said, though they had not met many times previously, "Izzy was just touched to tears by what you wrote about him; I never have seen him so moved, honestly. And this is our beautiful Martina, who pulled the whole project together. She still blushes when she talks about your fresh letter."

Bech grasped the slim cool hand proffered, which mustered a manly squeeze while her eyes levelled into his own. She was his height, perhaps an inch less. Her eyes were a grave shade of hazel. "At my age," he told her, "it's either fresh or frozen."

How strangely, unironically *there* this Martina was, though not quite beautiful; she had no sheen of glamour. She was all business. "I hope you noticed," she said, "that I defended your paragraph from the copyeditors. As you predicted, they wanted to break the flow." She spoke with the easy quickness of a thoroughly naturalized American, yet the words had an edge of definiteness, as if she did not quite trust them to convey her full meaning—a remnant, Bech guessed, of her immigrant parents' accents.

"Copyeditors do hate flow," he said. "I haven't looked into the book yet, actually. I thought it might make me too jealous. I'm all of sixty-eight, and nobody fests my schrift."

"You're too young, Mr. Bech. You must reach a round number."

"I'm not sure," he said, seriously—this steady-eyed woman was an invitation, received however late in life, to be serious; he checked their vicinity to verify that Pamela, the freckled, fabulous, still-girlish heiress, had moved on, having made this lit-tle conversational match—"that I have Izzy's gift for round numbers. Look at the bastard. The per-fect host, lapping up homage. He should have been a Roman emperor."

Thornbush, with the sixth sense that the literary jungle breeds, intuited from far across the room that Bech was talking about him; his protuberant eyes, with their jaundiced whites, slid toward his old colleague, even as a ring of adorers exploded into laughter at his most recent witticism, hot from his fat and flexible tongue.

In response to Bech's uncharacteristic serious-ness, Martina intensified her own. For emphasis she rested her cool fingers on the back of his hand, where it clasped a drink at his chest, a bourbon get-ting watery as he radiated heat. "People are afraid of you," she said in a scallion-scented gust of sincerity that tingled the hairs in his avid nostrils. "You're so pure. I think they think you'd laugh at the idea of a Festschrift. You'd scoff at the concept that people love you."

He considered the possible truth of this, as he contemplated the waxy white crimps of her ear. This ear was bared beneath a taut side of sensible brown hair, and was, as he had hazarded in their only previous communication, dainty. Fancy anticipates reality. He liked the old-fashioned severity of her hairdo, pulled back into a ponytail secured by a ringlet of silk, a pink cloth rose—an appealing cheap touch. He liked thrift in a woman, an ascetic self-careless streak; it showed the fitness needed to travel even briefly with him on his rocky road. "They're right, I would," Bech answered. "Praise that you squeeze out of people is worth about ten cents on the dollar. Enough about me. Tell me about you."

She let her level gaze drop while her sallow cheek, above her firm, excitingly antagonistic jaw, resisted a blush. "You had it only slightly wrong. My parents got out in '68, when I was three years old. My husband wasn't a gun-runner but in mergers and acquisitions, if you can see the difference."

"Was? Was in mergers and acquisitions, or was your husband?"

"The latter. I'm sorry I wrote 'unbuttoned.' I was nervous. Pamela was frantic to have you in the

Festschrift. I thought you'd spit on it. I was both grateful and disappointed when you didn't."

This, again, took them to a level of seriousness where neither was quite prepared to breathe. "I succumbed," he admitted. "To your blandishments. I've been to Czechoslovakia," he added.

"Of course. Everybody goes now. It's cheap, and Prague is raunchy."

"I was there when it was still real. Still Communist. That huge statue of Stalin. Those aging hippieish dissidents. It seemed like a very lively, tender place. Vulnerable."

"Yes, we are. The Czechs were put too close to fiercer peoples. Even when we got free, we smiled our way out."

"Nothing wrong with that. Would that we all could."

Her hands were clutched in front of her, one cupping the other, which held a glass of red wine tipped at a dangerous angle. He dared reach out and touch her. Her hand had seemed cooler when she had touched him. "Watch your back," he said. "Here comes the birthday boy."

Izzy Thornbush, the hairs of his bald head standing upright in the light, loomed. Standing beside Martina as if in military formation, he squeezed her shoulders hard enough to make her snicker in surprise. But she kept her wine from sloshing out. "She's some tootsie, huh, Henry, like we used to say?"

"The term hadn't occurred to me," said Bech gallantly.

"She's been my best buddy at Aesop," the much-honored scrivener went on. "The rest of those young slobs over there now are computerniks who think the written word is obsolete junk. They don't care about grammar, they don't care about margins. This young lady is a real throwback, to the age of us dinosaurs."

"I have always loved books," Martina said, with a little wriggle that loosened the wordmaster's bearlike grip. "I like the way," she said, "the reader can set his or her own pace, instead of some director on speed or Prozac, who sets it for you." Did Bech imagine it, or did her lips threaten a stammer, as her almost-native English stiffened on her tongue? Bech was annoyed to think that she was impressed, or intimidated, by Izzy.

The novelist's massive eyebrows—thickets, wherein arcs as red as burning filaments struggled to stay alight amid hairs from which all color and curl had been extracted—lifted in appreciation of this bulletin from the pharmaceutical generation. "There's never been enough organized thought," he announced, "on how a reader's input helps create the book. We have no equivalent to the art installation, where the viewer is also the orderer."

"Well, there was *Hopscotch*," Bech said. "And Barthes somewhere writes about how he always skips around in Proust."

"A computer system," Izzy was wool-gathering on, his eyes popping and bubbles of saliva exploding between his lips, "say, *À la Recherche* on CD-ROM, could generate a new path, an infinite series of new paths, through it, making a new novel every time—there could be one in which Jupien is the hero, or in which Albertine becomes Odette's lover!"

"A reader doesn't want decision-making power," Martina said, a bit testily, in the face of Thornbush's eminence. Perhaps she was showing Bech she was less intimidated than he had, onlooking, thought. "You read because no decisions are asked of you, the author has made them all. That is the luxury."

"But isn't this," Izzy said, displaying that he was not too old to have developed a Derridean streak, "a mode of tyranny? Isn't a traditional author the worst sort of maniacal Yahweh, telling us how everything must be?"

Bech glanced upward, wondering if Yahweh, who used to consider it a dreadful uncleanness to have His name in a mortal mouth, would strike Thornbush dead. Or had Izzy through marriage and promiscuously roving the world of ideas become so little a Jew as to enjoy a goyish immunity? A cool hard pressure on his hand recalled Bech to earth; Martina, formal and mannish, was shaking his hand goodbye. "I'll leave you two to settle these great matters," she said. "A pleasure to meet you, Mr. Bech. Thanks again for your wonderful contribution."

"Goodbye so soon? Perhaps," he ventured, "when and if I get my own Festschrift . . . "

Her serious deepset eyes met his; no smile crimped her unpainted lips. "Or sooner," she said sternly.

Sooner? Bech scented sex, that hint of eternal life. Her face, unadorned, held a naked promise that her figure did not deny. Izzy rotated his great neckless head to watch her gray-clad derrière, firm but a touch more ample than was locally fashionable, disappear into a smoky wall of animated cloth. "Cute," he muttered. "Bright. Knock the Commies all you want, they put some backbone into their brats you don't see in American kids that age—gone limp in front of the damn television."

"She came here when she was three, she told me," Bech said.

"You learn more by three than all the rest of your life," Thornbush rebutted. "Read Piaget. Read Erikson. Read anybody, for Chrissake—what the hell do you do all day in that empty loft downtown? Nobody can figure it out."

But he had an agenda. Now it was Bech's turn to feel the force of Izzy's grip, on his upper arm, through a patched tweed sleeve. "Henry, listen. How'd you like to head up the Forty? Do us all a favor and be the next president. Von Klappenemner's term's up, and it's time we got a younger guy in there, somebody from the literary end. These composers, they look good presiding, but they have no head for facts, and a few facts come up from time to time, even there."

The Forty—its number of members a wistful imitation of the French Academy—was one of the innumerable honorary organizations that the years 1865–1914, awash in untaxed dollars, had scattered throughout Manhattan. It was housed in a neoclassical, double-lot brick-front in the East Fifties, near the corner of Third Avenue, where the glass boxes—Citicorp! the Lipstick Building!— were marching north. An unwed heiress, Lucinda Baines, who, like Pamela Thornbush, fancied herself a patroness of the arts, had left her grand townhouse, with a suitable endowment, to serve as the gracious gathering-place of the hypothetical forty best artists—painters, writers, composers, sculptors—in the country. Her fortune had stemmed from a nineteenth-century nostrum called Baines' Powders, a fraud taken off the market by the Pure Food and Drug Act of 1906, but not before its illusory powers of palliation had eased many a rough-hewn death; the powders were gone but the fortune rolled on, keeping the mansion in heat and repair, feeding the faithful at the Forty's half-dozen ceremonial dinners a year, and funding a clutch of annual awards to the possibly deserving with which the organization preserved its tax-exempt status. A small paid staff fulfilled the daily duties, but by a romantic provision of Lucinda's will the

membership itself owned the building and controlled the endowment. "How come you're involved?" Bech asked, perhaps rudely.

When Izzy blinked, massive lashless eyelids
had to traverse nearly a full hemisphere of yellowing eyeball. "I'm on the board."

"What about *you* for president? Isaiah the prez:
that has a ring to it."

"You schmo, I *was* president, from '81 to '84.
Where were you? Try to pay attention—you never
come to the dinners."

"I'm watching my figure. Don't you find, once
you pass sixty-five—"

"Yeah, yeah. Listen, I got to circulate. The wife
is giving me the evil eye. But think of Edna—she'd
love it. She's dying for you. I'm asking on behalf of
Edna." Edna was the directress, a wiry little white-
haired spinster from Australia. "Don't make her
beg, at her age. The whole board is crazy about the
idea. They delegated me, since they thought we
were friends."

"Izzy, we *are* friends. Read your fucking Festschrift."

"People can be friends. Writers, no. Writers are
condemned to hate one another, doesn't Goethe
somewhere say? *Mit der Dummheit kämpfen Göt-
ter. . . .* Or was that Schiller? Forget it. I'm putting
this forward as a person. Loosen up. Remember the
good times we had in Albania? We were the first
Western writers in over the top."

"Slovenia, *not* Albania. Nobody got into Albania.

Ljubljana World Writers for Peace, in the Carter years. How could you have forgotten, Izzy—that frisky little blond poet from the Ukraine we had to do everything with in fractured French? Remember how she showed us the trick with a little tomato, biting it after tossing down a shot of vodka?"

It had been Bech, though, and not Thornbush that she had taken back with her to her cell of a room in the people's hotel. But much of the fervor of the encounter had been wasted in a breathless whispered discussion, in uncertain French, of birth control. She had kept rolling her eyes toward the corners of the room, indicating, as if he didn't know, that the walls were bugged. He knew but as an American didn't care. Perhaps she had been risking the gulag for him. How lovely in its child-like skinniness her naked body had been! Her pubic hair much darker than the hair on her head. The acid aftertaste of cherry tomato fighting with the sweetness of vodka in his mouth. She had halted him halfway in, with a stare of those wide scared eyes, eyes a many-petalled Ukrainian blue. For all the liquor she had consumed, she had been tight in the cunt, but he pushed on. She seemed relieved when he came, too soon. He had tried to wait, staring at a painting above the head-board. Shabby as the furniture was, the walls held real paintings, rough to the touch: the Socialist state supporting its hordes of collaborationist daubers.

As if he had accompanied Bech in his swift dip into memory, Thornbush sighed heavily and said, "They gave us a good time, the Commies. We're going to miss 'em."

"They soured me on writers' organizations. I don't want to be president of the Forty."

"Is that what you want me to tell Edna? You think I can go to her and tell her that? She's getting on, Henry. She's going to retire one of these days. Why do you want to break her heart?"

"Out of thirty-eight members not you or me," Bech patiently said, "there must be somebody else who can do it. How about a woman? Or a black?"

Once you start to argue with somebody like Thornbush, it becomes a negotiation. His painful grip on Bech's arm resumed. "There aren't forty of us, we're four or five short of the full body. Those that can do it have all done it. We're all old as bejesus. Any time a slot opens up in the membership, one old bastard puts up another, even older. As the Forty goes, you're a *kid*. Come *on*; I've done it; there's nothing to it. Two meetings a year, spring and fall; you can skip some of the dinners. All you've got to do is preside. Just *sit* there on your tochis."

Martina O'Reilly had emerged from the smoky wall of cloth, wearing an olive-drab loden coat, looking inquisitively everywhere but toward him. She was going to leave, Bech saw, and was giving him a chance to leave with her. If he missed this boat, who knew when there would be another? The docks were crumbling, like those off the West Fifties that had bustled with tugs and toughs when he was boy. "I'm not a presider," he told Izzy, more sharply, "I'm a—"

A learner rather, Stephen Dedalus had said, but Bech didn't finish, stricken by the way that Martina, resolving now to leave alone, glancing about with the reckless quickness of a woman in tears, reached up with both hands and lightly brushed back, in a symmetrical motion, some long strands straying from her severe hairdo.

"Cop-out," Izzy finished for him. "Above-it-all. That's the beauty of you for this post—you don't dirty yourself, generally, with being a nice guy. That's why we especially need you, after a string of these twelve-tone gladhanders. *Edna* needs you; she's got a bunch of senile fogeys on her hands."

"Izzy, let me think about it. I got to go."

"The fuck you'll think about it. Your check is in the mail, too. I know a brush-off." He had grabbed both Bech's forearms and the (slightly) younger author feared that he would have to wrestle the powerful older to escape. Martina was receding in the corner of Bech's squeezed field of vision. She was hatless, hurrying.

"O.K.," Bech said, "I'll *do* it. I'll do it, maybe. Have Edna call me and tell me the duties. Tell Pamela for me it was a great party, a great apotheosis."

"What's your rush? There's real eats coming. I wanted you to meet Pam's brother, he's a hell of a good egg, a genius in his line—moves real estate around like a chess player. And Pam wanted to talk to you about one of her pets, some benefit up at the Guggenheim."

"I bet she did. Another time. Izzy"—he found himself giving the man a hug, Communist-style, Brezhnev to Chou En-lai—"they don't make bull-shitters like you any more."

He hustled through a scrum of late arrivals in the foyer, whose walls were hung with silk prayer rugs from Kazakhstan, and saw ahead of him a pink cloth rose about to disappear. "Hey," he called. "Hold the elevator!"

Once they were sealed in together, softly plunging the fifteen stories down, he saw from the satisfied set of Martina's unpainted lips that she was not surprised by his pursuit; she had hoped for it. "Thanks," he said to her. "For holding the door." She had thrust her slender bare hand into its rubber-edged jaws. "Getting hot in there," he nervously added. "*Trop de* fest." He did feel warm, across his chest and under his arms: his exertions in coping with Izzy and escaping the party, but also a curious nagging satisfaction, a swollen sense of himself. President Bech. He had made, for wrong enough reasons, the right decision.

He rather liked presiding. Perhaps seven or eight of the Forty attended the biannual meetings. In what had been the solarium of the dainty Baines mansion, Bech sat at the massive president's desk—mahogany, with satinwood inlay—and in a facing row of leather wing chairs some of the most distinguished minds of his generation feigned respectful attention. Edna slipped the agenda to him beforehand on a sheet of paper and sat at his side with a tape recorder, taking notes on the proceedings. There might be a matter of repairs to the exquisitely designed building; or of the salary of Gabriel, the Hispanic caretaker who lived in the basement with his wife and three children; or of the insurance on the paintings and drawings that Reginald Marsh, John Sloan, William Glackens, William Merritt Chase, and the like had casually bestowed, as gentlemanly pleasantries, upon the place, and that by now had grown so in value that the insurance was prohibitive. And then there was the matter of new members—in the past two years death had opened up six new vacancies, and of thirty-four nomination requests mailed out this year only three had been returned. The array of sage and even saintly old faces confronting Bech politely, inscrutably listened. Edna adjusted the volume of her tape recorder and placed it closer to the edge of the desk, to catch any utterance from the quorum of the Forty. The quorum had once been ten but in response to poor attendance had been reduced to five. The meetings were held at dusk, before one of the dinners, so rush traffic was roaring north on Third Avenue, buses chuffing, trucks shifting down, taxis honking. It was hard to hear, even for those not hard of hearing. Across the street, trailer tractors moved in and out, laboriously backing, of a nameless bleak building that took up a third of the block.

J. Edward Jamison, whose novels of city manners had been thought sparklingly impudent as late as 1962, quaveringly spoke up: "There's this fellow Pynchon appears to be first-rate. At least, my grandsons adore his stuff. Computers is what they mostly care about, though."

"He'd never accept," croaked Amy Speer deLessups, one of the few female members and faithful in her attendance, perhaps because she lived in Turtle Bay, a modest hop to the south. Her rhyming confessions of her many amours had once created a sensation, thanks to her strict metrical defiance of the prevailing vers-libre mode. Now it was the amours themselves that seemed scandalous, in connection with this shrivelled, wispy body, lamed by arthritic joints. She walked with a cane, wore black velvet bell-bottoms, and carried her little wrinkled round face tipped up, a flirtatious habit left over from her days of comeliness. She went on, creakily turning in her chair to address Jamison and almost shouting in her pain, "He turns down *every*thing. These younger ones are like that. They think it's *smart,* not to belong. I was the same at their age."

Jamison perhaps had failed to hear her despite her effort, or had grasped only the most general import of her words, for he replied ambiguously,

"Not a bad idea. Then there's this Salinger my grandsons used to talk about. Not so much lately; now they've discovered the Internet, and girls."

"He won't accept either," Amy shouted.

This exchange awoke Aaron Fisch, a small and gnomish painter whose peculiar enamelled, fine-focus style of surrealistic political allegory had peaked in the late Thirties, plateaued for four popular years as war propaganda (no one could do Mussolini as he could, with five-o'clock shadow and jutting lower lip, and Hirohito in all his military braid, and Hitler's burning black eyes in a lean white poisoned-looking face), and then had, postwar, fallen swiftly into abysmal unfashionability, though Aaron himself lived on. A decade or more ago his work resurfaced in the art magazines as an anticipation of photorealism, but his recent paintings, as his eyes and fine motor control failed, were increasingly rough, more and more like Soutine. Blinking, pushing his thick black-framed spectacles back on his small nose, he looked toward Bech and asked, "Mr. President, have we ever given consideration to Arshile Gorky? Or did he never become an American citizen?"

"Aaron, he's *dead*," the other painter present, Limbaugh Seidensticker, gloomily erupted. "He committed suicide."

"Who?" the little surrealist asked, looking about in alarm, and almost piteously returning his pink-lidded gaze to the president, for guidance.

"Arshile Gorky, Mr. Fisch," Bech said.

"Oh, of course. I knew that. A wonderful sensibility. His onions and bulb-forms; very organic. He never understood why the Abstract Expressionists took him up."

This may have been deliberately tactless, since Seidensticker was an adamantly abstract painter, who worked entirely with commercial paint rollers and latex colors straight from the hardware-store can. Not since his moment of revelation in 1947 had he deviated from his faith that painting's subject was painting itself and even the rectangular shape of the canvas was an embarrassing tie with the picture/window fallacy. There were almost none like him left; the resurgence of figuration, among young artists who had no training in how to draw, had left him sputtering on his flat fields of chaste monochrome. "It's a scandal," he said now, "that Donald Judd isn't a member."

"Oh, Limby, don't you think if you've gone and seen one aluminum box you've seen them all?" Amy intervened, tipping up her wrinkled face to him like a round dish to be drained of its light, as the last rays of the spring afternoon bounced off the blank side walls of the truck depot opposite and sidled into Lucinda Baines' old solarium. As if still alive with plants, this skylit interior shimmered; the faces of the Forty seemed to Bech flowers, yellowish blooms of ancient flesh suspended against the Rembrandtesque gloom of the dark leather chairs.

"It would be a scandal if he were," said Aaron Fisch. "What about Andy Wyeth? He's been coming along lately. Those Helga things weren't as bad as people said."

Limbaugh Seidensticker snorted. "Oh, all that *hu*man interest! All those half-rotting fenceposts and flowering weeds, stalk by stalk! *Yukk,* as the young people say." Rage was galvanizing his body, lifting his head into the declining light so that his rimless glasses formed ovals of blind brightness. "Next we'll be entertaining purveyors of pictotrash like David Hare."

"He's dead," someone in the chairs said.

"He was just a boy," another softly exclaimed.

Edna cleared her throat and whispered something to Bech.

Bech said, "The directress informs me that Andrew Wyeth is already a member, though he rarely attends."

"In that case," Seidensticker rather boomingly announced, "I resign." But he did not get up from his chair.

Bech asked the group, "Is there any more discussion of possible new members?"

Silence.

"Does anyone wish to second the nomination of Donald Judd?"

Again, silence.

"Mr. President." Another old, especially dignified voice quavered into audibility, above the whir of Edna's tape recorder and the muffled rumble of circumambient traffic.

"Yes, Mr. MacDeane?" Amory Henry Mac-Deane was a historian, an avid chronicler of the dowdy, unsatisfactory stretches of national government between Jackson and Lincoln, when the United States, its founding successfully consolidated, ineffectually sought a compromise that would hold the South in the Union without giving everything, including all the West, over to the fiery proponents of black slavery. MacDeane, the son of an Ohio Scots-Irish factory owner, had several times abandoned the halls of academe for those of Washington, where he had advised Democratic administrations in their own compromises as they sought to contain Communism without engaging it in nuclear war. MacDeane knew Russian, French, German, and Italian, and had acted as ambassador to several ticklish, demonstration-prone countries; he wrote his histories and memoirs in elegiac Victorian periods imbued with the sadness of realpolitik, this consideration always balancing that. Bech admired him, as an intellectual who had willingly dirtied himself with decision-making in the realm of real, as opposed to coveted, power. Now he was old, over eighty, and scoop-faced, with a mustache the same faded tint as his gray skin, and lived in New York only because he had lost the way back to Ohio, the vanished Ohio of his youth. He spoke in quavery, fine-spun sentences. "The difficulty of obtaining nominations, so that the functioning membership of the so-called Forty is actually thirty-four, of whom the meagre quorum I count here as seven, eight with the president, leads me to wonder, Mr. President, if our beloved institution, so benignly conceived and pleasantly housed, is not perhaps destined to join those other institutions whose historical moment is past. One thinks, on a far larger scale of course, of the Grand Army of the Republic, so mighty and influential in its time, and the International Workers of the World, known as the Wobblies. There is no disgrace in death," the old diplomat went on in his faint, husky, but still superbly controlled voice. "The disgrace comes in prolonging life with artificial and unseemly means."

"I agree," Isaiah Thornbush announced from the end of the row, with uncharacteristic brevity. His position surprised Bech. Izzy soaked up honors and loved clubs; Bech had always rather despised him for it.

Eric Von Klappenemner, tall and bald and with a piercing flutelike delivery, said, "Oh, all my friends, it's so *bor*ing, they say they don't want this and they don't want that, they don't want oxygen and they don't want electronic resuscitators or whatever they are; I say to them, Why not? I want it *all*! Oxygen and IVs and bloody livers and bone marrow and all of it! What's the purpose of science, if not to prolong human life?"

"Klappy, you're so *greedy*!" Amy deLessups flirted. How did so addictively heterosexual a woman, Bech wondered, view a homosexual like

Von Klappenemner? Fondly, it seemed. As a fellow caster of the pearl of oneself before male swine.

"It's not *me,* it's not any senseless *hung*er for my personal existence, there's nothing I'd like better than a good long afternoon *nap,* a nap that never ends, it would be *splen*did. It's what I can still *give* people, all that beauty and majesty still locked up in me—suppose Beethoven had thrown it all in after that rather piffling Eighth Symphony; we'd have never had the glorious *Ninth!*"

Von Klappenemner had reached that stage of mental deterioration when verbal inhibitions lift, though the old habits of syntax are still intact. He had been, with his gleaming head and those curling Nordic lips spouting wicked drolleries from beneath his Saracen curve of a nose, a universal charmer; now the dimming solarium held, like a sound-swallowing baffle of nippled black foam rubber, the hush of his charm falling on deaf ears. The melody was still there, but the body's aged instrument could no longer play it. Bech felt he was coming to the babbling composer's rescue, saying, "Perhaps we're straying from the topic."

"What is the topic?" Aaron Fisch unabashedly asked.

"Isn't it time for cocktails?" J. Edward Jamison seconded.

"The topic is the dearth of new members," Bech told one, and then the other: "It is only ten minutes to six, Mr. Jamison. Let me say, before we proceed to the last item of the agenda"—Edna had cleared her throat and placed, suppressing a stab of impatience, a supremely sharp pencil-point upon the item still to be discussed—"that I am surprised to hear talk of dissolution, if that is what I have just heard. The purposes for which Miss Baines made her generous bequests are still valid. American society has not been so transformed since 1902 that the arts need no longer be honored, nor is there, to my knowledge, any other organization quite like ours—so purely and disinterestedly honorary. Are any of you suggesting that the artistic spirit—the appetite for truth and beauty—has suddenly died? If so, I missed the obituary in the *Times*. Many worthy prospective members exist, to fill up the spaces in our ranks; a meeting such as this serves, primarily, as an occasion to vent our views. Nominations should be submitted in writing, with the signature of one other member as a second. Then, in due course, we will vote, as our predecessors always have and our successors always will."

"Well said, Henry," Edna murmured at his side.

Indeed, his firmness in defending an organization he once viewed as superfluous surprised him. The words came out of him as crisply as if teletyped; the president within, whom he had never suspected was there, had spoken. And the elderly bodies seated before him—inspiration-scarred warriors in the battle for precision and harmony, for order in a world where the concept of divine order had become an obscene joke—fell silent under his conservative barrage, his rattling salute to continuity. "The last item on the agenda," Bech announced, his eyes bent on Edna's pencil-point, "is less existential and more practical. Gabriel Mendez, who, as you all know, lives in our basement as caretaker and watchman, has told Edna that he and his family must have more nearly adequate health benefits. Their youngest child evidently needs a great deal of specialized care."

Once it was ascertained that the endowment, benefitting from the steady rise in stock prices since the crash of October '87, could foot the bill, the benefits were voted, eight to none. A good deed done, with money not theirs. Yet, rising from his heady session of presiding, Bech felt the floor under him tip, the long dark desktop curve downward at both edges, and the emptying wing chairs defy perspective. The president was somehow on a slippery slope. Wasn't the Forty from its turn-of-the-century founding based on a false belief that art naturally kept company with gentility, both gracefully attendant on money—that money and power could be easily transmuted into truth and beauty, and that a club of the favored could exist, ten brownstone steps up from the pitted, filthy, sorely trafficked street? What was he doing here, presiding?

He lived on the west side of Crosby Street, that especially grim cobbled canyon of old iron-façaded industrial structures running south from Houston, one block east of lower Broadway. He occupied a loft so vast he had been able, finally, to get his books into a single set of shelves, a ramshackle rampart of pine planks on cinder blocks, Marx next to Marvell, Freud in all his frowning paperbacks between the slim poems of Philip Freneau and the leather-swaddled chronicles of Jean Froissart—picked up for four dollars when Bech was a GI-Bill student at NYU.

Bech could be said to be both a keen reader and the opposite; he nervously plucked at any journal or newspaper within reach of his hand, often leafing through back to front, a habit left over from his childhood, when mass magazines ran their cartoons toward the back. He pulled books from his shelves fitfully, quickly pleased or bored by a page, but he rarely settled to read a book through. This browsing was selfish and superstitious: he was looking for clues that would help him turn his own peculiar world into words, and he resisted submitting for long to another author's spell. After half an hour of reposing in his antique beanbag chair, in the carpeted island in the center of his single great room furnished in scattered islands, he would need to go outside, where the dour but populated streets fed another kind of scanning. Running-shoe-shod tourists cruising the galleries; art salesmen lugging wrapped rectangles; a fork-bearded, red-shirted geezer fresh, it seemed, from the hills of Kentucky; a young man with bleached-blond ponytail flying by on an absurdly small motorized scooter; a pair of young women totally in black prolongedly

embracing, either in passionate reunion or determined demonstration of gay pride, the shorter of
them wearing thrillingly brutal square-heeled
black boots dotted with silver studs; a plump social
worker leading on a knotted cord a quartet of the
blind, with their sunken sockets and undirected
smiles—all such bits of street theatre excited Bech
with a sense of human life, a vast inchoate atmosphere waiting, like the gray sky seen through the
fire escapes overhead, to be condensed and experienced as drops of rain or as letters of type.

For years he had lived at 99th Street and Riverside Drive, before a romantic excursion into marriage had taken him to a Westchester suburb and
another excursion (into the body of his wife's sister) had brought him ingloriously back to the city.
Within its confines, he had headed south, off the
numbered grid. Here in SoHo the flash and glitter
of youthful aspiration mingled with the clangor of
old warehouse enterprise. There were cobblestones
and elaborate dirty ironwork; there were still
greasy bicycle shops and men in bloody butchers'
aprons. The area below Houston—that light-filled
slash in Manhattan's close-woven fabric—had
once been known as Hell's Hundred Acres,
because of its infernal sweatshops and frequent
fires. Long black limousines out of Little Italy
prowled between aisles of graffiti-sprayed metal
shutters. Signs in Chinese popped up on its south-
eastern edge. From spots on Broome and Spring
Streets Bech could see both the gleaming needle of

the Chrysler Building and the looming outcrop of
the financial district, topped by the twin spireless
World Trade towers, box cathedrals. In the low-
lands of Soho Bech experienced an oddly big sky
and a sensation—important, he felt, for an artist—
of the disreputable, if not (there were too many art
galleries and cappuccino joints) of the proletarian.

Martina earnestly considered his confessed
queasiness in regard to the Forty. She brought to
every issue he raised an intent, unsmiling consideration he associated with Communist peace conferences, of which he had attended a few. "What is the
point, again," she asked, "of the Forty?"

"To exist, simply. A city on a hill, sort of. A
mountain seen from the plain. This woman,
Lucinda *Baines,* left her dandy townhouse and a lot
of ill-gotten *gains* for a kind of French Academy,
though we have none of their responsibilities. They
keep working away at a French dictionary, for one
thing, and have braided uniforms."

The long-dead Lucinda, he realized, had
become one of his love objects, and little efficient
Edna another. His imagination bred a needy flock
he lived to serve and placate—ewes who gave him
an identity as shepherd. He was an old-fashioned
gallant, Henry Bech; in all the women of his life he
was seeking truth and goodness. A great reservoir
of both must lie, he reasoned, with an entity able to
take his sexual agitation and turn it into a limpid,
post-coital peace. Martina moved around the car-

peted island, set in a sea of boards splintered by vanished industrial machinery, on solid bare feet, in a white terrycloth robe that an inamorata of Bech's, the volatile Claire Hoagland, had stolen long ago from their room in the Plaza, in one of her caprices. There was little capriciousness in Martina; she took literary giants seriously, even in their underwear.

"I wonder," she mused, "if it wasn't a dead idea even then. I mean, old guys sitting around drinking port and smoking cigars and telling each other what fine fellows they are—how William Dean Howells can you get?"

"Poor Howells," Bech said. "Everybody thinks of him as a toastmaster. In fact, the older he got, the more radical he became. I can't say the same for myself. You should have seen Edna's face when I defended the Forty so stoutly—her jaw dropped nearly back to Alice Springs."

It was charming when Martina laughed, the cautious dimpling and half-smothered eruption, her Socialist conscience checking her acquired American freedom to mock. "It is unlike you," she said. "You usually scoff at pomp and pretension."

"But the Forty is not pompous, it's *touch*ing. Almost nobody comes. Those that do are deaf or senile. The place has paintings on the wall we can't afford the insurance on. Everything inside is so exquisite and Grecian—high sculpted plaster ceilings and no two fireplaces carved alike—and across the street squats this huge uncaring flank of some building where dozens of trailer trucks seem to live."

"New York is full of uncaring buildings," she solemnly said. "What does your friend Isaiah Thornbush think about this Forty?"

"Who knows? He got me into the presidency, and then at the spring meeting he hardly spoke up. At one point he announced he agreed with MacDeane about something, but it could have been about dying, preventing extraordinary measures. We got onto that somehow. The discussion rambled."

"Why do you like presiding?"

Martina had spent the night, and so was there to greet the mid-morning sun as it threw golden rhomboids of warmth into the loft. She had curled her body in one of them, on a sofa opposite Bech's beanbag, across his glass coffee table and striped Peruvian rug. Bea, Bech's nicely domestic ex-wife, had covered a cracked old leather sofa of his with nubbly beige wool; nestled upon it, with her bare feet palely protruding from her robe, Martina suggested a big blintz—the terrycloth the enfolding crepe, her flesh the pure soft cheese. Her sunstruck toes wiggled in idle pleasure, and her hair swirled in a loose tangle all about her broad face, its brows, usually thick and straight and stern, interrogatively arched.

How good it was of women, Bech thought, not for the first time, to allow you intimacy with them, sharing their pleasure in the simplest elements of life. You can, through chinks in the male armor, feel a fraction of the bliss that must tumble in upon them all day long. "I suppose I like having the attention," he answered, "even as a formality, of men and women whose accomplishments I respect. Old poops now, it may be, they once put their minds and hearts on the line and tried to make something decent. Think of all that MacDeane knows about Millard Fillmore. Think of how he's made himself care about Calhoun. Even Von Klappenemner—all the Beethoven he's passed through his head and his arms, he's earned the right to call one of the symphonies piffling. I find that moving."

"I find it rather shocking," Martina said, "and likewise that you're so impressed. You saw the Writers' Unions perform their thuggery in Communist countries—why isn't the Forty more of the same?"

"Well, those were closed shops, and the politicians were pulling the strings. We're above politicians, or beneath their notice. Mailer a couple of years ago had George Shultz, when he was Reagan's Secretary of State, address a PEN conference, and everybody jumped all over him."

"And you didn't like that?"

"I didn't like the jumping, no. Free speech ought to be Shultz's right too. He gave a rather nice speech, but nobody listened. All that mob of intelligentsia cared about was hissing Reagan and the contras."

Martina slowly uncurled, pressing her feet into the cushion against the sofa's far arm. "Wasn't that clever of Izzy," she purred, "to know that you were presidential timber? Under that curly head of hair, behind those rumpled eyes, such a true-blue conservative."

"Oh, Izzy," he said, offended by her familiar use of the old phony's name. "He gives intelligence a bad name." Was she, he wondered in his most paranoid moments, a tool of Izzy's Stasi? His fingerprints were all over her.

She put her feet down, so for a moment they were viewed by Bech as if in a glass case, through the coffee-table top, their yellow heels and pink toes and blue instep veins mounted on red-and-black Peruvian stripes, and then she sidestepped languidly around the coffee table, her hands on the loose knot of her terrycloth robe. "Henry, I think it's so darling, that you have all these traditional sentiments. What did people used to say? Corny. It's a real turn-on." She lightly undid the belt. From within the parted folds of her robe, her naked body, displayed inches from his face, emitted the warmth and scent of food, a towering spread of it, doughy-pliant yet firm, lustrous, with visible mouthable details, tits pussy hips navel armpits, each with its flavor, its glaze, its tang of overwhelming goodness. Martina fucked administeringly, amused from a small distance and then the distance diminishing until she was lost in its absence. The Forty and its dainty mansion could not hold a candle to this.

The fall meeting was better attended than the spring's had been. Of the faithful, little Aaron Fisch had died; there would be no more nominations for Arshile Gorky. Seidensticker, MacDeane, Jamison, Von Klappenemner, Izzy, and Amy deLessups were there, along with six or seven more, not all of whom Bech knew. There were: Jason Marr, one of the two African-Americans among the Forty, a pale and suave preacher's son whose essays, long-lined poems, and surrealistic fictions were unremittingly full of rage and dire prophecy; X. I. Fong, a refugee from Mao's China whose large pale pencilled abstractions thrillingly approached invisibility; Isabella Úrsula "Lulu" Buendía Fleming, a Venezuelan diplomat's daughter whose many years as a girl and then young woman in Washington had led to fluent English, an American marriage, and a remarkable graft of magic realism upon the humdrum substance of suburban Maryland; and three or four others in the back row, probably composers, wearing dark suits. Edna read the minutes of the last meeting, which were approved. How could Edna's meticulous handiwork ever be disapproved? Several special repair requests—the copper flashing on the slate roof over the front portal had buckled in last summer's heat wave, and a bronze sundial, in the shape of a rampant griffin, donated by the late Paul Manship to stand in the ivy bed in the rear garden, had been bent and spray-painted by vandals—were passed. A tribute to Aaron Fisch was read, surprisingly, by Lulu Fleming; that was why, Bech realized, she had made the trip up from Bethesda. She found in Fisch's work a worthy Lower East Side equivalent of the idealistic mural art of Rivera and Siqueiros, with something of Salvador Dalí's hallucinatory high finish, itself derived from the ardent literalism of Catholic altar painting; it was in this broad and bloody stream of anonymous popular style that our deceased friend and colleague Aaron Fisch, she asserted, ultimately stood.

The report on election results was discouraging. None of the four candidates duly nominated and seconded over the course of the summer received a majority of the votes cast by mail ballot or the ten-vote minimum established by the by-laws. Oral nominations to fill the now seven new vacancies came sluggishly and begrudgingly. The name of William Gaddis, put forward by Thornbush, was batted aside with the phrase "Joycean gibberish" by J. Edward Jamison, and that of Jasper Johns met unenthusiasm in Seidensticker's summation of "Pop tricks and neo-figurative doodles—he had an abstract phase, but it turned out to be insincere." When MacDeane mentioned Susan Sontag, Amy pertly shot out her chin and said, *"Sonntagskind ist Montags Mutter,"* which made several of the shadows in the back—polyglot composers—laugh out loud.

Bech announced, rather desperately, "If we don't ever manage to elect anybody, the institution will dwindle to nothing."

The venerable MacDeane, his distinguished hangdog face tinged by the lingering tan of a Nantucket summer, pronounced in faint and quavery syllables, "As I took the liberty of suggesting at our last meeting, Mr. President, would that be an entirely unfortunate development? Perhaps our institutional body is trying to tell us something—that the moment for *gloire* is by. War ceased, in the trenches of 1914–1918, to be a path to *gloire* that any civilized man could condone, and now I wonder, with the passing of the Cold War, if *gloire* by even peaceful means is not an idle hope, a misbegotten vision based upon dissolved intellectual conventions. I raise this possibility quite without joy; but it is often a historian's duty to describe that which gives him—or her, of course—no joy."

Glwaar, Bech thought to himself, trying to wrap his mind around the juxtaposed consonants. Had it been to *glwaar* that he had been enslaved, denying himself a paying job, a spread of progeny, a life that was more than an excuse for those few minutes of each day when he was secreting words that might, possibly, harden to become, if not imperishable diamond, translucent amber, holding in it a captured moment like an extinct bug? An abyss of wasted minutes opened beneath Bech and

Edna, Edna his sterile partner in immortality management, Edna his presidential bride, here at the
great dark desk whose satinwood-rimmed top
stretched toward the horizon like the flight deck of
an aircraft carrier. In her neat but jagged hand,
relentless as a cardiograph, Edna was etching notes
on yellow legal paper, while the tape recorder at
her angular elbow purred. Beneath its top the desk
had a portly bowed shape, as if its sides were bending outward under invisible pressure from above.

A shadowy man in the back row half-stood,
waving his hands like a conductor during an alle-
gro movement. "There are no more composers!" he
called. "There is only electronic tapes! That is all
the young musicians care about! To elect one of
them would be to elect a machine!"

Seidensticker growled in agreement, "Painting
now is all crap—victim art with stick figures. Ever
since Kiefer and Kienholz hit it big, atrocities are
all you get—the Holocaust, the slave trade, rape,
ecology, blah blah. Everything is a protest poster.
Always excepting my distinguished colleague
here." X. I. Fong, who never spoke at meetings,
managed a beaming little kowtow without leaving
his seat. Seidensticker went on, trying now to be
gracious to the dead, "At least Aaron had the
excuse of when he was born, back in those American Scene dark ages—the kids now have no
excuse, and they know it. It's all gallery politics,
and gallery customers are all New York liberals

soaking up guilt, or else Japanese and Arabs wanting some soft porn for their dens."

"Shit," announced Eric Von Klappenemner, six months further gone into the de-inhibitions of dementia. "What they call art now is shit, smeared on the wall, smeared into your ears. Where is beauty? Trashed underfoot. Where is grace, discipline, self-denial? All gone up the boob tube. My young friends say, Watch TV, it's American meditation. But I say it's shit, I don't mince my words. They don't either. They tell me, You are a fucking old fool."

"Klappy, why do you have such rude young friends?" Amy deLessups asked, rolling her eyes roguishly at the composer, who was staring above her head to one side of Bech's head, where the tricolor (maroon, gold, and indigo) flag of the Forty hung limp on its standard, next to a portrait of Clarence Edmund Stedman, its first president, a Wall Street broker and a poet with a fleecy, trapezoidal beard. Not even Yahweh had had a whiter beard.

Bech, perched in Stedman's seat like a rat on a throne, surveyed the leather arc of immortals, looking for a friend. "We've heard from an artist, a composer, and a historian; how do the poets and novelists among us feel?"

"How do *you* feel, Bech?" J. Edward Jamison asked in peppery rejoinder. "Can you read any of these kids? I mean, the ones under sixty?"

"There is no magic," Lulu Fleming volunteered, with her enchanting small trace of Spanish
singsong. "There are these facts, this happened and
then that happened, all told in this killingly clean
prose. They have advanced degrees in creative
writing; they go to these workshops and criticize
each other, there is nothing left to criticize, but
something is missing, I don't know what it is—a
love of the world, some hope beyond the world."

"I read these younger women poets," Amy
deLessups said, "and it seems they've slept with
the same men I did, or the same women, but they
came to it ironically, wrapped in irony for protection and knew ahead of time it wouldn't work.
Perhaps," she admitted, her little round face seductively dimpling, "they had read my poems."

"I confess, ladies and gentlemen," Bech told
the chairs, "that new fiction makes me tired. All
that life that isn't mine. All that clamoring 'Look at
me!' But I thought the fault might be mine, the
effect of age. Izzy, what do you think? You still
read everything, you have the digestion of an ox.
When and where these days is fiction not weary?"
Izzy attended these meetings in a kind of watchful
sulk, ever since Bech had become president; he
deserved being put on the spot.

Slumped in the second row, Thornbush roused,
and pronounced, "If you'd asked me in the Seventies, I would have said Latin America; in the Eighties, Eastern Europe. Now, with the Nineties, the
whole globe seems on hold. Maybe the great stuff

is all on the Internet and we don't know how to access it yet. Mr. President, I'd like to propose a moratorium on new members until after the millennium clears the air."

"Second," said one of the composers in the back row.

There were a number of other seconds.

"Motion made and seconded," Bech had to say, though he knew it was all mischief. "Discussion?"

Edna cleared her throat beside him and said, in her thrilling Anglo-Australian twang, "If I may make a point. The by-laws are very clear about our electing new members. It's our main responsibility, virtually our *only* responsibility. I'm not sure we wouldn't be forfeiting our charter, and the endowment with it, if such a motion passed." Her white hair, cut in Prince Valiant fashion, trembled at the thought. Discreetly she bent her gaze back to her yellow pad, where she noted her own remarks. Bech fought an urge to pat her sleek head comfortingly.

"But we can't seem to find anybody," Amy sang out sweetly, "as wonderful as ourselves."

"We must *try*," Bech said, in his most severe presidential voice. "We must think back, to when we were on the outside, looking in. Suppose the then members had been as fastidious as we seem to be now?"

"Times are different," Seidensticker said. "Money and the media hadn't hopelessly corrupted everything at that point. You heard Eric say it—it's all shit."

"*Please,*" the president said primly.

X. I. Fong spoke up, smiling. "Lim, Lim, not that bad. Like always—some O.K., some not O.K. Things go in seasons. Change, never change."

Izzy Thornbush's stentorian voice cut across these melodic formulations. "Mr. President, there is a motion on the floor."

"We're discussing it, aren't we?"

"I move the question."

Bech was taken aback. He had forgotten the motion. Seeing this, Thornbush said, "The question is, Shall we declare a moratorium on new members until the millennium?"

"A lot can happen between here and the millennium," Bech observed. "It's eight years away. We could all be dead."

"The question, the question!" the dark suits in the back row insisted. Bech had always had a slight fear of composers. He couldn't understand what was in their heads—those key changes, those dominants and progressions and intervals, what did it all mean? They were men from outer space, and yet worldly, allied with money-men, artistic lawyers of a sort, so much of what they offered as created really mere boilerplate, the repeat sign saying *Here we go again. . . .*

"Our directress says we might forfeit our charter and the endowment," he pointed out to the membership.

"*Ayyye,*" Izzy thundered, and the back row chorused, and Seidensticker that puritanical prick also, and Von Klappenemner in his dementia, so Bech had to say, "The question has been moved. All those in favor of the moratorium raise your hands." Three from the back row, and Izzy and Seidensticker, but Von Klappenemner perhaps thought he had already voted. MacDeane, Bech was sorry to see, after a moment's thought raised his hand, perhaps acting on an old Cold Warrior's instinct that time gained is a victory, and any moratorium is a good one. That made six for. "Those opposed?" Bech asked, and his own hand went up. The writers, bless them, stuck with him—Jamison, Amy, Lulu, and Marr, who Bech might have thought would welcome damage inflicted on such a white man's club. But his brown hand was in the air, and so was the delicate yellow hand of X. I. Fong, master of pencil on paint. That made six against. In his confusion as to what was being decided, or perhaps captivated by a bygone ecstasy, Von Klappenemner made a flowery conductor's gesture, and Bech counted him in. "The motion fails," he announced, "seven to six. Membership in the Forty is still open."

Order had collapsed, everyone was jabbering; the hubbub subsided when Jason Marr indicated he would speak. "What this outfit needs," he said, "is a little affirmative action. Its spectrum needs to be broadened. I would like to nominate Toni Morrison, Henry Louis Gates, Cornel West, Albert Murray, and Lanford Wilson, right off the top of my head."

"I second them all," Amy exclaimed.

Edna interposed, "Toni Morrison is already a member."

"Then I nominate Rita Dove," said Marr suavely.

"Yes, women!" Amy cried. "There are so many these days! Wise women! Elaine Pagels! Ellen Zwilich! Eudora Welty! We no longer need swim on our backs, turning our foolish broken hearts into song, that was what we did in my day. Babies and songs—nothing else mattered enough. Even Dorothy Thompson and Martha Gellhorn, they thought they should be in love. I knew them both."

"Miss Welty is already a member," said Edna.

"I loved Gellhorn," Lulu interposed. "Even just the name. *Como una matadora.*"

"They were never members," Edna felt obliged to point out. She was getting tired. Her little cardiographs were trailing off into weak, irregular beats, and the tape recorder, if Bech read its little red light aright, was spinning a spool empty of tape. He was beginning to feel rescued, free. In his biggest, most presidential voice he announced, "These are all excellent nominations. We'll put them into writing. Send in any others to Edna, with seconds. We will get ballots in the mail by Christmas." One of Edna's young minions had come in, attractively breathless; her whispered secret was imparted from Edna to Bech. "I am informed," he announced, "that the caterer downstairs says the hot hors d'oeuvres are getting cold. Does anyone except me want a drink? If the answer is aye, I propose we adjourn. Thank you all for coming. It was an exceptional turnout." In the absence of a gavel, he rapped his knuckles on the wood, and the hollow, bow-sided desk resounded sonorously, like an African drum.

As the little elderly mob, growling and quarrelling and laughing, pressed toward the stairs, Edna at his side put down her pencil. "That was a bit of a scrape," she muttered, pronouncing it "scripe."

"Yeah, what's going on? What's eating Izzy? He twisted my arm to take this job, and now he gives off nothing but negative vibes."

"Deep waters, Henry," she said. He looked at her; she had never before employed a tone this intimate. His *éminence grise.* His First Lady. She was prim and efficient but with a lurking antipodean strangeness, an occasional hoot of laughter out of the outback. Her profile was a cameo, in eighteenth-century English style—precise pursed mouth, high-bridged Romneyesque nose. The white wings of her short page boy swung forward as she fussed, motherly, with the recording device and her yellow pad of jagged notes. While they all played at being the Forty, she *worked.* She was sixtyish, but, then, he was a year short of seventy. Spinsters preserve themselves, he figured. The buds of passion remain coiled tight. He had once been to Australia, and sampled the handsome native women there, but had never talked to Edna about it—the pale

parched land, the alkaline sky, the lacy iron balconies in Sydney, the opera house like a ship under
full sail. An America without Calvinism or
Judaism, just sunny brown space and the rough
male humor of a penal colony. He found himself, in
the wake of the battle they had breasted together,
quite close to Edna. What was it Izzy had told him?
She's dying for you. His dying for her wouldn't be
the worst fate. She had the requisite severity, a silver purity.

His relationship with Martina was deteriorat-
ing. Behind that Communist innocence lurked
a Nineties American woman—canny, ambitious,
condition-conscious, self-preserving. Bech could
hardly blame her for seeing men younger than himself (she would need the exercise, the multiple
orgasms he could no longer provide), but the suspicion that she and Izzy had something going
nagged. That polymathic slob, that kept man, that
pseudo-Talmudic maze-maker. Bech had an opportunity to spy on the situation when Pamela invited
him and, separately, Martina, to a Christmas party
in her penthouse. The artistic crowd that had
shrouded the Festschrift gala in smoke and stale
rivalries was in attendance only spottily—a plump
Princeton savant who believed that Genesis was
written by a woman; Vernon Klegg celebrating his
latest dryly written, alcohol-soaked *succès d'es-*

time; and a skinny, bespectacled poet whose poems all dealt, in cindery glints, with Ohio industrial depression. "I had pictured your husband as looking different," Bech confided to the poet's iron-haired but still-lissome wife.

"Oh? How?" she responded, too brightly. There was something giddy, on the edge of naughty, about this woman that Bech wearily ascribed to his ancient roguish reputation, which had preceded him.

"More blue-collar," he said. "He's always doing sestinas and pantoums about rusty I-beams and how he scrubbed out vats of acid in a rubber suit."

"That was his brother who did the vats. Jim worked in the mills only summers; he was the family dreamer. They all sacrificed so he could go to college."

"And is he grateful?"

"Very," she said. "But they hate his poems. They want him to write about higher things, not about *them,* and the mills."

Across the round table, delicate, pampered Jim in his rimless glasses nodded and cringed beneath the chattery, fluttery attentions of his hostess. He had won prizes, and Pamela liked that. But she noticed Bech noticing, and accosted him after dessert. The shining skin exposed by her low-cut Herrera gown of watered silk flashed like a breastplate; she pressed him into a conversational corner. He wanted, under the stimulus of the three colors of wine served with the meal, to reach down and fish up one of her tits, to see if her freckles extended to the nipple. Did she go topless, that is, in her and Izzy's privacy beside their East Hampton pool? As a girl she had surely sunbathed with minimum coverage on the salty, rainbow-ridden foredeck of her father's yachts as they ploughed the Sound and the turquoise Caribbean. She read these thoughts, or sensed their heat, and pressed her freckled décolletage two inches closer to his already rumpled shirtfront. "Henry, what's happening between you and Martina? She seems so distracted and sour."

"She does?" He searched out where in the little crowd of penthouse visitants Martina and her dull charcoal dress had lodged. She was, his secret garden fragrant of spices and overripe, leaf-embowered fruits, in close conversation with the blue-collar poet; without doubt Jim was the hero of the evening. "Well, maybe she doesn't like the way the Communist countries have adopted capitalism," Bech suggested. "They've taken the gangsters and the exploitation of the masses and left out all the rest."

"Henry, darling"—the "darling" meant that she knew he wanted to fish up her tits; she too had imbibed a tricolor of wine—"only you think of Martina as a Communist. She left Czechoslovakia when she was a toddler."

"As the twig is bent," Bech said.

"Isaiah and I thought you two were perfect for

each other. Lately she has dropped to him one or two hints that we were wrong."

"Being perfect for each other is itself an imperfection, don't you think, in the murky sexual arena? I mean, sado-masochism has to have some room for exercise. How do you and Izzy handle perfection, may I ask?"

Pamela tapped him on the sternum, deftly mirroring his desire to touch her in the corresponding, but naked, spot. Perky shiksa tits, without that sallow Jewish heaviness, that nagging memory of one's mother's. Pam's apple cheeks glowed; her teeth, small and round and tilted inwards like a baby's, were exposed by a flirtatious laugh back to the molars, which lacked a single metal filling. Had they been crowned? What is natural and what is not? With rich women one never knows. Were Pamela's eyes so wide-open because he was fascinatingly provocative, or because she had had lid surgery? He peered at the delicate skin beneath her arched brows, looking for tiny scars. "We share interests," she told him. "And we adore the children we've had by other marriages."

"Ah, children," Bech said, numbed by his memory of the three children of Bea Latchett's with whom he had for a time shared a Westchester County domicile—three little quick stabs, followed by a throb of loss. Ann and Judy, the twins, had married away from the East Coast, but Donald, their little brother, lived in New York, as a fashion photographer's assistant. Once a year he and his former stepfather had lunch. Donald was—to judge by his tight but tinted haircut and right-eared earring and failure ever to mention a girlfriend— gay, but Bech never inquired. If the boy had been warped, Bech blamed himself; when he and Bea had split up, Donald had been ten, and heartbreakingly willing to love them both.

"And on the rare occasions when we don't agree," Pamela was explaining, "we know how to fight healthily."

"Yes, I can see health written all over you. But sedentary old Izzy? Pamela, tell me"—he touched her bare arm, just under the freckled ball of her shoulder, a compromise—"don't you find him sometimes terribly, how can I say this, oppressive?"

Her face stiffened, intensifying Bech's suspicions of plastic surgery. She said, "Isaiah is the most sensitive and quick-witted man I have ever met. Don't be jealous, Henry. You have your own style. There's room enough in the world for both epic poets and writers of haiku."

"Is that what I write? Haiku? Even *Think Big*?"

Pamela, like many a woman before her, saw that it had been a mistake to get him on the subject of his writing: he took it too seriously, more seriously than sex or money. You cannot flirt with a writer about his books. She changed the subject: without even a shift of those wide-open eyes of hers, she grabbed a bulky man passing by in a double-breasted blue blazer. "Henry, I don't think you met my brother when you were here before. Zeke loves your books. He says you write rings around my darling husband."

"He's just teasing you," Bech assured her, shaking the big puffy hand extended into his. Zeke Towers, Jr., had one of those practiced handshakes that don't quite come into your grip but somehow withhold the palm, giving you just the fingers. The family freckles covered his big face so thickly he looked diseased, or clad in a Tom Sawyer mask.

"The Travellers," young Zeke pronounced, his boyish face betraying a deep mnemonic effort. "It knocked me out, back when I was in college. It was assigned in two different courses."

"Travel Light, I think you must mean. About a motorcycle gang cruising from town to town in the Midwest, raping and pillaging."

The fascinating face, which, like a plate of *nouvelle cuisine,* was bigger than it needed to be to contain what was on it, lit up with relief. "Yeah, terrific—I'd never been hardly west of the Hudson, and here was all this sex and violence."

"All made up," Bech assured him.

"And then that other one, set in New York, with the scene where the television crew—"

"Think Big. I've always been kind of embarrassed about that book—it became a best-seller."

"And that was bad?" Zeke Jr. asked in genuine puzzlement. Bech gathered that the man's brother-in-law didn't talk this perverse way. For Izzy, worldly success was a legitimate goal.

"Pretty bad. And then it ruined my perfectly fine marriage. My wife's sister was so indignant I had written a best-seller and appeared in *People* that she seduced me and her sister kicked me out." He confessed all this partly to interest and offend Pamela; but she, as was her way, had ducked off, leaving him with the conversational companion of her choosing.

It was hard to tell with Wasp males how old they were; they don't stop being boys. Zeke Jr. must have been fifty or so, and he blinked as if he had never heard self-deprecating doubletalk before. "That sounds rough," he said. "Hey, listen, I bet you've been asked this before, but what I've always wondered about you writer types is, Where the hell do you get your ideas?"

More and more, as Bech went out to parties, he found himself being interviewed. It was a mode of conversation he disliked but had become adept in. "A good question," he said firmly, repeating it: "Mr. Bech, where do you get your ideas?" Having given himself a moment to think, he now answered: "Your ideas are the product, generally, of spite. There is somebody you want to get even with, or some rival you want to outdo. The fiction then is what the psychiatrists call a working out. Or is it an 'acting out'?"

"You'd have to ask Pam about that. Until she got linked up with Izzy, she was on the couch five days a week."

"But she's the picture of health now." Rosy cheeks, buoyant dappled breasts, seamless plastic surgery. Was Bech falling in love yet again?

"Izzy's done wonders for her, I can tell you. My dad died happy, seeing his daughter in good hands at last."

"He sounds like an easy man to make happy."

Zeke Jr. was again puzzled, but had already built puzzlement into his expectations of Bech, and was determined to be polite. Why? Uneasily the unprolific author wondered what charm he held for this financial buccaneer, this boyish wielder of air rights and metropolitan acreage. "My dad had been lucky in life," young Zeke said reverently, as if taking a frat pledge, "and nothing was too good for his family. He would have spoiled the hell out of us, if he hadn't also exemplified the work ethic."

Before such piety, Bech was almost silent. "*My* father," he confessed, "thought nothing could be too bad for us. He was a spoiler. He managed to die in the subway at rush hour."

"My dad came from Queens," said Zeke Jr., taking the high road. "He began with just a couple of vacant lots, and then in the Depression he'd assume the mortgages of bankrupt commercial property, stuff nobody else'd touch. He never looked back. Even into his eighties he was working ten, twelve hours a day. 'I love the hassle and the wrassle,' he'd say."

What was this kid—kid, he could be sixty, if you factor in the rejuvenating effects of gym workouts and winter visits to the Fountain of Youth— trying to sell him? Maybe an earnest, innocent selling manner had become his only style, just like Bech could only do prose haiku. He wasn't used to such friendly attention from men in such expensive blazers, with a silk handkerchief tumbling from the breast pocket like a paisley orchid. "Where do you get *your* ideas?" Bech asked him.

"Ideas?"

"For deals."

Zeke Jr.'s candid eyes narrowed; the skin beneath his eyes took on a crêpey pallor, a tinge of corruption. "Oh—they just develop. It's a team effort. Not like what you do—think up all this stuff out of nowhere. That to me is awesome."

Thank God, Izzy came up to them, bringing the fresh air of familiar rudeness. "Henry *is* awesome," he said. "Especially in the sack."

"Who says?" Bech asked.

"Rumor hath it," said Thornbush smugly. "Henry, you are talking here to one of your foremost fans. Though it galls me to admit it, my main distinction in this lad's eyes is having a claim to your acquaintance."

"Not just a claim. You've done the mining."

"And pure gold it was. Is." The tenacious Izzy grip had closed around Bech's upper arm, which became a kind of tiller in these choppy currents. Bech found himself being steered toward a wall where an ice bucket and a militant array of bottles were being tended by a slender young mime sporting a nostril-ring.

"A privilege and pleasure to meet you, Mr. Bech," his alleged admirer's voice called after them.

Izzy turned in stately, politic fashion. "Zeke," he said, "I'd invite you to join us for brandy and cigars but I know you never let yourself be contaminated. Your better half was making noises in the dining room about the long ride back to Greenwich."

"You really feel at home with a shaygets like that?" Bech had to ask when he and the other writer were alone in a corner—the only such corner— containing bookshelves. Bech vainly scanned them for one of his own books; he knew their spines better than his past mistress's faces. Pamela must keep them in her bedroom.

"Don't underrate the boy," Izzy assured him. "He may not look it, but he's a genius at what he does. New York real estate has been rocky lately, but young Zeke never gets caught holding the bag. *Very* impressive. He's as ruthless as his old man, and smoother. You can be glad old Zeke isn't here any more. A fucking monster—never got past eighth grade, and with every prejudice in the book. Came out of the South Jersey pine woods— Appalachia without the mountain air. He would have blocked the marriage if I hadn't told him I would rescue his daughter from Jewish shrinks. Takes a Jew to chase a Jew, I knew he'd think."

Izzy had lit up a cigar, a smuggled Havana, and Bech was holding the brandy. His third sip of the raw cognac put him in touch, via a knight's move of the consciousness, with the volatile essence of truth. "How would he have blocked it?" he asked.

"Disinherit," Izzy said.

"But surely," Bech protested, "you didn't marry Pamela for her money?"

"It was part of the picture. Just like her tits. Would you want to marry a woman if they sawed off her tits? Stick with her, sure—but take her on? Hey, what's with you and La O'Reilly?"

"She's souring on me. She ever talk to you about it?"

Under those prodigious eyebrows the old wizard's eyes veiled meretriciously. "She and I don't talk romance, just the word business. I was surprised you put such a move on her. You don't generally go for bluestocking, methodical types; you like destructive."

"Martina has her sweet destructive side," Bech said. He must not finish this brandy, he vowed to himself.

"I think she's jealous of Edna," Thornbush volunteered.

"Edna? Dear little birdy, virginal Edna?" Yet the very name had conjured up the chaste inner spaces of the Forty's mansion, and the distinguished dim visages over whom he now and then presided as if over a congress of the ghosts of the dignity, the integrity, the saintly devotion that had once attached to the concept of the arts in the American republic. Edna had as pure a profile as Miss Liberty on the old dime.

"She says you talk about her. You talk about the Forty all too tenderly, in Martina's view. She thinks you've gone establishment. I tell her, 'Not Bech. He's the last of the desperadoes. *Dérèglement de tous les sens,* that's his motto.'"

"Well, thanks. I guess. You and Martina have these intimate consultations about me often?"

"No, just at lunch the other day. We had business. Aesop is bringing out a collection of my out-of-print essays, including a bunch I did for *Displeasure.* Remember *Displeasure?*"

"How could I forget?" For all his egregious faults, Izzy had what few people left in the world had: he remembered *Displeasure.* Its crammed second-floor offices in Chelsea, its ragged right margins, its titles in lower-case sans. The black-haired internes from the Village, girlfriends of associate editors, who helped out, their triangular brows furrowed by the search for typos, which tended to multiply when corrected.

"Old Fritzi Egle in his bedroom slippers," Izzy was saying, "with that funny sweet smell around his head all the time. We were so frigging innocent we didn't know he was sucking opium. We thought it was his hair tonic."

"How big is the collection?" Bech was jealous.

The Vellum Press had let his miscellany *When the Saints* go out of print, and his second novel, *Brother Pig,* existed only in quality paperback, available, maybe, at college bookstores. He used to see himself on drugstore racks and in airports, but no more. If he wasn't assigned in a college seminar on post-war anti-realism, he wasn't read.

"Too big," Thornbush allowed with mock modesty. "Over a thousand pages, unless they cheat me on the leading. These young editors keep asking for this and that favorite they remember, and Aesop doesn't want to leave any real gem out."

"Heaven forbid," Bech said, and decided to see the brandy through after all. He swirled the dark-amber residue in the bottom of the snifter and dizzily reflected that no doubt there were strict laws, known to mathematicians and specialists in the study of chaos, to describe exactly its elliptical gyrations. Then he tossed it down. It burned, lower and lower in his esophageal tract. "Listen, Izzy," he said. "You got me into being president of the Forty, it's not something I was dying to do. Now you're acting like there's something dirty about it. At the fall meeting, when MacDeane began to talk about what sounded like dissolution, you egged it on: you proposed that moratorium on new members that just about would have scotched the whole institution. Who of us is going to be around in the year 2000? Edna was horrified. So was I."

"I was saving the situation," Izzy suavely said. "Those goons from music were out for blood."

"Yeah, why?"

"You heard them. They don't like the electronic crowd that might get elected. Seidensticker doesn't like representational revisionism. MacDeane hates the revisionist historians that make us the bad guys in the late Cold War. Also, he's out of the Washington power loop and it hurts."

"So, kill the whole thing. The whole idea of the Forty, never mind what Forty. Is that what the arts in America have come to? Is that what Lucinda Baines laid down her fortune for? A lot of people died, taking Baines' Powders, so the Forty could exist."

Izzy with his clownish side-wings of snowy hair was playing an imaginary violin, so convincingly that his jaw sprouted multiple chins. Bech could see the strings, hear the vibrato. "You're breaking my heart," Izzy said. "Anyway, my motion saved the situation. Glad I could help out. You can thank me later."

"If that was help, I'll take opposition. Hey," Bech said, "I got to go. Martina's making motions of her own." She was, as over a year ago, moving about in her loden coat, preparing to leave without him.

Izzy was enjoying the conversation. "It's like prizes and prize committees," he said. "Do *you* want to be a literary judge? Reading all that crap, and then getting no thanks?"

"No," Bech admitted. "I always duck it."

"Me, too. So who accepts? Midgets. So who do they choose for the prize? Another midget."

There was an analogy there, but Bech felt he was missing it. He knew that Thornbush hadn't won a prize since a Critics Circle for the *LB-Bull* in 1971. Sour grapes, the champagne of the intelligentsia. Martina had put on that shapeless green coat over her gray wool dress and as she bent forward to give Pamela an unsmiling kiss, a peck on each cheek European-style, she seemed to brandified Bech a schoolgirl refugee from those pre-war public-school classrooms where he had sat learning the rudiments of history, biology, and mathematics. P.S. 87, a bleak brick building at 77th and Amsterdam, had been staffed in that laggard time mostly by unmarried Christian women who, hindsight told him, were very young. Girls, really. They had seemed enormously tall and mature and wise. They had taught him to read, and that had been the making and unmaking of him. "I feel like my feet are stuck in buckets of brandy," he told Izzy, trying to break free of the other writer's powerful gravitational field.

But Martina moved across his field of vision, green, a bit of Birnam wood removing to Dunsinane. *I say, a moving grove,* the messenger told Macbeth. The power of sexual attraction snapped Bech loose from Izzy's spell; he sailed across the room and came up against Martina with a bump. "What are you doing?" he asked.

"Going."

"Without me?"

"Why not? You've ignored me all night."

"I didn't want to cramp your style."

"I have no style, Henry. I'm just a lowly copy-editor, correcting other people's styles and getting small thanks."

Small thanks seemed to be a theme of the evening. "That's not true. You have tons of style. You're Colette in a loden coat. Listen, you. We may not have come together, but we go together. That's how we do it." His stomach sagged and burned beneath the brandy-soaked possibility of losing this fragrant, solid, slightly un-American woman. He was bad at the business of life, which is letting go. In the elevator he pleaded, "Come back to the loft. We got to work on our relationship."

"Ha," Martina said. "Relating to you is like wallpapering an igloo."

"That bad?" The phrase didn't sound like her; it was too good, too intricate, too Thornbushian.

Martina went on, "I saw you with our hostess, trying to crawl down the front of her dress. She's all show, Henry, I tell you this as a friend. All show and no performance. Like any rich bitch. She fucks badly."

"How do you know that? Let me guess. The husband. Holy Isaiah, with his suction-cup mouth. At age seventy-one, he wants performance?"

The plunging elevator hiccuped to its stop, and they put on straight faces for the doorman, who warned them, in his jolly Russian-refugee accent, that it was cold outside—calder than vitch's teet.

When Bech lived up on West 99th Street, he would feel, heading across West End Avenue toward Riverside Drive and the Hudson, safe at last; now he felt that way when the taxi crossed Houston's rushing car-stream. The industrial streets reflected scattered wan lights on their old paving-stones; the incidence of habitation here reverted to prehistoric times, when man was outnumbered by lions and timber wolves, and his lonely fires flickered at the backs of caves halfway up iron-stained cliffs. Bech's second-floor (third, counting the ground floor) loft lay in the rickety block between Prince and Spring. His neighbors were, below him, a struggling gallery of Sahel art and crafts, and, above him, a morose little sweatshop where a pack of Filipinos wove and bent baskets, rope sandals, floor mats, and rattan animals. At night his nearest active neighbor was a jazz club at the back of a building up the block; its weakly applauded riffs and cymbal-punctuated climaxes filtered through his walls. Bech, a bit sickened by the cognac and the sweet smell of Izzy Thornbush's sell-out to the rich, poured himself a cleansing Pellegrino, but Martina decided to stick with white wine. She found some recorked Chardonnay in the back of his refrigerator. "Henry," she said, settling into the exact center of the little sofa opposite his beanbag chair, so that there was no space for an amorous drunk on either side of her, "I don't intend to quarrel or make love. We've done both for all they're worth."

"Done and done? Isn't there a recurrent need? Pamela thought you seemed distracted and sour lately."

"Oh, Pamela. Those wide-open little-girl eyes. Unlike her, I have more in life than to play. All my books at work are problem books. A lot of necessary revision, fighting prima-donna authors, and not much payoff on the bottom line likely."

He thought of sawing away at an imaginary violin, but instead asked, "What do you and Izzy talk about all the time? He said you're bringing out a collection of all the essays he's ever written. That's some load."

"Some of them are quite amazing," she said, tucking her stocking feet up under her solid haunches on the old leather sofa that Bea in Ossining had covered in nubbly almond-colored wool before she sent both Bech and the sofa back to New York and desolation. Strange, but, thinking of fabrics, Bech perceived that Martina had managed to find in the United States pantyhose of the less-than-fine, gray-brown knit that Communist women used to wear. "Such intellectual curiosity!" she was going on, of the deplorable Thornbush's written effusions. "There was nothing he wouldn't tackle—chess, the international meaning of Ping-Pong, Adlai Stevenson as Hamlet versus

Eisenhower's Fortinbras, these Persian and Chinese and Ethiopian novelists nobody else has heard of or read—"

"Wonderful, wonderful. The walking brain, later to be known as Mr. Potato-Head. What did you mean when you told him at lunch that you thought I was going establishment?"

Her face—the deepset eyes, the unplucked brows, the lipstickless lips—was startled by the betrayal. A clarinet swooped up an octave in the jazz club many walls away, then slippingly descended the scale via flats and sharps. "I didn't say it exactly like that. I'm surprised he told you."

"That's how Izzy is. A communicator. If you thought you and he had any secrets, forget it."

The restless, slightly guilty way she adjusted her stocking feet under her haunch's warm weight was driving him tenderly wild. "What I may have said was that ever since you became president of the Forty you've been acting a little different. Not self-important, exactly, but . . . more declarative. Dictatorial, even. When you come back from meeting all afternoon privately with Edna you're quite impossible—I don't think you're aware of it."

"Well, yes, I dictate. I've never had the use, before, of a secretary, to take down my words and type them all up on cream-colored stationery. For the first time I see what all these men with power are clinging to."

"And you've never had a professional harem before, possibly," she said, working on it with him therapeutically. "They all grovel, Edna and her help. You're the catch, the living immortal."

"Author of prose haiku," he said. It still rankled.

"What do you care what a flutterbrain like Pamela Thornbush says? How greedy you are, Henry, to have every woman in the world on her knees in front of you."

The image was pure blue movie. Now the drummer, his brushes and high-hat cymbals tingling, had launched a solo, coaxing a spatter of applause from the desultory little crowd. "Flutterbrain," he said. "Is that a word you made up, or what the smart young people now are all saying?"

"You know what I meant. Birdbrain. Don't deflect. I think it's sad, that an absolutely meaningless organization like the Forty, just because it has some endowment to play with and the staff flatters you, would take up any of your time and energy. In the days when you had integrity, you would have sneered at it. It is decadent capitalism at its most insidious."

"Don't you mean triumphant, not decadent? Read the papers."

"It's just not *real,*" Martina said. "A bunch of mostly New York City has-beens electing each other. It's worse than the Writers' Unions—at least they had a kind of policing function. They could reward and punish."

"What do you want me to do, get it to dissolve?"

"Yes." The simple syllable was paired with a distant collapse of multiple instruments into the climactic, finalizing set of chords. "It's pointless," she said, "and an insult to young artists. The only positive thing it does is make work for Edna and her sleek little lackeys."

How did she know the assistants were sleek? Their brushed hair, their respectful smiles, their little golden granny glasses. As in some ceiling vision by Tiepolo they ministered, bare legs dangling, to the arc of befuddled old faces, shiningly clean from their lifelong bath in the higher verities. "Imagine the Forty," he told Martina, "as a Festschrift all year long."

"That was my job. I thought you were stupid, contributing to it, by the way. I thought it was beneath you. And your irony didn't save it."

"Then why was your letter so seductive?"

She took her feet out from under her haunch and sat up as if to go somewhere. "Was it?"

"I thought so."

"My pantyhose feel hot."

"They look heavy. You should break down and buy the finer-gauge."

"Those run," she told him, pushing her pelvis toward the loft ceiling to hook her thumbs around the pantyhose's waistband.

"You've said," he pointed out, "unforgivable things to me."

Her voice was milder, though she still didn't smile. "Just that you're silly to be seduced by something like the Forty. You scorn Izzy and his rich wife, but you're knocked silly by this dead woman's money, what was her name, Lucinda Baines?" In stripping off her pantyhose she had flashed old-fashioned plain white non-bikini underpants; the old-fashionedness hit Bech hard, hurtling him back to boyhood glimpses of underpants at P.S. 87. Did his memory betray him, or did wisps of pubic fuzz peek out of the loose leg-holes, the elastic limp in the Depression?

"You should see the house Lucinda gave us," he boasted. "So lovely—no two mantelpieces alike, and a solarium that's like a high oval birdcage. We meet in there. The president's desk has bowed-out sides like a Spanish galleon, and upstairs, there is this terrific library with carved animal heads, lions alternating with lambs, full of everybody's books, which nobody reads."

She was stuffing her pantyhose into her purse and perching forward on the sofa to leave. "I'm sorry," she said, "I just cannot sleep with a man who takes a birdcage or dollhouse or whatever like that so seriously. Who would care about becoming a member except midgets?"

"Midgets," he said. "There's a word I've heard already tonight. According to Izzy, we're all midgets, except him."

"Not you, Henry." She seemed sincere, her serious eyes, darkened by the lateness of the hour, boring into his. "You can do magical things Izzy can't. You can make characters breathe and walk on their own. His, he has to move them around himself; all their energy is his."

"Really?" he said. Was it he or the brandy blushing? He was deeply gratified. Farther along in the drab recesses of Crosby Street, the jazz group took up another set, with a tenor sax laying out the tune—"April in Paris"—in halting, introspective phrases. "You believe that?"

She stood loomingly above him, the little fuzzy pills of wear on her gray skirt a more appealing texture to him than the most shimmering watered silk: the drab texture of virtue. "Everybody knows it," she said, and he could hear her voice resonate in her belly. He leaned his face, his ear against that flat belly. It was warm through the worn wool. Skin and hair were within kissing distance.

"You're right," he said. "The Forty is a farce. It just seems to me a harmless farce."

"Nothing is harmless," said Martina sternly, "if it takes up space. Mental and spiritual space. You must get it out of your mind."

"I will. It is. Out." He struggled up from the clammy grip of the beanbag chair to wrap his arms around her thickest part, the haunch and rump whose muscle and fat were braced by the flaring pelvis. He thought of all her layers, bones out to clothes, and foresaw a profound satisfaction in removing just the outermost ones. They hadn't made love for weeks, because of this edgy political tension always between them. "Do stay tonight," Bech begged, hoarsely. "I'll swear off presiding forever." Did he imagine it, or was the scent of musk pressing through the wool lap of the skirt, along the horizontal seam where, if Martina were a mermaid, her fishy half would begin?

"You can preside," Martina said. She made an impatient motion within his arms, of wanting to be free. "Just don't be so proud of it. It makes you absurd, like some poltroon."

"Now there's a word you must have got from one of your prima-donna authors," he said, sinking back into the beanbag. He was tired, but he just had to relax and it would all happen, as water flows downhill; already she was out of her jacket and undoing the little pearly buttons of her blouse. *Chestnuts in blossom,* the saxophone was repeating. "Do you really think I'm a better writer than Izzy?"

"Better *writer,*" Martina said, shedding her clothes and slowly filling the loft with her scents, as apples rotting in the long wet grass perfume an entire orchard. "He's the better *thinker.* Most of the time, Henry dearest"—she was drawing closer—"you don't seem to be thinking at all."

The spring meeting of the Forty, though the day turned out to be a rainy one, attained an all-time high: twenty-three members were in attendance. The buzz was up; the white-haired old heads bobbed one toward another as the rain drummed on the panes of the solarium, arching above their heads in a high half-shell. Over the winter, the stately MacDeane had died and also, her avidly flirtatious heart unexpectedly giving out after one last poetry reading at the 92nd Street "Y," Amy Speer deLessups. Bech would miss them both. He had read them when young; they took with them some of the glamour of the post-war years, when the New York School was eclipsing Paris, and at any minute the new *Farewell to Arms* would appear, and it seemed everything would pick up and go on as it had before the war, only better, without the poverty and racial cruelty. You ate lunch in drugstores, and books cost two dollars, and college students wore neckties, and typewriters were the most advanced word processors there were. Amy had been smart and slender and wore big straw hats and slept with Delmore Schwartz and Philip Rahv in rumored conjunctions as exalted and cloudily chaste as the copulations of the Olympian gods. She was gone now, with Schwartz and Rahv and Wilson and Trilling and all those other guardians of Bech's youthful aspirations.

When the rudimentary business of announcements and minutes was over with, the shapely brown hand of Jason Marr was lifted for recognition. Bech imagined he would be commenting on the unprecedented number of African-American candidates brought forth into nomination. But no, it was on a graver, more general matter that Marr spoke. "Mr. President," he said, in his rich slow voice reminiscent of the pulpit, "as we discovered at our last meeting, there is an element within this institution that for unfathomable reasons of their own wishes to see it dissolved. I would like to give expression to my righteous horror at this development. Since I was a boy on the mean streets well north of here, I had heard of the Forty; the streets were not so mean, nor was our ignorance so complete, that word was denied to the least of us that somewhere on this rocky island the pinnacle of artistic accomplishment could be located—as it turned out, in the very building where I am now privileged, unto my everlasting wonder and gratitude, to sit. I have often heard the other members complain that this institution serves no distinct purpose, save that of self-glorification. But of how many institutions can it be said that, even if their distinct good deeds do not make a legion of headlines, they do symbolize in their very being something eternal and unquestionably to be valued? Are love and respect for the arts so dead—are we so far gone in electronic degradation and the lust for monetary profit—that we can seriously contemplate writing 'finis' to a dream born at the outset of this cruellest of centuries, in the heart of a refined lady of means, one Lucinda Baines, who dared hope to redeem her drug-peddling family's unsavory fortune by devoting a fraction of it to the establishment of a golden hill, a hill to be set before the eyes of the nation's young as a Mount Sinai, a Mount Olympus, a Mount Everest of the spirit existing to be climbed by them? Mr. President, I would welcome a comment from the chair, and an

endorsement or a refutation of these sentiments."
He sat down.

Bech's head spun a little; there was more going
on here than he knew. What did "the lust of monetary profit" have to do with it? He said cautiously,
"Mr. Marr, your sentiments endorse themselves, by
virtue of the eloquence of their expression. But
someone playing the devil's advocate could ask,
Might we not embody an idea whose time has
come and gone, with its distinct savor of elitism
and of outmoded establishment values? Values, I
need not tell you, established by a white male hier-
archy whose comfortable idealism rested on the
unconfessed exploitation of women, workers, and
people of color." Martina, he felt, would have especially liked the insertion of "workers" in the litany
of abused minorities.

Marr was on his feet indignantly. "Mr. President, I did not speak as a person of color. I spoke as
a person of sensibility, one elected to this body on
the strength of my work. If the content of my work
is rage, black rage, its form is timeless, of the ages.
As a poet I claim fellowship with Sappho, with
Whitman, with Shakespeare—yea, with Kipling
and Tennyson and the singers of the white empire
of their day. If the Forty is disbanded, I will be
denied one of the few venues in which I can
express that everlasting fellowship—I, and all my
brothers and sisters of color. We are set to climb the
golden hill; now some would take the golden hill
away!"

"But," Bech pointed out, "there is no motion to disband the Forty."

"I so move, Mr. President," a voice boomed from within the several rows of heads, shadowy beneath the thrumming rain. Bech recognized the voice of Isaiah Thornbush, its topping of English accent on a base of local gravel. There was a host of eager seconds.

"Would Mr. Thornbush," Bech asked, striving to keep a level head, "like to speak to the motion?"

"You've already nailed it, Henry," Izzy said with impudent coziness. "Elitist. Edwardian. Establishment. Extinct. You're either in the march of progress or you're obstructing it. This luxurious, idle, *honorary*"—scornfully emphasized and prolonged—"organization is an obstruction. It's cultural clutter, if I may coin a virtual anagram."

At Bech's elbow Edna's pencil was stabbing frantically on her yellow pad. *Charter by-laws don't provide for dissolution,* he made out. The spinning in his head had increased; he was feeling helicoptered high above the fray. The members' heads looked like eggs in a carton. His desk looked the size of a shoebox. "The directress," he stated to the meeting from on high, "informs me that the by-laws have no provision for dissolution."

"Laws are for men, not men for laws," one of the composers in the back row shouted.

Seidensticker in his vast abstract irritability announced, "Don't elect anybody, don't elect the crap artists, that's the way to end this boondoggle.

Bad as the NEA, supporting all this performance art, some woman shaving her cunt in public, smearing herself all over with chocolate pudding, all this so-called earth art, some big ditch bulldozed in the desert, who needs it? Photorealism— what a crock. Any fool with a Polaroid and an enlarger can do it! That's not drawing, it's *tracing!*"

Others, too, vented the injustices and slights endured in a lifetime of practicing the arts. Frauds, phonies, pedants, narcissists—that had been the competition, garnering prizes and acclaim. Izzy's orotund voice rolled through the hubbub: "Could the directress kindly answer a simple question: Who owns this building?"

Bech glanced aside at Edna; color was high in her cameo profile. A raspberry tinge had crept up, like a stain in litmus paper, to color her throat. The membership grew quiet. "The terms of the will," she said, her upper lip lifting in disdain at this invasion of institutional privacy, "are somewhat imprecise. The lawyer who drew it up was a close friend of Miss Baines who himself administered the trust until he died a good many years later; since then his Wall Street firm, Briggs, Parsons, and Traphagen, has acted as trust officers and overseen the financial details."

"But in trust," Izzy pressed, "for whom?"

"Well," Edna admitted, her throat slowly regaining its whiteness, her upper lip now stiffening as if frosted, "it would seem from the phrasing that Miss Baines was leaving it directly to the Forty, as the group would be constituted after her death. But this is a legal impossibility."

"I don't see why," Izzy said. He no longer had to raise his voice to be heard; such an alert silence had fallen over the solarium that the caterers could be heard downstairs setting up their bottles and slamming the stainless-steel doors of their steam cabinets. "The Forty owns the building, with the endowment for its upkeep, and if there were a dissolution, the proceeds would be divided among the forty members. Since—how many memberships are open now, Edna?"

"Nine, actually."

"Since nine are open, among a mere thirty-one. A pretty penny, I would estimate—way uptown in Lucinda's day, this lot has come to be prime midtown real estate. And let's not forget the pictures on our walls. Chase and Sloan ain't exactly chopped liver."

An excited furor ensued; Bech faced it, but with an irresistible sense of drifting away, of being disconnected. Halfway through his three-year term, he was tired of presiding. J. Edward Jamison spoke with quivering outrage of breaking with tradition; his gray smudge of a Brian Aherne–style mustache seesawed as he sneeringly mouthed his opinion of those who would sell their father's mansion for a mess of pottage; Jason Marr had set a convenient Biblical tone. Von Klappenemner, his bald head ridged like a quartz hatchet-head, stood

and enunciated thoughts upon group euthanasia
that had become, in his advanced dementia, totally
unintelligible, though all of his compellingly
graceful conductor's gestures remained. Lulu
Fleming said that in her opinion all of the little
nobility that was left in the United States was right
here in this room; disbanding would be an atrocity,
though since she was also an honorary member of
the Academia Brasileira de Letras and the Academia Venezolana it wouldn't really be the end of her
world.

The antis, the pros, they sounded alike—the
same stridency, the same ready recourse to the first
person singular, the same defensive encirclement
of imaginary prerogatives. Bech thought of Martina opening her bathrobe to release zephyrs of car-
nal odor, her face stern and unsmiling atop her
sturdy nudity, and everything else seemed vanity
and maya. His quiescence, his psychological
absence during the rhetorical storm, was slowly
sensed as an insult by the agitated members. Izzy
called, "Mr. President, I move the question."

"What is the question, Mr. Thornbush?"

"To be or not to be, that is the question.
Whether or not the Forty should disband, sell the
mansion, and divide the proceeds among the members as an encouragement to the living best in
American art."

"Second!" snorted Seidensticker.

The vote was eleven to disband, eleven to continue as before. Bech himself had not voted. All

eyes turned on him. Edna's were alarmed, above her suddenly hectic cheeks. She was pure nerves, and Bech had always vibrated in response to the nervousness of women, their iridescent aura of potential hysteria. Adrift, he tried to haul himself in and to dock at the distasteful and awkward matter at hand. "Well, you do wonder," he began, "if half of an organization is willing to sell itself out, what purpose there is in the other half denying them the pleasure. I would like to resign, and let my esteemed old friend and colleague Isaiah Thornbush come preside in my stead. He seems to be running things anyway, from the back bench."

Edna wrote on her pad, in handwriting that seemed to be tracing a cardiac seizure, "Can't be done. New elections necessary."

Bech regained a presidential timbre: "But since it can't, evidently, be done, I will stay in my chair and vote against the motion and propose that our able directress consult Briggs, Parsons, and Traphagen as to the financial and legal parameters of the case and give us a full report at the fall meeting."

Von Klappenemner's long waving arms were unignorable, and he was getting to his feet whether or not Bech recognized him. "Oh no you don't, Mr. sassy Presi-dent," he fluted in his demented but still musical voice. "Oh no you don't, you literary wiseacre. You're not cheating me out of my share of this mansion—we're talking millions, all my fellow composers have just assured me. Millions for everybody! I change my vote. I vote Yes, yes, let's for common decency's sake put ourselves out of our misery and disband. Die, everybody! This place has been on life supports for years. No intubation, no respirator, no plastic hearts, no liver and lung transplants. Let's all die! Die rich!!"

Bech asked Edna quietly, "Did he vote against it before?"

"I'm afraid he did, Henry."

"Ah," he announced, with an unconscionable relief. "Very well. With Mr. Von Klappenemner's change of vote, the motion then stands twelve to eleven for disbandment and liquidation and division of the spoils. On such a drastic decision, however, the entire membership must be notified and the matter put to a paper ballot. The lawyers must be consulted. The U.S. Congress should be consulted, since they granted us our charter in 1904. All this will take time. Now is the time, however, ladies and gentlemen, for us to go downstairs and drink and dine. *Carpe diem*, the night is coming." Still lacking a gavel, he rapped his knuckles several times on the resounding desk.

"Well said, Mr. President," Edna murmured as the jostling, thirsty, hungry shards of the dissolving organization filed out.

"But, Edna, it doesn't look good. Once word gets out that there's money to be had . . . "

She hooted: a brawling, what-the-hell noise emerged from her refined small face, a sort of a snort confessing that the two of them had been, as it were, in bed together. An aboriginal wilderness lurked in that hoot. Then her face snapped shut again, upon its own composure. A decisive fatigue veiled the chalk-blue eyes and pursed the chiselled lips. "I've been thinking of retirement, Henry. This has been a long haul, thirty-five years with the Forty. I came to Manhattan when I was twenty-two—graduate work at Columbia in anthropology of all things—and never intended to stay. You were born here, I believe; it doesn't sit on your chest the way it does on mine. For years, when I woke up, I felt I was caught in some enormous machine rattling all around me. Grace Paul took me on as an assistant when I was at loose ends and she was growing dotty, and the year to get out never quite came. I was well enough paid. I enjoyed the building; I liked as well as admired the members, and, the oddest thing, I think I fell in love with Lucinda Baines. You've seen the portraits and photographs of her that we have about the place; poor thing, she was terribly plain. I pitied her, fancying myself *not* plain, but, looking back on my life, I see that I might as well have been. I've led the life of a very plain woman. Anyway, love, don't mean to be bending your ear."

"Bend away. The sphinx speaks."

"You're a good sort. Most of you are. You all have to be self-centered, I realize that, if you're going to do anything worthwhile."

From downstairs arose the din of the members talking and wolfing down the free drinks and watercress sandwiches. The nearly deserted solarium was gathering the spring dusk in its high inverted bowl of leaded panes. Pollen and pale-green catkins tinted the gutters and car roofs, in the Manhattan spring, and the smell of tar underfoot intensified. *Pollen and catkins / tint gutters and car roofs green. / Underfoot, sweet tar.*

Edna touched a spot below one eye, and then looked at her fingertip to see if it were wet. "Sorry, old Henry. This is an emotional moment for me, evidently. My widowed sister has an enormous spread in the hills north of Adelaide. For years she's been wanting me to come and help her manage the vineyards. And the sheep." She brushed back a silken strand of white hair and returned to stroking the spot below her eye, as if she were awakening to simple sensation. "It will be a strange thing, after New York, being able to see the horizon. My memory of it is, there's a dreadful amount of horizon."

It has been said—meaning no derogation, of course—that Henry Bech writes American haiku. But, though some of his precious paragraphs, distilled molecule by molecule like dewdrops, give the studied impression of his having counted the syllables, I do not see Bech as belonging to the company of Bashō, Buson, and Issa. *Travel Light,* the novel with which he burst upon the mid-Fifties like a leather-jacketed biker into a party of gray suits, surely

finds its affinity in the tales of the raffish demi-
monde of the compassionate and uninhibited
Ihara Saikaku, and his next, *Brother Pig,* in the
grotesque fantasy of the splendid Ueda Aki-
nari. *The Chosen,* with its undercurrent of
moralism no less irresistible for its being saline
with sardonic irony, evokes yet another Tokugawa master, the copious yet high-minded Tak-
izawa Bakin, and *Think Big,* if not quite Bech's
Genji monogatari (to give the famous tale its
precise title), certainly contains scenes that, in
their easy warmth of stylization and elegant
candor, might not have embarrassed Lady
Murasaki. But it is to a poet far too little
known, Tachibana Akemi, who was born the
year when Napoleon was defeated and died the
year in which Ulysses Grant was elected President, that Bech has his closest affinities, so
powerful they are foreshadowed anagrammati-
cally. For it was, of course, Tachibana, along
with Ōkuma Kotomichi and the Buddhist
priest Ryōkan, who wrested the tanka—a form
two lines more capacious than the haiku—
away from court poets and wrought it into a
vehicle for describing not just the autumn
moon and cherry blossoms but the ineluctable
details of daily happenstance, including political developments and otherwise unheard rum-
blings within the sealed room of the Tokugawa
era. This is the Bech of inestimable value—he
who hustles toward us like a waiter laden with

not just the tureen of soup made from the tortoise upon whose back the universe legendarily rests but the meat, potatoes, and peas of quotidian fare, transformed into ambrosia by its painstaking cookery. If Bech had taken less pains, the shelf of his books would be thrice as long, but we might be but a third as grateful for his exquisite *yugen,* to use the Japanese term most easily translated "mystery and depth." Congratulations, indispensable Henry—seventy is but a number to conjure with, for those who still possess the conjuror's boyish spirit!

Thus read Isaiah Thornbush's cagey contribution to Henry Bech's Festschrift volume, which had been assembled, over Bech's objections, by the assistant to his editor, Jim Flaggerty. The assistant that Bech had first known, petite, black-haired Arlene Schoenberg, with the shadow of whose fine female hands on the photocopying machine he had briefly fallen in love, had long since moved on; her latest replacement, with the New Age name of Crystal, had done an adequate job assembling the volume, but the overall production values, not to mention the fervor of the tributes, fell considerably short, Bech felt, of what Thornbush had received two years earlier. The Festschrift party, instead of being held in a Park Avenue penthouse, was held in some back rooms of Michael's Pub. A pianist and bassist mutteringly played, but Woody Allen, though invited, had declined to sit in. Nor did Donald Trump come, though Pamela Thornbush had extracted from him and Marla what she had thought had been a promise.

Thornbush himself was trying to ease his bulk inconspicuously through the Bech-oriented crowd, but his reflective bald head, winged like a swan alighting on a pond, was hard to miss. Bech swiftly sidled over to him, knifing through a trio of Armani-clad agents. "Izzy, I didn't know you knew Japanese," he said.

"I don't. I consulted the *Britannica.* The '69 edition, the last solid one before they ruined it with that micro/macro crap. Pam had told me you seemed offended when she told you you wrote haiku."

"Am I that kind of sorehead? Have I ever even complained about the vile way you panned *Think Big* in *Commentary*? At the age of three score and ten, who should hold a grudge? Where *is* Pam? I'll give her a hug that'll make her tits squeak."

Izzy seemed a shade depressed. "She couldn't come—some Christian good cause her brother got her on the board of. Canned milk for starving Ethiopians—who knows? Zeke Jr. turns out to be a kind of holy Joe. She said she'd hope to drop by but these do-gooder meetings go on forever."

"No Pam, huh? Well, how about Martina?"

Thornbush looked distinctly frayed. There were yellow bags under his eyes, and beneath his

outspread wings of hair his ears were red as stoplights. *Eyes with yellow bags. / Beneath wings of
hair outspread, / ears red as stoplights.*

"Haven't you heard?" he asked Bech. "She's
left Aesop to help get out the bimonthly newsletter
of a conservative Washington think tank. They
offered her more money than she'd known existed
and a crack at the editorship in two years, if she
learns to sing their neocon tune. This with my
mega-collection of criticism and opinion pieces still
up in the air. I kidded her about becoming an apolo-
gist for capitalism but she got very solemn, the way
she can, and said, 'What else is there left to believe
in?' But you must have heard all this from her."

"No. As *you* must have heard, we broke up
when the Forty began to come apart. I know I
shouldn't have blamed her, but I did. I saw her as a
temptress. It got worked around in my mind that
Edna stood for everything noble and she'd been
raped. That made Martina the rapist. And you, of
course."

"Me? *Me*? I was the least of it. It was the composers and artists, they can't stand anybody's shit
but their own. I could have swung either way. The
Forty was a fun place to go now and then, but,
frankly, Edna always struck me as a bit out of her
depth. How's she doing, have you heard?"

"She dropped me a postcard. She says the
sheep seem pretty sensible, after all those years
with us."

The ballot by mail in the summer past had

totalled up five against, six not voting, and twenty for disbandment and dispersement of the realized assets. The Baines heirs—a flock of distant cousins resident in Indiana and Oklahoma—had filed motions contesting the interpretation of Lucinda's will, demanding that all the proceeds not consumed by lawyers' fees be distributed to living Baineses. It would be years, if ever, before the matter was legally settled. The fall meeting consisted of Bech announcing these developments and that a specially struck gold-alloy medal was being awarded to Edna for her decades of service. At dinner there were spontaneous toasts and even some singing; several members said it was the best dinner for ages and they certainly looked forward to next year's. They didn't understand that there would be no next year's. Bech had served for only two of the three years of a president's usual term. He was the end of a list of which Clarence Edmund Stedman, hand-picked by the dying Lucinda, was the first. The mansion had already found a buyer, for something in eight figures. The lawyers on all sides had agreed to let the sale go through, rather than have the upkeep whittle at the endowment.

Izzy asked him, "How do you like *Summa Saeculorum* for a title?"

"For what?"

"For my book, you *farmishter.* See, it's my summing up, and *saeculum* means an age, our age, as well as world, worldly, you know, as opposed to *theologica.*"

"You and Aquinas, together again. You don't think it's a little, how can I say, grandiose?"

"Thus speaketh the old haikumeister. But listen, seriously"—here was that grip on the tender part of the arm again—"you did a great job with the Forty. A number of us saw the demise coming, and you gave it dignity; I figured you would. Edna agreed."

"She saw it coming too?"

"Maybe not consciously, but in her gut. You know women. Hey, who's this little mother's joy?"

A girl in a very short silver dress, with platinum hair a nappy half-inch long covering her beautifully ovoid skull, had appeared at Bech's side. "Izzy," he said, "I'd like you meet Crystal Medford, Jim Flaggerty's assistant over at Vellum and the editor and organizer of my Festchrift volume. It offended my modesty, but nothing I said could dissuade her from her salaried duty."

"Crystal," Izzy repeated. "Of course. *Adored* your letter; you got me to do something I swore I never would—heap more praise on this bastard's swelled head. So your mother called you Crystal. I bet it came to her in a vision."

"My parents told me it was my dad's idea," said the assistant editor politely, her little hand lost and evidently forgotten within the old maze-maker's heavy grip. "He's the one more into extra dimensions."

"Yes, those extra ones. Still with us, is he, your dad? On our earthly plane?"

"Oh yeah, he's doing real well. He makes these special birdhouses in Vermont. They're like apartment buildings, for the purple martins, to put out in the marshes and on golf courses."

"Enchanting," Izzy said, and Bech could feel his old rival's creative gears turn a worn cog or two—apartment building, birds, a city of such cages, a mock epic satirizing modern society, feather by feather. A muscle in Bech's jaw ached from suppressing an anticipatory yawn.

"Crystal has both feet on the ground," he said protectively.

"Not, I hope, every single hour of the day," Izzy said with roguish gallantry, releasing her hand from his enveloping grip as if slowly disclosing a humid secret.

Crystal gazed at her creased palm and told Bech nervously, "Mr. Flaggerty says there are some German book-club people here he'd like you to meet." As they threaded their way toward these sacred guests, Bech tried to comfort her; her hand was bright pink from the prolonged pressure. "That's America's most portentous writer," he said. "Didn't they assign you some Thornbush in college?"

"Something about Nixon," she said. "Or was that Philip Roth? I didn't get very far in it. Is Nixon the President who kept hitting people with golf balls?"

"Try Izzy when you're older. He's what is called professionally *un sacré monstre. Guten*

Abend, meinen Herren," he smoothly continued,
they having arrived at the smiling Germans, who
spoke English so beautifully that it seemed to Bech
that a polished metal language-machine hung in
front of their faces.

With the help of two old-fashioneds and a frequently refilled wineglass, he felt the party as an
enormous success, a spontaneous outpouring of
love for his person and of respect for his slim but
agile oeuvre. Even those who were not here were
here: his mother, dead a generation ago but her
faith in him still a live goad, and Norma Latchett,
his mistress and fruitful irritant for many years, and
Bea Latchett, his wife and mollescent muse for,
alas, too brief a period, and all the women he had
burningly coveted and (a much smaller number)
fleetingly possessed, and, having joined the piano
and the bass, Woody Allen himself, hitting one
high note after another on the old licorice stick, as
we used to call it. In his imagination Bech presided
over this gathering—*Dieser ist mein Endfest,* he
had told the Germans, to their puzzled, civil guf-
faws—with superhuman energy and charm, glid-
ing from one conversational knot to another,
intruding the deft words which let each guest know
that his or her presence was especially meaningful.
Each brought to him, as the worms brought
Badroulbadour up from her tomb in the Wallace
Stevens poem, a piece of himself, from his scamp-
ish boyhood on the Upper West Side to his heady
days as a negotiable item of American cultural

exchange abroad. Skip Reynolds was there, now retired from the State Department and the president of a bankrupt Long Island college, and Angus Desmouches, the ubiquitous fashion photographer, whose wide head of wiry black hair had turned as white as coal in a negative, and Lucy Ebright, who had put Bech into one of her innumerable novels but unrecognizably to himself, and Tad Greenbaum, the six-foot-four, highly personable hero of *Think Big,* Bech's lone best-seller. Even Pamela Thornbush showed up, as she had promised but Bech had not dared hope, on the arm of her boyish brother, Zeke Towers, Jr.

Bech hugged Pamela but her breasts did not squeak. Her cheek under his kiss was like an upstate apple, cool and smooth from the refrigerator truck. "Has Izzy been misbehaving?" she murmured breathlessly, flirtatiously into his ear.

"Sugar, when isn't he?" He loved that in himself, how smoothly corrupt he could sound.

"Who's the girl in the silver dress he's got cornered?"

"Her name is Crystal, but relax. He's cruising not for nooky but for some gullible slave to edit the biggest book since the dictionary. *Summa Summorum.* Why don't you tell him to think small for a change? It would be good for his cardiovascular system."

"Henry, please—you're manicky. My brother has something serious he wants to say to you."

Young Zeke looked Bech straight in the eyes,

lovingly, and said, "Mr. Bech, I really want to thank you for all you did to help make the Baines property available."

"The Baines property? Oh. I didn't do a thing, did I?"

"Don't you go denying it, sir. My brother-in-law says you're the only one who could have swung it, with the requisite sensitivity and tact. We've been needing that piece for five years, to complete our parcel. Now we have the whole half-block and if the city goes along we'll be putting up a building ten feet taller than Citicorp."

"Ten feet?" Bech felt as if his two feet had been dragged down from twinkling like Tinker Bell's through his party and abruptly planted on the soggy soil where real things rest.

"That's not counting the flagpole and airplane-warning lights. The Towers Building—the dream of my dad's lifetime. We'll have our own tunnel into both the 53rd Street station on the Queens line and the 51st Street on the Lex. Some day, when they renovate, we might even get the name of a station. As you pull in you'll see towers spelled out in tiles on the wall."

Pamela broke in, adding, "We're all so thrilled and grateful, Henry." Her blue eyes were bright as amethysts; the freckles exposed on her bosom danced; her round cheeks flamed. Money does that, he thought—promotes health and strong family feeling.

"We're going to express our appreciation some way, you can count on that," Zeke assured the septuagenarian author. Bech winced under the glare of that frat-boy sincerity, that dazzling Wasp blankness which comes of never having been persecuted and scorned.

"I don't deserve a thing, honest Injun," Bech protested, at the same time wondering, with a tingle that numbed him from head to toe, what this expression of plutocratic appreciation might consist of. A Mercedes? A cottage in the Hamptons? *After a lifetime / of dwelling among fine shades / a payoff at last.*

Bech Pleads Guilty

Now, AND ONLY NOW, can it be told. Until recently, possible legal ramifications have laid a seal of silence on the three weeks that Bech once spent in Los Angeles, being sued for libel. The year was 1972. Vietnam was winding down, and the seeds of Watergate were nestled warm within Nixon's paranoia. Bech was a mere forty-nine, wallowing in the long trough between the publication, in 1963, of his rather disappointingly received chef d'oeuvre, *The Chosen,* and, sixteen years later, the triumphantly sleazy best-seller *Think Big.* He lived in dowdy bachelor solitude in his apartment at West 99th Street and Riverside, and, though continuing royalties from his 1955 semi-Beat near-classic *Travel Light* dribbled in, along with other odd sums, his need for money was acute enough to drive him out into the sunlit agora of a wider America: he went around impersonating himself at colleges and occasionally accepted a magazine assignment, if it seemed eccentric enough to be turned, by a little extra willful spin, into art. Art—

as understood in the era of his boyhood, which extended through the Depression and World War II, in which he boyishly fought—was his god, his guiding star.

When a new New York biweekly called *Flying Fur,* in hopeful echo of *Rolling Stone,* asked him to write an "impressionistic sort of piece" on the new, post-studio Hollywood, he consented, imagining that he would be visiting the site of the black-and-white melodramas that had entranced his adolescence. Alas, he found instead a world in full and awful color, like reels of fermenting, bleached Kodachrome stock—cans and cans of worms, of agents and manipulators voraciously trying, in the absence of the autocratic old studios, to assemble blockbuster-potential "packages" within the chaotic primal soup of underemployed actors, directors, stuntmen, and all such other loose hands once kept busy within the film industry when its assembly lines moved and television hadn't yet kidnapped its mass audience. Bech had described what he saw and felt, and got sued for his trouble. Admirer of Hollywood melodrama though he had been, he couldn't believe it. "You mean I actually have to go out there again, to sit in a courtroom and be sued for just writing the truth?"

"What is truth?" his New York lawyer asked over the phone, each syllable ticking into the meter running at, in those days, $110 an hour.

Bech had been paid $1,250 for the article, plus the expenses of his week on the West Coast doing research. In the two years since it had appeared, *Flying Fur* had gone belly-up. Its editors and lay-out artists had dispersed to other frontiers, and its old offices on East 17th Street—canary-yellow walls hung with Pop Art prints—were given over to a team of young tooth-implant specialists. This lawsuit, however, survived, an unkillable zombie stalking its prey through the mists.

"You'll love our West Coast team," the lawyer said, mollifyingly. "Tom Rantoul may not look it, Henry, but he is a legal wizard. I don't know when he last lost a case; my memory doesn't go back that far."

Rantoul proved to be a huge and hearty former athlete of Southern background, with an inward slope to the back of his head and meaty though manicured hands. At a lawyer-client luncheon on Bech's fourth day in Los Angeles, Rantoul announced, "Well, lady and gents, it looks like we done finally got ourselves a judge." He gestured with one of those manicured hands toward the browned filet of sole on the defendant's plate. "He's about the color of that there fish."

Bech hesitated with his fork, then stabbed and parted the white meat. Racial issues did not seem, offhand, to be at stake. He was being sued because he called the plaintiff, a venerable Hollywood agent named Morris Ohrbach, an "arch-gouger" who for "greedy reasons of his own rake-off" had "widened the prevailing tragic rift between the literary and cinematic arts." He knew the phrases by heart, since they had been the subject of fitful and increasingly dire communications ever since his article had appeared, under the title (supplied by a vanished sub-editor) "The Only Winners Left in Tinseltown." Ohrbach was claiming that he had suffered five million dollars in personal distress and humiliation, and another five million in loss of professional credibility. In the course of Bech's week, two years ago, of bilious-making lunches and pay-phone calls and hot waits in the nightmarishly constant California sun, Ohrbach's name had repeatedly surfaced, with a spume of that mingled outrage and admiration with which the carnivores of the film world hail an especially spectacular predator. It was Ohrbach who had invented the 15-percent agent's fee, with a non-returnable down payment by the client; it was Ohrbach who had devised a discretionary clause whereby, above the 15 percent, up to half of the client's earnings was to be invested at the agent's discretion, with a 3-percent investment commission withdrawn semi-annually from the capital. It was related to Bech how, having bled the great pop singer Lanna Jerome and her gullible husband at the time (a former pet hairdresser, famous for his poodle cuts) of millions of her earnings, Ohrbach demanded a half-million more to prop up the teetering edifice of porkbelly options and dry oil wells he had constructed, and promptly sued her when she and her new husband (a former disco bouncer) at last moved to stop the bleeding. Ohrbach was lightning-quick to sue. He would even, as a scorpion when aroused will supposedly sting itself, sue his own lawyers, if he felt a suit had been inadequately prosecuted.

As to Bech, he had a soft spot for Lanna Jerome. He and Claire Hoagland, a skittish blond love object he had romanced when his heart was relatively young and uncallused, had met to the background music of Lanna's first hit, "Comin' On Strong," and had separated, four years later, while the singer's "Don't Send Me Back My Letters" ("Keep them in their envelopes / Holding my forsaken hopes") dominated the airwaves. This soft spot of Bech's, painfully touched by the tales of Ohrbach's predatory inroads into Lanna Jerome's sentimentally generated fortune, may have been what landed him here, in the iron grip of lawyers. Even when he wrote the word, "arch-gouger" seemed a touch extreme, with a bit of extra, artistic spin. But hardly, he thought, actionable. A creeping sense of unreality enveloped him as, bit by bit, the certified letters on legal stationery piled up, and a lawyer of his own had to be obtained, and depositions were taken in an awkward atmosphere blended of jollity and menace, and various forestalling actions and moves for dismissal from his side were consumed in an inexorable munching process on the other side. Finally the legalities required Bech to make another continent-spanning visit to Los Angeles, the capital of organized unreality. The law was at home here, with its slow motion and spurious courtesy—a world of pretend where amid the plaster pillars and masked trapdoors a freakish monster of unpredictability roamed. Rantoul, having raised the spectre of race, now touched upon the hazards of regional prejudice, allowing solemnly that there was no telling how the jury might respond to Bech's reputation as a sophisticated Easterner.

"Ohrbach is a Westerner, then? Some cowboy," Bech said. His lawyer only slowly smiled.

"Yes, in a way, Morris is one of ours," he conceded. His was a hybrid accent wherein Georgia still controlled the vowels.

"So are the rats in the Santa Monica dump," Bech snapped; a long buildup of indignation lay repressed in him. "He's the kind of vulture that's drowning Hollywood in crassness and cocaine." Even as he spoke, he wondered if he hadn't, finding boyish refuge each Saturday afternoon and many a weekday evening in the hypertrophied cinema palaces of upper Broadway, idealized the old Hollywood, the Dearborn of tintype dreams.

The lawyer's assistant spoke up. He was named Gregg Nunn, and wore a Dutch-boy haircut and thick aviator-style glasses. His voice had an irritating timbre, a near-squeak, like the semi-musical sound produced by rubbing the rims of a glass with a wet finger. "Oh, I think he's quite a puritan," he said. "He works these incredibly long hours and lives quite modestly, over in Westwood, behind the university. In his own image of himself, he's a conscientious slave to his clients' interests."

Irritated by this underling's elfin shine of perverse admiration, Bech said to Rantoul, "To get back to your point: I can't believe a jury of L.A. working men and women is going to identify that much with a ruthless Hollywood wheeler-dealer."

"Oh, they identify," was the drawled answer. "Everybody thinks movies out here. They're as proud of their local product as the good folks in Iowa are of corn. The opposition is sure as shooting going to present this as an effete Eastern smart-aleck maligning a worker in the fields. What you call gouging the plaintiff will endeavor to construe as the going rate and simple honorable enterprise."

Bech's voice, after Rantoul's, sounded rather anxious and hurried in his own ears—high-pitched and, he supposed, effetely Eastern. "But what about what he did to poor Lanna Jerome? He absolutely disem*bow*elled her money." Violent gory images—buzz-saws ripping through stacks of dollar bills, vultures and hyenas tugging at the ribbed carcass of a succulent chanteuse beneath a blazing desert sun—assaulted the defendant's head. Perhaps the lawsuit was right; he was too suggestible to be a trustworthy journalist. His father had always scoffed at Bech's dreams of being a writer. Writing a hard-boiled exposé like "The Only Winners Left in Tinseltown" for a fly-by-night rag like *Flying Fur* had been an attempt, perhaps, to convince the old man that he could turn a dollar when he needed it. Abraham Bech had died last year, in the subway, under the sliding filth of the East River. At least he hadn't lived to crow over this debacle.

"Now you're talking the local language," the lawyer said, his eye moving from his very clean plate to Bech's half-eaten sole. "You get Lanna Jerome up on the stand, the jury's yours. But she's hiding out in Palm Springs and has dodged every summons we've put out on her."

"Anyway," said Gregg Nunn, "there's no telling how the jury would react. That long affair she had with the governor of Nevada didn't sit too well with a lot of fundamentalists."

Rantoul explained, "L.A.'s a lot like Persia these days; everybody's either a fundamentalist or a whore. And then there's this: if we seem to have Lanna on our side, the jury may figure there's tons of money and why not throw poor old Morris a sop of a million or so?"

My non-existent million, Bech thought. The fish he had swallowed bit the tender lining of his stomach, and he devoutly wished he were back in the twelve-table Italian restaurant he knew, just off upper Broadway on 97th, sitting solitary with a plate of spinach fettuccine and that afternoon's *Post*. Not even in his idealistic post-war *Partisan Review* and *Accent* stage had he dreamed that words, mere words, had so much power—the power to pull him across the continent and dump him in this sumptuous restaurant with these three expensive strangers. The restaurant was wide and deep and dark, in that heavy baronial style that had possessed Hollywood at the height of its grandeur. There were carved dadoes and corbelled stones and leaded windows with Gothic arches. Errol Flynn and the sheriff of Nottingham (played by Basil Rathbone) might stroll in at any minute.

The fourth person at the table, the "lady" of Rantoul's jocular announcement, was a female paralegal named Rita: tightly pulled-back long black hair, carmine lips, hoop earrings, and an unsmiling Latina intensity. On a blue-lined pad beside her plate she sporadically took rapid notes.

Flying Fur had carried some libel insurance but bankruptcy had cancelled it. If the jury found for the defense, Rantoul planned to countersue for legal expenses. In the meantime, Bech had drawn out his savings and borrowed from his publisher on a novel he felt much too distracted and put-upon to write. Four pricey days had already been spent waiting for the Los Angeles legal system to find a judge with space on his docket for this case. Ohrbach's attorneys had asked for a jury trial and that would take more days. Biting, nibbling, churning hatred of Morris Ohrbach robbed Bech of his appetite, and he asked his lawyer if he'd like to try his sole. "Just a taste," the big man obligingly drawled, reaching with his fork. "There was quite a to-do in the Food Section of the L.A. *Times* when they hired this chef all the way from Grenoble, France, and Ah confess Ah couldn't much tell from my pork chop what the fuss was all about."

The judge was really more the color of a pale briefcase, and surprisingly young, and amazingly, Bech thought as the days in court wore on, patient. The judge sat for hours without saying a word, leaning a bit to his left, as if away from the winds of justice blowing out of the slowly filling jury box. When he did speak, it was firmly and softly, with an excessive fairness, Bech felt, to the inept, time-wasting shenanigans of Ohrbach's counsel, a short and excitable man called Ralph Kepper. The defense team named him Sergeant Kepper. He always wore khaki pants and baggy sports jackets, which amounted to a statement: he was no fancy-Dan pinstriped Eastern-establishment cat's-paw, he was an honest workaday legal man.

In questioning the prospective jurors, Kepper would ask them if they had ever read a magazine called *Flying Fur* (they answered, invariably, no) and if they had any prima-facie prejudice against "sophisticated, cynical, New York–style journalism." Sometimes he would ask them if, when they heard the words "Hollywood agent," they suffered any pejorative input. Language did strange things in Kepper's mouth, and he frequently announced himself as having "misspoken"—"Yeronner, I misspoke myself."

Nevertheless, this rumpled clown was regarded by the pale-brown judge with unwinking gravity, and his endless peremptory challenges caused juror after juror to leave the box, humiliated. The tactic, Bech's team explained to him, was merely to prolong the proceedings and make the defendant all the more willing to offer a settlement as the cheapest way out.

"Well?" Bech asked. "Would it be? The cheapest way out."

Rantoul was stunned enough to stop chewing. He swallowed and rested a thick hand on Bech's sleeve. "Even if it were," he said, "this team won't let you. Now, don't tell me that you lack team spirit."

A spacious cafeteria occupied the top floor of the Los Angeles Courthouse, and here the defense team gathered for lunch every day, during the long recesses. Protocol dictated that, but for curt, prim nods of recognition, they ignore Kepper as he ate in morose solitude, gnawing at a sandwich that kept getting lost under sheaves of legal paper. Ohrbach, over a week into the proceedings, had not deigned to appear yet. Rantoul thought the jury, when at last in place, would resent this show of indifference, whereas Nunn thought it might, on the contrary, signify an impressively crowded schedule and enhance his eventual appearance. "Not being here,"

Nunn fancifully continued, his little hands flickering and his elfin face gleaming under the even
blond bangs, "makes him the central figure of our
drama, the awaited Godot, the Kafkaesque deity
whose minions carry on on behalf of his obscure
but majestic authority. Absence is an awesome
statement, as the world's religions testify."

"He lets hisself get arrogant," Rantoul allowed,
shifting in his chair before engulfing a thick wedge,
topped with whipped cream, of cafeteria pecan pie.
"That's come out in some of his other trials. He
goes along real smooth on the stand, and then he
gets cute. He stops minding the store. It's hurt him
before, and it'll hurt him again."

The description touched a furtive chord of sympathy in Bech. "Cute" and "not minding the store"
were phrases his late father would have used for
what his only son had chosen to do in life. Young
Bech didn't have his feet on the ground, he didn't
know his ass from his elbow. It was true. Just writing "arch-gouger" showed a kind of dreaminess; he
should have let the facts and the percentages speak
for themselves. He had been inflamed by mis-
placed love for Lanna Jerome, confusing her with
dear lost Claire. He had tried to get her attention
with the fervor of his denunciation of her despoiler.
But how could Lanna Jerome care about him and
what he wrote in a doomed 17th Street rag? She
received three million plus some points of the
unadjusted gross for a feature film, and her last
album went platinum within a week of issue.

Outside the cafeteria, the roof held an open-air promenade, from which one could see vast hazed tracts of pastel housing, glass skyscrapers, merging ribbons of freeway, and far hills dried to the gold of the southern-California winter. On a near hill perched the shiny blue stadium where the once-Brooklyn Dodgers played, and, down below, across the street, stood a gold-trimmed opera house, with a small green park around it. Though it all looked nothing like his idea of a metropolis, Bech felt at home on this roof. When he was an awkward thirteen his family moved from the Upper West Side to Brooklyn. The West Side was getting too full of blacks and spics, his father felt, and Brooklyn was where two of Abe Bech's brothers, Ike and Joe, had lived for years. His father was a dealer in diamonds and precious metals on West 47th Street. Though the materials were precious, the competition was stiff and the profit margin ever more finely shaved. Life was a struggle. Even in Brooklyn, it turned out, it was a struggle. The kids weren't necessarily tougher than those on the Upper West Side, but they were provincial—intolerant of outsiders, un-understanding of nuances. Henry was already a creature of nuances. For fresh air the easiest thing for him, rather than walking the eight blocks to Prospect Park and risking getting hassled by bigger teenagers, was to go up on the roof of their 9th Street brownstone. The other rooftops of Brooklyn spread out in a vast dark plain thickly planted with chimney pots; on one edge of the plain, like a rectilinear mountain hazed by carbon dioxide, Manhattan unreally rose. Now, on the opposite side of the continent, he found himself remembering those monotonous tarpaper vistas and again, as when an adolescent, yearning to fly away, to launch himself from the roof into another life, an airy, glamorous life of literature.

The trial finally got under way. The plaintiff's side had exhausted all its challenges. Rantoul tried to expedite matters by challenging almost nobody: only one old dignified Chicano gardener, whose command of English appeared halting (he was insulted; he protested, "I understand good, I am citizen since twenty years!"), and a snappily dressed Bel Air matron who had once been married to a lawyer. "You never know how she might react," Rantoul explained. "Ex-wives just aren't rational where the law is concerned."

The solemnly impanelled twelve jury members, with the two alternates, sat on the left of the courtroom. Bech and what spectators there might be—a stray street person; a courthouse office worker taking a break—faced the judge's high desk across an area of chairs and tables; here the lawyers, the agonists, performed and the court stenographer, like an unspeaking Greek chorus, rippled out yards and yards of typed notes. The paper folded itself, accordion-style, into a cardboard box on the far side of his shorthand machine.

The stenographer was a thin pale bald man with a yellow toothbrush mustache and an unfocused blue gaze. He dressed like the old vaudeville comedians, in checked suits and polka-dot ties. When the lawyers held a conference with the judge, he hurried with his machine to eavesdrop and kept on tapping. When the judge declared some passage of procedure off the record, his tireless long white fingers dropped to his lap and his glazed stare rested on a blank wall near the American flag. He was the only person in the room who seemed to Bech not to be wasting his time.

Though by modernist prescription artists live on the edge of respectability, in a state of liberating derangement, Bech had never before been hauled into court. He had heard that the wheels of justice ground fine, but he had not expected those wheels to be so wobbly, so oddly swivelled in every direction but that of the simple truth.

The first witness for the plaintiff was a mincing professor of English at Southern Cal who responded at length to Sergeant Kepper's questions about the words involved. The prefix "arch," by way of Anglo-Saxon and Old French, derives from a Greek verb meaning "to begin, to rule," and signifies either the highest of its type, as in "archbishop" or "archangel" or, to quote Webster, "most fully embodying the qualities of his or its time." Mr. Bech's article asserted, then, that Mr. Ohrbach was the chief, or most fully developed, gouger in the entire Los Angeles area. "Gouge," authorities tend to agree, is a word of Celtic origin, by way of Late Latin, referring to a chisel of concave cross section. Had the word Mr. Bech chosen been "chiseller," it was interesting to note, the implication of wrong-doing would have been more distinct, and the connotation of brute strength rather less. The phrase "greedy reasons of his own rake-off" is less easy to decipher, and for a time the expert thought there might be a typographical error or an editorial slip involved. The expression "rake-off," of course, stems from the old practice in gambling houses of the croupier with his rake taking the gambling house's percentage out of the chips on the table. "Widened the prevailing tragic rift between the literary and cinematic arts" is also far from clear, since the two arts have never been close and the tragedy of their separation would seem to lie only in the eye of the beholder, in this case a writer of modestly paid fiction and journalism who might have had in mind the much greater financial rewards of film work.

"Objection: conjecture," Rantoul automatically growled.

"Sustained," the judge as automatically responded.

All this semantic disquisition was putting the jury to sleep. They sat there, in their two sextuple rows (five men, seven women; five whites, four blacks, two Asian-Americans, and a part-Cherokee) plus the two alternates, who sat beside but not in the elevated jury box, all hoping to see

Lanna Jerome, with her rice-powder makeup, her
artificial mole, her slinky, slimmed-down figure,
her hair dyed soot-black and moussed into short
spikes. "Slinky, slimmed-down": as was common
knowledge among her millions of fans, Lanna had
a weakness for Dr Pepper and junk snacks. After
her relationship with the governor of Nevada had
broken up she put on thirty pounds in mournful
bingeing. Bech had loved her all the more for that
vulnerable, blubbery side of her.

Rantoul and the word-expert batted the prefix
"arch" around, the latter finally conceding, minc-
ingly, that its use here might signify merely a relatively high standing as a gouger, not a supreme and
ruling status in an organized group of them.

The next witness for the prosecution, a self-
styled "expert in media," discoursed on the circula-
tion figures of *Flying Fur* during its eighteen
months of existence. Though the subscriptions in
southern California were only forty-two in number,
of which eighteen went to libraries, the influence of
those few copies would be hard to overestimate;
the magazine, as the latest "hip" word from New
York City, was avidly read by agents, actors, pro-
ducers, and other persons active in Mr. Ohrbach's
business, and an adverse reference in its pages
would certainly do him incalculable professional
damage.

Rantoul had a field day with that witness, and
ate an especially hearty lunch in the sky-view cafeteria. The trial was under way, and still Ohrbach

had not showed up. However, Bech did have a glimpse, one afternoon, of the judge out by the elevators, going home. He was wearing a denim suit the tasty shade of honeydew melon, with bell-bottom pants and a lapel-less jacket. Out of his robes, he looked like a smooth young dude heading into the pleasures of the evening. He studiously avoided Bech's eye.

In the legal world, eye avoidance is an art. Morris Ohrbach turned out to be a master of it. When, the next day, he at last appeared, he entered the courtroom bobbing and smiling in all directions, but his smiles landed nowhere, like the fist-flurry of a boxer warming up. His gaze, as benign and generalized as that of a Byzantine icon, flicked past Bech's face. One of Ohrbach's well-known eccentricities was a virtually religious avoidance of being photographed, so Bech had had no idea of what his archenemy looked like. The elderly plaintiff, of middle height, hunched over like a man about to break into a run; he had this vaguely smiling mouth, a large nose, and a shock of wavy white hair thrust forward by a cowlick that reminded Bech of his own stiffly wiry, hard-to-control hair. Bech's hair was still basically dark, and his posture had not yet acquired an elderly stoop, but the resemblance was nevertheless strong. Ohrbach looked enough like him to be his father.

The jury stirred, excited by the presence of

someone who, if not exactly famous, had bilked the famous. The judge momentarily sat up straight, and paid scrupulous attention to the morning's witnesses, a series of character witnesses on Ohrbach's behalf. They were women, Hollywood hostesses, who, at first timidly and then irrepressibly, testified to the plaintiff's humanity—his courteous manners, his unfailing good humor and even temper, his personal and financial generosity to a host of causes ranging from the state of Israel to a little-league baseball team of impoverished Mexican-American youngsters.

"Morrie Ohrbach is a su*perb* human being!" one especially pneumatic widow cried, in an abrupt release of pressure; she had been previously stifled by Rantoul's objections to her breathy account of how, during her bereavement some years before, the agent had been assiduously attentive and beautifully considerate. Further, she added defiantly, as Rantoul half-stood to object again, *all* the investments he had talked *her* into had made money— *scads* of it.

Another woman, squarish and brown and bedecked with Navajo jewelry, testified that when she heard that her dear friend Morris had been called a gouger in one of these snide Eastern magazines she broke down and cried, off and on, for days. He would drop by the house in the late afternoon and looked an absolute wreck—he got so thin she was afraid he'd sink, just a bundle of bones, in her swimming pool and drown. Morrie himself, poor soul, didn't have a swimming pool any more; he lived in this tiny two-bedroom condo in Westwood and had had to sell all but one of his sports cars, that's how much of a gouger he was.

Rantoul in cross-examination elicited that the move to Westwood and the sports-car sales had followed the adverse legal judgment in the Lanna Jerome case. "Oh, that *hide*ous woman!" was the unabashed response. "Everybody knows how she chased after the governor of Nevada until she broke up his lovely home and absolutely *wrecked* his career! He could have been *Pres*ident!"

At lunch, Bech confessed he was getting scared. Ohrbach was being painted as a saint, and in fact he did look awfully sweet, and rather touchingly shabby. He had worn a linen suit with a yellow sheen, and a sad little bow tie that called attention to his neck wattles.

Rantoul snorted, "And Ah bet you think a Gila monster has a friendly face." He had taken off his coat and turned back his sleeves to dig into some cafeteria corn on the cob. Flecks of starch dotted his jaw.

"There *is* something friendly about his face. Something sensitive and shy. When he came in, he seemed so outnumbered. Just poor old Sergeant Kepper and him, against all of us."

"Us-all ruthless Eastern-establishment types," Rantoul filled in. "You got the message he was sending. Ah'm sure glad, Henry, you ain't on that there jury."

Rita laughed, showing dazzling sharp teeth. "It is you who are sweet, Henry, to see in such a way." Like Lanna Jerome, she had a mole near her chin. In Rita's case, it looked genuine.

"To me," said Gregg Nunn, "his face is weird. I get queasy and dizzy, looking at it. There's no center. It's like he's a hologram. And his eyes. What color are his eyes? Nobody knows—we're all too spooked to look, and if you notice, even when he seems to be smiling at you, his eyes are downcast, like he's trying to see through the lids. He's an alien—he can see through his eyelids!" As the boy expanded on his fantasy, his small round hands made wider and wider circles, and his voice attained so excited a pitch that several heads in the cafeteria turned around.

Kepper and his client were not here; they were off, perhaps hatching more character witnesses. Or witnesses to expose Bech, his whole discreditable career. His refusal to learn the diamond trade at his father's knee. His restless resistance to his mother's intrusive love. His failure to become a poet, like Auden and Delmore Schwartz, both of whom he had met in his post-war phase of haunting the Village, or a critic, like Dwight Macdonald and Clement Greenberg, who also had been caught in his skein of acquaintance. He had felt that what critics did was too pat, too dictatorial; he preferred, lazily, to submit to his subjective inklings and glimpses, and to turn these into epiphanies briefer than Joyce's and less grim than Kafka's. He had failed his publisher, hearty, life-loving, travel-tanned Big Billy Vanderhaven, by refusing to deliver, in the wake of *Travel Light*'s mild *succès d'estime,* the "big" novel just sitting there, in the realm of Platonic ideas, waiting to take the public and the book clubs by storm; he had failed his first editor, dapper, fastidious Ned Clavell, by refusing to remove from the sprawling text of *The Chosen* all those earthy idioms and verbal frontalia that chilled, in still-prissy 1963, the book's critical and popular reception. Bech had just refused to pan out, as author, son, and lover. One woman after another, having given her naked all, stridently had pointed out that he was unable to make a commitment. Behind him stretched a chain of disappointments going back to his grade-school teachers at P.S. 87—kindly Irish nuns *manquées,* most of them—and his professors at NYU, whom he felt he had usually wound up disappointing, after a flashy first paper. He failed, or declined, to graduate. He was not a superb human being. He was a vain, limp leech on the leg of literature as it waded through swampy times. In the courthouse cafeteria, he lost his appetite, and left half of his tuna-salad sandwich untouched, and all of the butter-almond ice cream he had taken for dessert, homesick for the Italian restaurant's spumoni. Rantoul, having consumed a platter of meatloaf, gravy, mashed potatoes, and peas, delicately inquired after these remnants, and made them disappear.

The next character witnesses were other

agents, who praised Ohrbach as their mentor and
inspiration, as an immensely creative and concerned thinker on behalf of the film industry. It was
Ohrbach, claimed one rough beast in a tieless silk
shirt and a number of gold chains, who had origi-
nated the valuable concept of total agent involvement—no longer could one rest content with
forging advantageous deals for the client, but one
should follow up and make sure that the rewards, in
the always uncertain and sometimes abbreviated
career of a performing artist, were secure and
themselves performing up to capacity. Not just
career management, but total life-assets management was the basis of the concept, traceable (in the
rough beast's view, his ringed hands chopping the
air and chest hair frothing from between his
chains) to the genius of Morris Ohrbach. Then sec-
retaries—ex-bimbos with plastic eyelashes and
leathery, bone-deep tans—testified to Ohrbach's
generosity as a boss, and told of days off granted
with pay when a mother died, of bonuses at both
Christmas and Passover, of compassionate leaves
of absence during spells of health or man trouble.
Clients—sallow, slightly faded and off-center male
and female beauties—confided how Morris would
tide them over, would reduce his cut to 12½ percent, would give them fatherly advice for free, out
of his own precious time.

Throughout this torrent of homage, its object,
who sat beside Sergeant Kepper at a table six feet
in front of Bech, actively pursued his good works,

scribbling away on pieces of paper and annotating small stacks of correspondence and financial statements and occasionally dashing off and sealing a letter, with a licking and thumping of the envelope so noisy as to cause the court stenographer to glance around and the judge to direct a disciplinary stare. Was the judge, from his angle, receiving the same piteous impression, of vulnerable elderliness, that Bech was gathering from behind? The cords of Ohrbach's slender neck strained, the shirt collar looked a size too big and not entirely fresh, the overgrown ears had sprouted white whiskers. The entire frail skull gently wagged in decrepitude's absent-minded palsy.

Abe Bech had not allowed himself to appear old, though he had been seventy when he died. He had used a rinse to keep his hair dark, sat in the winter under a sun lamp, and gone off to the diamond district each day in a crisp white shirt laundered at a place that sent them back to you uncreased, on hangers. Like all salesmen, he gave his best self to his prospective customers, and saved his rage, sarcasm, and indifference for his family. Though circulatory problems had for some time been affecting his legs and hands, his cerebral hemorrhage had come out of the blue. In death as in life he had been abrupt and hard to reach. His last impact upon the metropolis—the only one to make the newspapers—was a half-hour delay underground at rush hour, inconveniencing thousands. Since the service elevator at the Clark Street

station in Brooklyn Heights was out of commission, the stretcher bearers had brought his father,
inscrutable and implacable in his body bag, up all
those dirty tile steps, through the flood of exasper-
ated commuters. In Bech's mind it had the
grandeur of a pharaoh's funeral procession up from
the Nile, into the depths of a Pyramid where the
soul's embalmed shell would lie forever intact.

By leaning forward and reaching with his arm
he could have tapped Ohrbach's thin hunched
shoulder and asked his forgiveness for calling him
an arch-gouger. But the gesture would have admitted ten million dollars' worth of guilt, and betrayed
his team.

The team was less impressed by the plaintiff's
accumulating case than Bech was. Rantoul even
rose to indignation about Ohrbach's chiropractor,
an autocratically bald man who from the witness
stand claimed to have observed a marked psycho-
somatic deterioriation in his patient immediately
after the *Flying Fur* article had appeared. Solemnly
turning over leaves from his files, in a cumbersome
ring binder, the chiropractor described lower-back
spasms and attendant pain that incapacitated the
sensitive agent for months thereafter and perhaps
permanently impaired his professional effective-
ness. Rantoul had asked to examine the pages that
the chiropractor consulted and saw terms like
"mental-stress-induced" and "spastic depression"

inserted in a smaller handwriting, in a fresher ink, into the records of two long years ago, when "The Only Winners Left in Tinseltown" had appeared. At lunch, Rantoul boasted, "Ah asked the judge to admit the file in evidence and Kepper turned pale as a goose's belly. He withdrew the testimony. We would have had 'em for perjury sure as sugar."

The last word was a modification, in Southerncourtly fashion, for Rita's benefit. As his stay in Los Angeles moved into its third week, Rita had become clearer to Bech. Her Hispanic rat-tat-tat way of thinking and talking had been softened by North American entrepreneurism, its willingness to smile and to explore possibilities. One day when Rantoul and Nunn had some other legal fish to fry, he and she had gone out to lunch at a Mexican restaurant a few blocks away from the courthouse. To her he had unburdened himself of his qualms, his growing sympathy and pity for the plaintiff, who seemed to be the defendant. "I feel so *guilty,*" he said.

"That is a luxury you are allowing yourself," Rita explained. "Some kind of Jewish thing, identifying with the people trying to destroy you. A way of making yourself superior to a fight. That's fine, Henry. That's very lovable. That's why you have us, to do the fighting for you."

"Ohrbach's Jewish, too. Maybe he feels the same way about me."

"Don't you wish."

"How do you think it's going?"

She shrugged, making her hoop earrings wobble. "Their case is *basura,* but that doesn't mean the jury won't buy it. Juries go for underdogs and you haven't yet established yourself as one. Ohrbach is doing that. We think he's buying his shirts with the collar a size too big deliberately, and has developed on purpose that piteous head-waggle."

"Really? Then that does make me mad. Rita, let's nail the slippery bastard. May I call you Rita? Tell me, what do you do nights?"

His own nights stretched long and empty, moseying about his skyscraper hotel—a futuristic round tower arisen where two freeways met—with its many levels of underpatronized restaurants. One night he would sit at a counter watching nimble Japanese in chef hats slice steak and vegetables into a kind of edible origami; the next night he patronized the Chinese in their trickling grotto, with its small arched bridge guarded by a silk-clad hostess. He tried walking out into the night, but the downtown was eerily empty, and felt dangerous. There was only the rustle of palm trees and the roar of freeway traffic. He could never figure out where the movie houses were, or the little Italian restaurants, or the corner newsstands so ubiquitous in New York. In the mornings, however, as Bech climbed up a concrete hill above a chasm where cars vibratingly pummelled the earth and made the air quiver with carbon dioxide, he could feel in the fresh sunlight, faithfully delivered from a cloudless sky, what had fetched and held millions here: a desert clarity, a transparency that ascended from the fragile panorama of pastel buildings to the serene glassy nothingness at the heart of the heavens. No amount of reckless development and ruthless exploitation could hopelessly besmog such sublime air. This was the Promised Land; this was what Israel should have been, not some crabbed, endlessly disputed sliver of the Arab world. The Spanish had been ousted, yet remained, in the architecture, the place names, the ochre tint, the fatalism of this splendid mirage. He would arrive at the courthouse steps with a light sweat started across his shoulder blades, and a faint breathlessness of expectation.

"Oh, you don't care," Rita told him. "You must have a lot of girls back east, terribly clever and attractive East Coast girls."

"I care," he assured her.

"I do legal homework and cook for my parents and take care of my sister's kids," Rita answered. "She performs nude water ballet in a big tank at a businessmen's bar over in Venice."

"How about my taking you out to dinner, some night when she's drying off?"

"Henry, let's wait until after the verdict. You may not have enough left to pay for a single taco."

Back in court, the plaintiffs had produced their most amusing witness, who had the jury laughing until tears came; he even elicited a smile from the court stenographer as he pattered away, his fingers falling—like a pianist's more than a regular typist's—in chords. The witness was an enormously fat and beautifully spoken process server, a virtuoso of court testimony who, in attempting to subpoena Lanna Jerome, had hid in the bushes and howled outside her condo wall in Palm Springs like a dog, mewed like a kitten, and chirped like a wounded bird. The singer and screen star was notoriously fond of animals, and he had thought thus to create a window of opportunity and slap the papers at her over the sill. No soap. She never stuck her head out. He demonstrated the howl, the mew, and the chirp.

"What is the relevance of all these sound effects?" the judge asked, when the jury's laughter—slightly forced and sparse at the end, like canned laughter—had died down.

Sergeant Kepper was on his feet. "We have reason to believe, yeronner, that Ms. Jerome has changed her mind and now harbors a more favorable opinion of Mr. Ohrbach's professional services on her behalf than she did at the time wherein on advice of her unscrupulous counsel he sued her. I mean *she* sued *him.* I misspoke myself, yeronner."

"Objection. Irrelevant and immaterial and unproven hearsay," Rantoul said.

"Sustained." The judge directed the jury to forget the exchange they had just heard, and the process server pulled himself from the witness chair with the practiced skill of a wine steward easing out a champagne cork.

Up in the cafeteria, Rantoul was jubilant. "They keep opening up that Jerome can of worms like dogs returning to their mess," he gloated. "She show up, their case is *toast*."

Gregg Nunn said excitedly, "Did you all notice how through that whole fantastic performance, with the animal noises and everything, Morrie never looked up and kept scribbling notes to himself? He's given up on this one and is working on his next finagle. The guy never rests; he's a spider, he spins lawsuits!"

Bech was grateful to Nunn for voicing, in his fey way, his own sense of the plaintiff as a transcendent phenomenon. At night, lying unsleeping and agitated in his hotel room, he felt Ohrbach enclosing him suffocatingly. This room was in the shape of a slice of pie. Bech's head lay in the narrow end, near the shaft at the core of the round tower, in which elevators throbbed and hummed at all hours: high-priced hookers riding up with their junketing clients from the Pacific Rim, and then riding down alone. Beyond Bech's twitching feet, gold curtains hid a forest of other glass skyscrapers, in L.A.'s eerily empty and abstract downtown. Ohrbach and his implacable lawsuit had brought Bech here, wedged into this unreal corner of the continent, just as his father had irascibly moved him, on the delicate cusp of puberty, to Brooklyn. The parallel made Ohrbach seem vast, and somewhat benign, as all the forces that create us must, in our instinctive self-approval, seem benign. In spite of his legal team's warrior spirit, Bech harbored the sneaking suspicion that he and his enemy could strike a deal—indeed *were,* beneath all the vapid legal machinations, invisibly striking a deal. Ohrbach, Bech knew from the way the elderly man's misty, evasive gaze tenderly flicked past the defendant's face every morning, loved him; his apparent mercilessness hid a profound, persistent mercy.

Sure enough, the white-haired agent, brought to the stand to testify, oddly dissolved. He scotched his own case. In Rantoul's phrase, he stopped minding the store. His eyes were now as shy of the jury as they had been of the defense team; he kept gazing down at some three-by-five cards he had brought to the stand, and as the lawyers and the judge sought to resolve some question of procedure, he would compulsively begin annotating them, with an old-fashioned fountain pen that audibly scratched. Kepper tried to lead him through the mental agony of being libelled in *Flying Fur,* but Ohrbach seemed no longer much interested; rather, he wanted to speak of Lanna Jerome, how much he had loved her and her then husband for the many years of their association, how wounded he had been when she inexplicably sued him at the instigation of her new, bouncer husband, and how entirely his affection and admiration for her had survived the mere "legal wars" that he and she had been obliged to wage. He would lay down his life for her, Ohrbach confided to the jury, and down deep he was sure that she felt the same about him.

Had she ever, Kepper asked him, sweatily trying to keep the testimony on track, called him a "gouger"?

"Oh, she might have, but only in fun. In affectionate fun. Exaggeration was her style—a performer's stock in trade."

Kepper blanched. Had any of his clients, he asked Ohrbach, ever accused him of gouging, to the best of his recollection?

"There's always a discussion," Ohrbach smilingly allowed, "before the exact terms of any arrangement are ironed out. Things are said in heat that neither party actually means."

Had anybody in his entire life, Kepper asked, almost shouting in exasperation, ever called him a "gouger," let alone an "arch-gouger"?

These were creampuff pitches, Bech could see, meant to be knocked out of the park; but Ohrbach was letting them pop into the catcher's mitt.

His waggling white-crowned head thrust even lower from his oversize collar as the talent agent said, in a shaky, slanting voice that still kept an edge of New York accent, "Well, in fifty years of working the Hollywood mills I've been called any number of things. I don't recall ever seeing it in print, though, until the article by this nice young man." And his shifty eyes dared follow his withered hand, for a second, in its shy gesture toward the place where Bech had been sitting and stewing day after day. Ohrbach was reaching out. David and Absalom. Joseph and his brothers. The

Prodigal Son. Forgiveness, the patriarchal prerogative. Bech fought an impulse to leap up and go kneel before the witness and bow his head for the touch of the blessing his own father had denied.

"Shit," said Sergeant Kepper. His stubby arms lifted from his sides and slapped back down, like a penguin's flippers. "I give up." To the electrified court he apologized, "Sorry, yeronner. I misspoke myself."

"Didn't that break your heart?" Bech asked Rita that Saturday night, at a Polynesian restaurant in Venice Beach, where great flaming things were hurried back and forth on platters that sounded wired to amplify the sizzle. "His own lawyer giving up on him."

"No, Henry," she said. "My heart is as fragile as any other woman's, but that did not break it. One shabby performer crossing up another, it happens all the time. I think our plaintiff's brain has been scrambled by too many years of *escamoteo*."

"He seemed to miss Kepper's signals entirely."

"Your pet gouger is not in his prime—why should that sadden you so?"

The restaurant door was open to the soft California twilight, its pacific silence gashed by the grating sound of skateboards and roller skates hurtling muscular young bodies along.

"Speaking of people in their primes," he said,

"where is the place where your sister does her underwater act?"

"Far from here, in terms of both distance and ambiance. I did not want you to ogle my sister. I want you all for myself, Henry. I am more jealous than your New York sophisticated girls." With a volcanic burst of flame and a thunderous cascade of scalding fat, their appetizer, Pork Strips à la Molokai, arrived. A pack of Rollerbladers cascaded past. Bech saw, with a simultaneous rising and sinking sensation, that his date had primed herself to go all the way.

The case for the defense was brisk and anticlimactic. Rantoul had found more witnesses than he needed to swear that Ohrbach was no angel. A revered octogenarian mogul from the old studio days, crowned by even more snowy hair than the plaintiff, answered, when asked what Ohrbach's reputation was in the industry, with a single phrase, "The pits." Another witness, an actress whose smooth, almond-eyed face was vaguely familiar to millions for having played female co-pilots, androids, and extra-terrestrial princesses in low-budget space movies, wept as she described the shockingly fractional fortune left to her after Ohrbach's ministrations.

Bech found her performance a bit overwrought, but it froze all the profiles of the jury—compacted, from his angle, like one of those patriotic posters Norman Rockwell had crammed with a cross-section of Americans. Not quite all profiles, actually, because one of the two alternates, a large round-faced woman in a series of unfortunate pants suits, had taken to staring at him. Her luminous moon face bothered the corner of his eye all day. Whenever he happened to glance toward her, she gave him a wink. He would have been more heartened by this if she hadn't been only an alternate. It was a sign, he supposed, of habituation when a locality's females began to zero in. He had been out here nearly three weeks, at the cost of a thousand or more a day. If he winked back at the alternate juror, the judge might declare a mistrial. Bech determinedly refocused on the back of Ohrbach's head, and noticed a pathetic little bald spot, a peek of defenseless pink amid the snowy waves, where a cowlick swirled. When he had viewed his father at the Brooklyn morgue, Bech had been struck by how thin his hair had become; as long as Abe Bech was alive, the Grecian Formula, the year-round tan, and his ferocious will had enforced the illusion of a full and bristling head.

At the end of that day's testimony, when the plaintiff quaveringly stood near the door and let his cloudy, sad, reflexive smile skid here and there across the courtroom faces, Bech accidentally caught his eye and, with winks on his mind, gave him one.

Or did he? He couldn't believe he would do a thing so disastrous. His enemy's eyes filmed over with fishiness; they were virtually colorless, dragged up from some depth of the sea where light made no difference. Bech blushed in embarrassment, and tried to picture ten million dollars, stacked up in bundled tens and twenties. That's what that wink could cost him. Recalled to the stand, Ohrbach could testify, "Your honor, and ladies and gentlemen of the jury, the defendant winked at me. Surely that proves beyond the shadow of a doubt, if further proof were needed, that he views me as a pal, a fellow spirit and soulmate, and by no means as an arch-gouger!"

But Ohrbach, instead of pressing his sudden advantage, reverted to not showing up in court. Bech's imprudent wink, if it occurred, had perhaps mortally offended him. The old finagler had felt mocked; the machinations of the law were not to be winked at. In his absence the trial dragged in a trance toward its termination. Circlets of gray hair had begun to appear in the judge's Afro, and his list to the left approached the supine. Lanna Jerome did not come out of hiding in Palm Springs, but an accountant and a lawyer in her employ testified with a stultifying double-entry particularity as to financial wrongs and half-wrongs she had suffered. Her relationship with Morrie Ohrbach had begun with "Comin' On Strong" and had ended with "Don't Send Me Back My Letters, My Lawyer Will Be in Touch with Yours."

Bech himself took the stand. The courtroom, seen at last from so different an angle, had a surreal pop-up quality—the judge looming close, the jury

fanned out like a grandstand viewed from the playing field, the scattered marks on the court stenographer's spewing paper almost legible. In his old
high-school debating voice, as clear as footprints in
the mud, Bech testified that the epithet in question
had seemed to him, after much time spent gathering evidence from responsible sources, both apt
and fair. He had meant "arch" in its second, more
common dictionary sense of "extreme: most fully
embodying the qualities of his or its kind."

He had always imagined that it would be very
difficult to lie in court, after taking an oath on the
Bible, but nothing, he discovered, would be easier.
One becomes an actor, a protagonist in a drama,
and words become mere instruments of the joust.
Words: how could he have dedicated his life to anything so flimsy, so flexible, so ready to deceive?
Asked by Rantoul if he had meant to express it as
his *opinion* that Ohrbach was an arch-gouger or as
a *fact,* he said that he had meant to express it as his
opinion. Bech had been amply coached in this legal
distinction, upon which mighty First Amendment
matters somehow hinged, though it made no real
sense to him. What good is an opinion if it doesn't
express a fact? But he refrained from saying this,
and his thick-necked lawyer gave him an approv-
ing grimace.

Sergeant Kepper rose to cross-examine.
"Would you describe yourself, Mr. Bech, as infatu-
ated with Lanna Jerome?"

The little courtroom went so quiet Bech heard a juror's shoe scrape; the stenographer's machine tapped what seemed two measures of skeletal melody. "No," he lied. "I admire her talents, of course, but so do millions."

"Never mind the millions," Kepper said raspingly. "The tone of your description of her relations with the plaintiff reminded me, may I say, of a jealous would-be lover."

"Objection," Rantoul cried. "Conjecture. Irrelevant."

"Overruled," the judge said quietly. "It could be relevant. Proceed, counsellor."

"Might it be fair to say," Kepper proceeded, "that your infatuation with Miss Jerome led you to show, in print, hatred, ill will, and spite toward Mr. Ohrbach?"

Bech recognized the legal language, the poison on the tip of the lance. "Not at all," he said, with an invincible sincerity. "I feel now and felt then no ill will toward Mr. Ohrbach. I have never met him, and have had no dealings with him." He suppressed the insane urge to confess that, far from ill will, he had come in these days in court to feel a filial affection.

He was ready to plead guilty, had they only known it. But Sergeant Kepper's pokes toward the chinks in the defendant's armor became listless, and Bech was soon allowed to step down. There were no more witnesses.

Next day, Kepper's summation of Ohrbach v. Bech was distracted and jerky, with much miss-peaking and idle oratory about the dangers of unbridled media. He spoke of east and west coasts, the West being the open-hearted seat of creativity and entertainment, and the East of cavilling, nega-tivistic criticism. Who is this Henry Bech, a mod-estly paid litterateur (with emphasis on the last syllable, pronounced *toor*), to understand the ins and outs of agent-client relations in a vastly suc-cessful popular art? Yet, though his stubby arms sawed up and down, his heart and mind seemed to have moved on. In Rantoul's opinion, Kepper had been persuaded to take Ohrbach's case on a contin-gency basis, and knew the jig was up when no out-of-court settlement was reached beforehand. All this—all this expense and terror—had been simply going through the motions.

Ohrbach had absented himself from the denouement. The ghost had evaporated from the machine.

Rantoul, striving to rouse the case from its tor-por, drawled out almost a comically eloquent word-picture of the preposterous injustice of this claim of libel, in view of the plaintiff's notorious reputation; if in this great country an honest opin-ion, supported by a rich array of evidence, that a man is an arch-gouger can't be expressed in a jour-nal of information, what is the point of the Consti-tution and all the wars fought to defend it against tyrannies of both the fascist and Communist persuasion?

It took the jury, though, four whole hours, while caterpillars becoming butterflies chewed at the lining of Bech's stomach, to arrive at the verdict of not guilty. One of the Asian-Americans, Gregg Nunn later discovered and confided in a gossippy letter to Bech, thought *Flying Fur* was a pornographic publication, and as a born-again Christian he wasn't so crazy about Lanna Jerome's affair with the governor of Nevada either, or her well-publicized statements in defense of abortion rights and single motherhood.

Bech's father, Abe Bech, had had terrible varicose veins in the last decade of his life, symptomatic of the circulatory difficulties that eventually killed him. Nevertheless, he walked off to the subway each morning, the Atlantic Avenue station, and stood on his feet in the gloomy, glittering diamond store all day, when he wasn't limping up and down 47th Street looking for a deal. Dealing is what fathers do, so that sons can disdain it and try to fly away, over the rooftops. But in the end we are brought back to reality and find ourselves tossing a man and his whole life of dealing—doing the necessary, by his own lights—into the hopper for the sake of a peppy phrase. For $1,250 plus expenses. "I feel so guilty," he told Rita.

"Why on earth why? The plaintiff, he was one *podrido* son of a bitch."

Her voice had lost its paralegal primness and relaxed back toward a maternal Latina rhythm. They were naked in his bed in the futuristic hotel, side by side, sharing a joint. She had biscuit-brown shoulders and spiralling dark down on her forearms and a tousled short hairdo just like the prepunk Lanna Jerome's. They had been discussing Bech's countersuit, not only for the legal expenses but for his mental anguish and time lost and the inestimable damage to his professional reputation. Tom Rantoul was licking his chops. "We'll nail that turkey," he vowed, "so he'll never gobble again." The case, to be financed on a contingency basis, would take months to prepare, and it seemed that Bech's life was here now, on this coast. He had been asking around, looking up the contacts he had made two years before, and even got a few nibbles. Could he do TV scripts? A lot of the sitcoms take place in the Northeast, because of the audience demographics, and yet there was a whole generation of Hollywood writers to whom New York was just a fable, an Old World from which their fathers and grandfathers had immigrated. The fee named for a trial script equalled half of Bech's earnings for all last year. He said he'd have to think it over.

"I loved him," he told Rita. "The stooped way he moved and kept bobbing his head, asking everybody's pardon and not expecting to get it. When my father died," he went on, "we found in his bureau drawers these black elastic stockings I had bought him, so his legs wouldn't hurt so much. He had never worn them. They still had the cardboard in them. Pieces of cardboard shaped like feet."

"Sweetheart, O.K. I see it. The cardboard feet. Dying down in the subway. Life is rough. But that other *judío* was trying to eat you. You eat him, or he eats you. Which would you rather?"

"Hey, I don't know," the defendant responded, touching two fingers to the erectile tip—the color of a sun-darkened, un-sulphur-treated apricot—of her nearer breast. "Neither seems ideal."

And neither coast is ideal; Bech in a few more weeks of consultation and courtship returned to our own, while on that far shore a broken female heart slowly mended, and legal wheels, like masticating jaws, ground on and on and then, one day when nobody was looking, stopped.

Bech Noir

BECH HAD A NEW SIDEKICK. Her monicker was Robin. Rachel "Robin" Teagarten. Twenty-six, post-Jewish, frizzy big hair, figure on the short and solid side. She interfaced for him with an IBM PS/1 his publisher had talked him into buying. She set up the defaults, rearranged the icons, programmed the style formats, accessed the ANSI character sets—Bech was a stickler for foreign accents. When he answered a letter, she typed it for him from dictation. When he took a creative leap, she deciphered his handwriting and turned it into digitized code. Neither happened very often. Bech was of the Ernest Hemingway save-your-juices school. To fill the time, he and Robin slept together. He was seventy-four, but they worked with that. Seventy-four plus twenty-six was one hundred; divided by two, that was fifty, the prime of life. The energy of youth plus the wisdom of age. A team. A duo.

They were in his snug aerie on Crosby Street. He was reading the *Times* at breakfast: caffeineless

Folgers, calcium-reinforced D'Agostino orange juice, poppy-seed bagel lightly toasted. The crumbs and poppy seeds had scattered over the newspaper and into his lap but you don't get something for nothing, not on this hard planet. Bech announced to Robin, "Hey, Lucas Mishner is dead."

A creamy satisfaction—the finest quality, made extra easy to spread by the toasty warmth—thickly covered his heart.

"Who's Lucas Mishner?" Robin asked. She was deep in the D section—Business Day. She was a practical-minded broad with no experience of culture prior to 1975.

"Once-powerful critic," Bech told her, biting off his phrases. "Late *Partisan Review* school. Used to condescend to appear in the *Trib Book Review,* when the *Trib* was still alive on this side of the Atlantic. Despised my stuff. Called it 'superficially energetic but lacking in the true American fiber, the grit, the wrestle.' That's him talking, not me. The grit, the wrestle. Sanctimonious bastard. When *The Chosen* came out in '63, he wrote, 'Strive and squirm as he will, Bech will never, never be touched by the American sublime.' The simple, smug, know-it-all son of a bitch. You know what his idea of the real stuff was? James Jones. James Jones and James Gould Cozzens."

There Mishner's face was, in the *Times,* twenty years younger, with a fuzzy little rosebud smirk and a pathetic slicked-down comb-over like limp Venetian blinds throwing a shadow across the dome of his head. The thought of him dead filled Bech with creamy ease. He told Robin, "Lived way the hell up in Connecticut. Three wives, no flowers. Hadn't published for years. The rumor in the industry was he was gaga with alcoholic dementia."

"You seem happy."

"Very."

"Why? You say he had stopped being a critic anyway."

"Not in my head. He tried to hurt me. He did hurt me. Vengeance is mine."

"Who said that?"

"The Lord. In the Bible. Wake up, Robin."

"I thought it didn't sound like you," she admitted. "Stop hogging the Arts section. Let's see what's playing in the Village. I feel like a movie tonight."

"I'm not reading the Arts Section."

"But it's under what you are reading."

"I was going to get to it."

"That's what I call hogging. Pass it over."

He passed it over, with a pattering of poppy seeds on the polyurethaned teak dining table Robin had installed. For years he and his female guests had eaten at a low glass coffee table farther forward in the loft. The sun slanting in had been pretty, but eating all doubled up had been bad for their internal organs. Robin had got him to take vitamins, too, and the calcium-reinforced o.j. She thought it would straighten his spine. He was in his best shape in years. She had got him doing sit-ups and push-ups. He was hard and quick, for a man who'd had his Biblical three score and ten. He was ready for action. He liked the tone of his own body. He liked the cut of Robin's smooth broad jaw across the teak table. Her healthy big hair, her pushy plump lips, her little flattened nose. "One down," he told her, mysteriously.

But she was reading the Arts Section, the B section, and didn't hear. "*Con Air, Face/Off,*" she read. This was the summer of 1997. "*Air Force One, Men in Black.* They're all violent. Disgusting."

"Why are you afraid of a little violence?" he asked her. "Violence is our poetry now, now that sex has become fatally tainted."

"Or *Contact,*" Robin said. "From the reviews it's all about how the universe secretly loves us."

"That'll be the day," snarled Bech. Though in fact the juices surging inside him bore a passing resemblance to those of love. Mishner dead put another inch on his prick.

A week later, he was in the subway. The Rockefeller Center station on Sixth Avenue, the old IND line. The downtown platform was jammed. All those McGraw-Hill, Exxon, and Time-Life execs were rushing back to their wives in the Heights. Or going down to West 4th to have some herbal tea and put on drag for the evening. Monogamous transvestite executives were clogging the system. Bech was in a savage mood. He had been to MoMA, checking out the Constructivist film-poster show and the Project 60 room. The room featured three "ultra-hip," according to the new *New Yorker,* figurative painters: one who did "poisonous portraits of fashion victims," another who specialized in "things so boring that they verge on non-being," and a third who did "glossy, seductive portraits of pop stars and gay boys." None of them had been Bech's bag. Art had passed him by. Literature was passing him by. Music he had never gotten exactly with, not since USO record hops. Those cuddly little WACs from Ohio in their starched uniforms. That war had been over too soon, before he got to kill enough Germans.

Down in the subway, in the flickering jaundiced light, three competing groups of electronic buskers—one country, one progressive jazz, and one doing Christian hip-hop—were competing, while a huge overhead voice unintelligibly burbled about cancellations and delays. In the cacophony, Bech spotted an English critic: Raymond Featherwaite, former Cambridge eminence lured to CUNY by American moolah. From his perch in the CUNY crenellations, using an antique matchlock arquebus, he had been snottily potting American writers for twenty years, courtesy of the ravingly

Anglophile *New York Review of Books.* Prolix and *voulu,* Featherwaite had called Bech's best-selling comeback book, *Think Big,* back in 1979. Inflation was peaking under Carter, the AIDS virus was sallying forth unidentified and unnamed, and here this limey carpetbagger was calling Bech's chef-d'oeuvre prolix and *voulu.* When, in the deflationary epoch supervised by Reagan, Bech had ventured a harmless collection of sketches and stories called *Biding Time,* Featherwaite had written, "One's spirits, however initially well-disposed toward one of America's more carefully tended reputations, begin severely to sag under the repeated empathetic effort of watching Mr. Bech, page after page, strain to make something of very little. A minor talent in a minor key makes for very faint music indeed."

The combined decibels of the buskers drowned out, for all but the most attuned city ears, the approach of the train whose delay had been so indistinctly bruited. Featherwaite, like all these Brits who were breeding like woodlice in the rotting log piles of the New York literary industry, was no slouch at pushing ahead. Though there was hardly room to place one's shoes on the filthy concrete, he had shoved and wormed his way to the front of the crowd, right to the edge of the platform. His edgy profile, with its supercilious overbite and artfully projecting eyebrows, turned with arrogant expectancy toward the screamingly approaching

D train, as though hailing a servile black London taxi or gilded Victorian brougham. Featherwaite affected a wispy-banged Nero haircut. There were rougelike touches of color on his cheekbones. The tidy English head bit into Bech's vision like a branding iron.

Prolix, he thought. *Voulu.* He had had to look up *voulu* in his French dictionary. It put a sneering curse on Bech's entire oeuvre, for what, as Schopenhauer had asked, isn't willed?

Bech was three bodies back in the crush, tightly immersed in the odors, clothes, accents, breaths, and balked wills of others. Two broad-backed bodies, padded with junk food and fermented malt, intervened between himself and Featherwaite, while others importunately pushed at his own back. As if suddenly shoved from behind, he lowered his shoulder and rammed into the body ahead of his; like dominoes, it and the next tipped the third, the stiff-backed Englishman, off the platform. In the next moment the train with the force of a flash flood poured into the station, drowning all other noise under a shrieking gush of tortured metal. Featherwaite's hand in the last second of his life had shot up and his head jerked back as if in sudden recognition of an old acquaintance. Then he had vanished.

It was an instant's event, without time for the D-train driver to brake or a bystander to scream. Just one head pleasantly less in the compressed, malodorous mob. The man ahead of Bech, a ponderous black with bloodshot eyes, wearing a knit cap in the depths of summer, regained his balance and turned indignantly, but Bech, feigning a furious glance behind him, slipped sideways as the crowd arranged itself into funnels beside each door of the now halted train. A woman's raised voice—foreign, shrill—had begun to leak the horrible truth of what she had witnessed, and far away, beyond the turnstiles, a telepathic policeman's whistle was tweeting. But the crowd within the train was surging obliviously outward against the crowd trying to enter, and in the thick eddies of disgruntled and compressed humanity nimble, bookish, elderly Bech put more and more space between himself and his unwitting accomplices. He secreted himself a car's length away, hanging from a hand-burnished bar next to an ad publicizing free condoms and clean needles, with a dainty Oxford edition of Donne's poems pressed close to his face as the news of the unthinkable truth spread, and the whistles of distant authority drew nearer, and the train refused to move and was finally emptied of passengers, while the official voice overhead, louder and less intelligible than ever, shouted word of cancellation, of disaster, of evacuation without panic.

Obediently Bech left the stalled train, blood on its wheels, and climbed the metallic stairs sparkling with pulverized glass. His insides shuddered in tune with the shoving, near-panicked mob about him. He inhaled the outdoor air and Manhattan anonymity gratefully. Avenue of the Americas, a sign said, in stubborn upholding of an obsolete gesture of hemispheric good will. Bech walked south, then over to Seventh Avenue. Scrupulously he halted at each red light and deposited each handed-out leaflet (girls! college sex kittens topless! bottomless after 6:30 p.m.!) in the next city trash receptacle. He descended into the Times Square station, where the old IRT system's innumerable tunnels mingled their misery in a vast subterranean maze of passageways, stairs, signs, and candy stands. He bought a Snickers bar and leaned against a white-tiled pillar to read where his little book had fallen open,

> Death, be not proud, though some have callèd
>   thee
>   Mighty and dreadful, for thou art not so;
>   For those whom thou think'st thou dost over-
>   throw
> Die not, poor Death, nor yet canst thou kill me.

He caught an N train that took him to Broadway and Prince. Afternoon had sweetly turned to evening while he had been underground. The galleries were closing, the restaurants were opening. Robin was in the loft, keeping lasagna warm. "I thought MoMA closed at six," she said.

"There was a tie-up in the Sixth Avenue subway. Nothing was running. I had to walk down to Times Square. I *hated* the stuff the museum had up. Violent, attention-getting."

"Maybe there comes a time," she said, "when new art isn't for you, it's for somebody else. I wonder what caused the tie-up."

"Nobody knew. Power failure. A shootout uptown. Some maniac," he added, wondering at his own words. His insides felt agitated, purged, scrubbed, yet not yet creamy. Perhaps the creaminess needed to wait until the morning *Times*. He feared he could not sleep, out of nervous anticipation, yet he toppled into dreams while Robin still read beneath a burning light, as if he had done a long day's worth of physical labor.

ENGLISH CRITIC, TEACHER DEAD / IN WEST SIDE SUBWAY MISHAP, the headline read. The story was low on the front page and jumped to the obituaries. The obit photo, taken decades ago, glamorized Featherwaite—head facing one way, shoulders another—so he resembled a younger, less impish brother of George Sanders. High brow, thin lips, cocky glass chin. . . . *according to witnesses appeared to fling himself under the subway train as it approached the platform . . . colleagues at CUNY puzzled but agreed he had been under significant stress compiling permissions for his textbook of postmodern narrative strategies . . . former wife, reached in London, allowed the deceased had been subject to mood swings and fits of creative despair . . . the author of several youthful satirical novels and a single book of poems likened to those of Philip Larkin . . . Robert Silvers of The New York Review expressed shock and*

termed Featherwaite "a valued and versatile con-
tributor of unflinching critical integrity" . . . born
in Scunthorpe, Yorkshire, the third child and only
son of a greengrocer and a part-time piano teacher
. . . and so on. A pesky little existence. "Ray Featherwaite is dead," he announced to Robin, trying to
keep a tremble of triumph out of his voice.

"Who was he?"

"A critic. More minor than Mishner. English.
Came from Yorkshire, in fact—I had never known
that. Went to Cambridge on a scholarship. I had figured him for inherited wealth; he wanted you to
think so."

"That makes two critics this week," said Robin,
preoccupied by the dense gray pages of stock
prices.

"Every third person in Manhattan is some kind
of critic," Bech pointed out. He hoped the conversation would move on.

"How did he die?"

There was no way to hide it; she would be reading this section eventually. "Jumped under a subway train, oddly. Seems he'd been feeling low,
trying to secure too many copyright permissions or
something. These academics have a lot of stress.
It's a tough world they're in—a lot of bitter faculty
politics."

"Oh?" Robin's eyes—bright, glossy, the living
volatile brown of a slick moist pelt—had left the
stock prices. "What subway line?"

"Sixth Avenue, actually."

"Maybe that was the tie-up you mentioned."

"Could be. Very likely, in fact. Did I ever tell you that my father died in the subway, under the East River in his case? Made a terrible mess of rush hour."

"Yes, Henry," Robin said, in the pointedly patient voice that let him know she was younger and clearer-headed. "You've told me more than once."

"Sorry."

"So why are your hands trembling? You can hardly hold your bagel." And his other hand, he noticed, was making the poppy seeds vibrate on the obituary page, as if a subway train were passing underneath.

"Who knows?" he asked her. "I may be coming down with something. I went out like a light last night."

"I'll say," said Robin, returning her eyes to the page. That summer the stock prices climbed up and up, breaking new records every day. It was unreal.

"Sorry," he repeated. Ease was beginning to flow again within him. The past was sinking, every second, under fresher, obscuring layers of the recent past. "Did it make you feel neglected? A young woman needs her sex."

"No," she said. "It made me feel tender. You seemed so innocent, with your mouth sagging open."

.   .   .

Robin, like Spider-man's wife, Mary Jane, worked in a computer emporium. She not so much sold them as shared her insights with customers as they struggled in the crashing waves of innovation and the lightning-swift undertow of obsolescence. The exorbitant memory demands of Microsoft's Windows 95 had overflowed two-year-old 4-RAM and 8-RAM IBMs and Compaqs. Once-mighty Macintosh had become a mere tidal pool, crawling with slowly suffocating Apple addicts. Simply holding one's place in cyberspace required more and more megabytes and megahertzes. Such pell-mell dispensability uncomfortably reminded Bech of his possible own, within the cultural turnover. Giants of his youth—A. J. Cronin, Louis Bromfield, John Erskine, Pearl Buck—had slipped over the horizon of living readership into the limbo of small-town book sales. Like a traveller in one of Einstein's thought experiments, he could be rapidly shrinking in such a recession and be the last to know it. Bech found himself described in scholarly offprints as "Early Postmodern" or "Post-Realist" or "Pre-Minimalist" as if, a narrowly configured ephemerid, he had been born to mate and die in a certain week of summer.

Nevertheless, it pleased him to view Robin in her outlet—on Third Avenue near 27th Street, a few blocks from Bellevue—standing solid and calm in a gray suit whose lapels swerved to take in her bosom. Amid her array of putty-colored monitors and system-unit housings, she received the petitions of those in thrall to the computer revolution. They were mostly skinny young men with parched hair and sunless complexions. Many of them forgot, Robin confided, to sleep or to bathe, in the intensity of their keyboard communions. She spoke their foreign language. It seemed exotic to Bech, erotic. He liked to stare in the display windows at her, while she was copulating, mentally, with a rapt customer. She had a rough way of seizing her own hair, bushy as it was, and pulling it back from her face for a moment, before letting it spring back again around her features, which were knotted in earnest disquisitions on the merits, say, of upgrading a modem from 14.4 kilobytes a second to 33.6 kbps. Sometimes Bech would enter the store, like some grizzled human glitch in its electronic hum, and take Robin to lunch. Sometimes he would sneak away content with his glimpse of this princess decreeing in her realm. He marvelled that at the end of the day she would find her way through the circuitry of the city and return to him. The tenacity of erotic connection presaged the faithful transistor and microchip.

Bech had not always been an evil man. He had dedicated himself early to what appeared plainly a good cause, art. It was amusing and helpful to others, he imagined as he emerged from the Army, to turn contiguous bits of the world into words, words which when properly arranged and typeset possessed a gleam that in wordless reality was lost beneath the daily accretions of habit, worry, and boredom. What harm could there be in art? What enemies could there be?

But he discovered that the literary world was a battlefield—mined with hatred, rimmed with snipers. His first stories and essays, appearing in defunct mass publications like *Liberty* and defunct avant-garde journals like *Displeasure,* roused little comment, and his dispatches, published in *The New Leader,* from Normandy in the wake of the 1944 invasion, and then from the Bulge and Berlin, went little noticed in a print world drenched in war coverage. But, ten years later, his first novel, *Travel Light,* made a small splash, and for the first time he saw, in print, spite directed at himself. Not just spite, but a willful mistaking of his intentions and a cheerfully ham-handed divulgence of all his plot's nicely calculated and hoarded twists. A New York Jew writing about Midwestern bikers infuriated some reviewers—some Jewish, some Midwestern—and the sly asceticism of his next, novella-length novel, *Brother Pig,* annoyed others: "The contemptuous medieval expression for the body which the author has used as a title serves only too well," one reviewer (female) wrote, "to prepare us for the sad orgy of Jewish self-hatred with which Mr. Bech will disappoint and repel his admirers—few, it is true, but in some rarefied circles curiously fervent." And his magnum opus, *The Chosen,* in which he tried to please his critics by facing the ethnicity purposefully sidestepped in *Brother Pig,* ran into a barrage of querulous misprision, not a barbed phrase of which had failed to stick in his sensitive skin. "Ignore the cretins," his wise acquaintance Norman Mailer had advised him. "Why do you even read such crap?" Joseph Heller sagely asked. Bech had tried to take their realistic advice, and in mid-career imagined that he had developed, if not the hide of a rhinoceros, at least the oily, resplendent back of a duck. He thought the reviews ran off him, chilly droplets swallowed in Lethe's black waters.

However, as he aged into the ranks of the elderly, adverse phrases from the far past surfaced in his memory, word for word—"says utterly nothing with surprising aplomb," "too toothless or shrewd to tackle life's raw meat," "never doffs his velour exercise togs to break a sweat," "the sentimental coarseness of a pornographic valentine," "prose arabesques of phenomenal irrelevancy," "refusal or failure to ironize his reactionary positions," "starry-eyed sexism," "minor, minorer, minormost"—and clamorously rattled around in his head, rendering him, some days, while his brain tried to be busy with something else, stupid with rage. It was as if these insults, these hurled mud balls, these stains on the robe of his vocation, were, now that he was nearing the end, bleeding wounds. That a negative review might be a fallible verdict, delivered in haste, against a deadline, for a few dollars, by a writer with problems and limitations of his own was a reasonable and weaselling supposition he could no longer, in the dignity of his years, entertain. *Any* adverse review, even a single mild phrase of qualification or reservation within a favorable and even adoring notice, stood revealed as the piece of pure enmity it was—an assault, a virtual murder, a purely malicious attempt to unman and destroy him. What was precious and potentially enduring about Bech was not his body, that fraternal pig, with its little oink of an ego, but his oeuvre. Any slighting of his oeuvre attacked the self he chiefly valued. After fifty years of trying to rise above criticism, he liberated himself to take it personally. A furious lava—an acidic indignation begging for the Maalox of creamy, murderous satisfaction—had secretly become Bech's essence, his angelic ichor.

The female reviewer, Deborah Frueh, who had in 1957 maligned *Brother Pig* as a flight of Jewish self-hatred lived far from New York, in the haven of Seattle, amid New Age mantras and medicinal powders, between Boeing and Mount Rainier. He could not get her ancient review out of his aging mind—the serene inarguable complacency of it, the certainty that she grasped the ineffable reality of being "covenanted" and he, poor pseudo-Jew, did not. He began to conceive of a way to reach her with the long arm of vengeance. She was still alive, he felt in his bones. She had been young when she dealt the young Bech her savage blow, but had emerged in 1979 to write, for the *Washington Post,* a stinging, almost pathologically sour review of *Think Big* beginning, "Somehow, I have never been persuaded to hop onto the Bech bandwagon. Even (or maybe especially) at its flashiest, his prose seems flimsy, the nowhere song of a nowhere man, devoid of any serious ethnic identification and stimulated by only the most trivial, consumeristic aspects of the United States. . . ." She, the spot bio accompanying this onslaught revealed, taught English poetry and the post-colonial novel at the University of Washington. From this remove her dismissive, pompous criticism ever more rarely reached the book-review columns of the Northeast Corridor. Perhaps academia had seduced her into Derridean convolution, culminating in self-erasure. But she could not hide from him, now that he had been aroused and become, on the verge of dotage, a man of action.

Though she was grit too fine to be found in the coarse sieve of *Who's Who,* he discovered her address in the *Poets & Writers'* directory, which listed a few critical articles and her fewer books, all children's books with heart-tugging titles like *Jennifer's Lonely Birthday* and *The Day Dad Didn't Come Home* and *A Teddy Bear's Bequest.* These books, Bech saw, were her Achilles' heel.

The renovated old factory where he lived assigned each of its tenants a storage room in the basement. But these partitioned, padlocked chambers by no means included all the basement space: exploration discovered far, dim-lit, brick-walled caverns that held rusted stitching machines and junked parts whose intricate shape defied speculation as to their mechanical purpose at the other, clanking end of the century. In a slightly less neglected recess, the building's management—a realty corporation headquartered in New Jersey—kept some shelved cans of paint and, hung on pegboard, plumbing supplies and carpentry tools and other infrequently wielded implements of upkeep. The super had about a dozen SoHo buildings in his care and was seldom in the basement, though a split, scuffed Naugahyde armchair, a stack of musty *Hustler*s, and an antique, gray-encrusted standing ashtray, long ago lifted from a hotel lobby, testified to a potential presence capable of, in the era before downsizing, some low-down leisure. In one of his furtive forays into these lower levels of Manhattan's lost Industrial Age, Bech found around a grimy corner a narrow wooden closet fitted between waste pipes and an abandoned set of water meters. The locked door was a simple hinged frame holding, where glass might have been, chicken wire rusted to a friable thinness. Peering inside, he saw a cobwebbed cache of dried dark jars, nibbled cardboard boxes, and a time-hardened contraption of rubber tubing with a tin hand-pump, coiled and cracked and speckled with oxidation. His attention fastened on a thick jar of brown glass whose label, in the stiff and innocent typographic style of the 1940s, warned poison and displayed along its border an array of dead vermin, roaches and rats and centipedes in dictionary-style engraving. Snapping the frail brown wire enough to admit his hand, Bech lifted the bottle out. The size of a coffee can, it sloshed, half-full. In the dusty light he read on the label that among the ingredients was hydrocyanic acid. Fearful that the palms of his hands might become contaminated, Bech carried the antique vermicide up to his loft wrapped in a *News* the super had tossed aside (headline: KOCH BLASTS ALBANY) and did not unscrew the rusty lid until he had donned Robin's mint-green rubber kitchen gloves. He exerted his grip. His teeth ground together; his crowns gnashed on their stumps of dentine. The lid's seal snapped a second before his carotid artery would have popped. Out of fifty intervening years of subterranean stillness arose the penetrating whiff, cited in many a mystery novel, of bitter almonds. The liquid, which was colorless, seemed to be vaporizing eagerly, its ghostly essence rushing upward from the gaping mouth of the jar.

He replaced the lid. He hid the jar in the drawer of his filing cabinet where he kept his old reviews. He did some research. Hydrocyanic, or prussic, acid was miscible with water, and a minute amount—a few drops of even a mild solution—would slow the heart, inhibit breathing, dilate the pupils, promote violent convulsive movements, cause loss of consciousness, and asphyxiate the victim with a complete loss of muscular power. Cyanides act within seconds, halting tissue oxidation and suspending vital functions. The victim's countenance turns a bluish color, not to be

confused with Prussian blue, an inert precipitant of
the poison.

    Bech wrote Deborah Frueh a fan letter, in a
slow and childish hand, in black ballpoint, on blue-
lined paper. "Dear Debora Freuh," he wrote, deliberately misspelling, "You are my very favrite
writer. I have red your books over 'n' over. I would
be greatful if you could find time to sign the two
enclosed cards for me and my best frend Betsey
and return them in the inclosed envelop. That
would be really grate of you and many *many* thanx
in advance." He signed it, "Your real fan, Mary
Jane Mason."

    He wrote it once and then rewrote it, holding
the pen in what felt like a little girl's fist. Then he
set the letter aside and worked carefully on the
envelope. He had bought a cheap box of one hundred at an office-supply store on lower Broadway
and destroyed a number before he got the alchemy
right. He put on the rubber gloves. They made his
hands sweat. With a paper towel he delicately
moistened the dried gum on the envelope flap—not
too much, or it curled. Then, gingerly using a glass
martini-stirring rod, he placed three or four drops
of the colorless poison on the moist adhesive. Lest
it be betrayingly bitter when licked, and Deborah
Frueh rush to ingest an antidote, he sweetened
the doctored spots with some sugar water mixed
in an orange-juice glass and applied with an eye-

dropper. Several times he stopped himself from absent-mindedly licking the flap to test the taste. He recoiled, it was as if he had been walking the edge of a cliff and nearly slipped and fell off, down toward the Prussian-blue sea of asphyxia and oblivion. In the midst of life, death is a misstep away.

The afternoon waned; the roar of tunnel-bound traffic up on Houston reached its crescendo unnoticed; the windows of the cast-iron façade across Crosby Street entertained unseen the blazing amber of the lowering sun. Bech was wheezily panting in the intensity of his concentration. His nose was running; he kept wiping it with a trembling handkerchief. His littered desk—an old army-surplus behemoth, with green metal sides and a black plastic top—reminded him of art-class projects at P.S. 87, before his father heedlessly moved him to Brooklyn. He and his peers had built tiny metropolises out of cereal boxes, butterflies out of colored papers and white paste, scissored into being red valentines and black profiles of George Washington, even made paper Easter eggs and Christmas trees, under their young and starchy Irish and German instructresses, who without fear of protest swept their little Jewish-American pupils into the Christian calendar. Back then, the magazine covers on the newsstand rack, the carols on the radio, the decorations on the school windowpanes all bespoke one culture, stuck in the Depression and the tired legend of that goyish young Jew who had made his way from Bethlehem to Golgotha, a life-journey children still celebrated with paper, cardboard, and paste.

Bech thought hard about the return address on the envelope, which could become, once its fatal bait was taken, a dangerous clue. The poison, before hitting home, might give Deborah Frueh time to seal the thing, which in the confusion after her death might be mailed. That would be perfect—the clue consigned to a continental mailbag and arrived with the junk mail at an indifferent American household. In the Westchester directory he found a Mason in New Rochelle and fistily inscribed the address beneath the name of his phantom Frueh fan. Folding the envelope, he imagined he heard a faint crackling—microscopic sugar and cyanide crystals? His conscience, dried up by this century of atrocity and atheism, trying to come to life? He slipped the folded envelope with the letter and four (why not be generous?) three-by-five index cards into the envelope painstakingly addressed in the immature, girlish handwriting. As he licked the stamp he thought of the Simpson trial and the insidious intricacy of DNA evidence. Semen, blood, saliva—all contain the entire person, coiled in ribbons of microscopic code. Everywhere we dabble or dribble or spit, we can be traced. Bech stuck the tongue-licked stamp thriftily on a blank envelope and moistened the one for Frueh on a corner of paper towel held under a running faucet, then squeezed.

The tall old wobbly windows across Crosby Street cast a sketchy orange web of reflected light into his loft. Before Robin could return from work and express curiosity about the mess on his desk, he cleaned it up. The paper towels and spoiled stationery went into the kitchen trash, and the lethal jar into the back of the cabinet drawer with the old reviews, which only he cared about—only he and a tiny band of Bech scholars, who were dying off and not being replaced by younger recruits. Even the caretaker of his archives at NYU had expressed a lack of interest in his yellowing clippings—which included such lovingly snipped tidbits as Bech sentences cited in the *Reader's Digest* feature "Picturesque Speech and Patter"—claiming that old newsprint posed "a terrible conservancy problem."

Bech took off the rubber gloves and hurried downstairs, his worn heart pounding, to throw Mary Jane Mason's fan letter into the mailbox at Broadway and Prince. A lurid salmon-striped sunset hung in the direction of New Jersey. The streets were crammed with the living and the guiltless, heading home in the day's horizontal rays, blinking from the subway's flicker and a long day spent at computer terminals. The narrow streets and low commercial buildings imparted the busy intimacy of a stage set, half lit as the curtain goes up. Bech hesitated a second before relinquishing his letter to the blue, graffiti-sprayed box, there in front of Victoria's Secret. A delicate middle-aged Japanese couple in bulbous sightseer's sneakers glanced at him timidly, a piece of local color with his springy white hair, his aggressively large nose, his deskworker's humped back. A snappy black woman, her beaded cornrows bristling and rattling, arrived at his back with an armful of metered nine-by-twelve envelopes, impatient to make her more massive, less lethal drop. Bech stifled his qualm. The governmental box hollowly sounded as its lid like a flat broad tongue closed upon the fathomless innards of sorting and delivery to which he consigned his missive. His life had been spent as a votary of the mails. This was but one more submission.

Morning after morning, the *Times* carried no word on the demise of Deborah Frueh. Perhaps, just as she wasn't in *Who's Who,* she was too small a fish to be caught in the *Times* obituary net. But no, they observed at respectful length the deaths of hundreds of people of whom Bech had never heard. Former aldermen, upstate prioresses, New Jersey judges, straight men on defunct TV comedies, founders of Manhattan dog-walking services—all got their space, their chiselled paragraphs, their farewell salute. Noticing the avidity with which he always turned to the back of the Metro section, Robin asked him, "What are you looking for?"

He couldn't tell her. His necessary reticence was poisoning their relationship. We are each of us sealed containers of gaseous fantasies and hostilities, but a factual secret, with its liquid weight, leaks out, if only in the care with which one speaks, as if around a pebble held in the mouth. "Familiar names," he said. "People I once knew."

"Henry, it seems morbid. Here, I'm done with Arts and Sports."

"I've read enough about arts and sports," he told this bossy dame, "to last me to the grave." Mortality was his meat now.

He went to the public library, the Hamilton Fish Park Branch over on East Houston, and in the children's section found one of Deborah Frueh's books, *Jennifer's Lonely Birthday,* and checked it out. He read it and wrote her another letter, this time in blue ballpoint, on unlined stationery with a little Peter Max–ish elf-figure up in one corner, the kind a very young girl might be given for her birthday by an aunt or uncle. "Dear Deborah Frueh," he wrote, "I love your exciting work. I love the way at the end of 'Jennifer's Lonely Birthday' Jennifer realizes that she has had a pretty good day after all and that in life you can't depend on anybody else to entertain you, you have to entertain and preoccupy your own mind. At the local library I have 'The Day Dad Didn't Come Home' on reserve. I hope it isn't too sad. I liked the positive ending to 'Jennifer's Lonely Birthday.' 'A Teddy Bear's Bequest' they never heard of at the library. I know you are a busy woman and must be working on more books but I hope you could send me a photograph of you for the wall of my room or if your too busy to do that please sign this zerox of the one on the cover of 'Jennifer's Lonely Birthday.' I like the way you do your hair, it's like my Aunt Florence, up behind. Find enclosed a stamped envelope to send it in. Yours most hopefully, Judith Green."

Miss Green in Bech's mind was a year or so older than Mary Jane Mason. She misspelled hardly at all, and had self-consciously converted her grammar-school handwriting to a stylish printing, which Bech slaved at for several hours before attaining the proper girlish plumpness in the "o"s and "m"s. He tried dotting the "i"s with little circles and ultimately discarded the device as unpersuasive. He did venture, however, a little happy-face, with smile and hair ribbon. He intensified the dose of hydrocyanic acid on the envelope flap, and eased off on the sugar water. When Deborah Frueh took her lick—he pictured it as avid and thorough, not one but several swoops of her vicious, pointed tongue—the bitterness would register too late. The covenanted bitch would never know what hit her.

The postmark was a problem. Mary Jane up there in New Rochelle might well have had a father who, setting off in the morning with a full briefcase, would mail her letter for her in New York, but two in a row from Manhattan and Frueh might smell a rat, especially if she had responded to the last request and was still feeling queasy. Bech took the ferry from the World Financial Center to Hoboken, treating himself to a river ride. He looked up

Greens in a telephone booth near the terminal, and picked one on Willow Street to be little Judy's family. Hoboken made him nostalgic for the Depression. In this densely built port from the past, lacy with iron balustrades, he went into an old-fashioned greasy spoon on Washington Street; there were wooden booths and stools at a counter and the selections and prices up in movable white letters on a grooved blackboard. He sat in a booth. He needed a table to write the return address on. In case he spoiled one envelope he had brought a spare, with a pastel elf in the lower left corner. But the address went well, it seemed to him. For a flourish he added a smiley face underneath the zip code.

Art excited his appetite. He ordered liver and onions from the lunch menu, a dish he hadn't had for years. The fried slab of gut came framed in oblong bubbles of blood-tinged grease. He ate it all, burped, and tasted the onions again. He deposited his letter in a small box on a concrete post—he hadn't known boxes like that still existed—and took the ferry back to lower Manhattan. His nerves hummed. His eyes narrowed against the river glare. The other passengers, too, felt the excitement of waterborne transition; they chattered in Spanish, in Chinese, in ebonics. What did Whitman write of such crossings? *Flood-tide below me! I see you face to face!* And, later on, speaking so urgently from the grave, *Just as you are refresh'd by the gladness of the river and the bright flow, I was refresh'd, / Just as you stand and lean on the rail, yet hurry with the swift current, I stood yet was hurried.* That "yet was hurried" was brilliant, with all of Whitman's brilliant homeliness. Soon, Bech reflected, he too would be dead, looking up through the flowing water to the generations as yet unborn, his bloodless visage sadder than Whitman's, because for all his striving and squirming he had—according to Lucas Mishner, himself recently enrolled in the underworld's eddying throng—never been touched by the American sublime.

The fuck he hadn't. Bech's hurried heart hummed all the way up Church Street to Warren, then over to City Hall and on up Broadway and home. *I too walk'd the streets of Manhattan island . . . / I am he who knew what it was to be evil, / I too knotted the old knot of contrariety, / Blabb'd, blush'd, resented, lied, stole, grudg'd . . .*

A week went by. Ten days. The death he desired was not reported in the *Times.* He wondered if a boy fan might win a better response, a more enthusiastic, heterosexual licking of the return envelope. "*Dear Deborah Frueh,*" he typed, using the clunky Script face available on his IBM PS/1:

You are a great writer, the greatest as far as I am concerned in the world. Your book titled "The Day Dad Didn't Come Home" broke me up, it was so sad and true. The way little Katrina comforts her baby brother Sam and realizes that they all will have to be Dad for each other now is so true it hurts. I have had a similar experience. I bet thousands of your readers have. I don't want to waste any more of your time reading this so you can get back to writing another super book but it would be sensational if you would sign the enclosed first-day cover for Sarah Orne Jewett, the greatest female American writer until you came along. Even if you have a policy against signing I'd appreciate you're returning it in the enclosed self-addressed stamped envelope since I am a collector and spent a week's allowance for it at the hobby shop here in Amityville, Long Island, NY. Sign it on the pencil line I have drawn. I will erase the line when you have signed. I look forward to hearing from you soon.

Yours very sincerely,

Jason Johnson, Jr.

Boys did seem a bit more adventurous and thrusting in their thinking than girls, Bech discovered through this act of ventriloquism. Maybe he should cut down on Jason's verbal braggadocio. The word processor, its frictionless patter, encouraged, as academics had been complaining for years, prolixity. But Featherwaite had pronounced Bech prolix when he was still using a manual, a Smith-Corona portable. He decided to let the boy have his say.

It was a pleasant change, in the too-even tenor of Bech's days, to ride the Long Island Rail Road out to Amityville and mail Jason Johnson's letter. Just to visit Penn Station again offered a fresh perspective—that Roman grandeur from Bech's youth, that onetime temple to commuting Fortuna, reduced to these ignoble ceilings and Tartarean passageways. And then, after the elevated views of tar-roofed Queens, the touching suburban stations, like so many knobbed Victorian toys, with their carefully pointed stonework and gleaming rows of parked cars and stretches of suburban park. Each stop represented happiness for thousands, and reminded him of his own suburban days in Ossining, married to Bea, stepfather to female twins and a small boy. He had felt uneasy, those years, a Jew with three acres and a dog and a car, as though occupying someone else's dream; but wasn't America after all the place to live in a dream, a dream determined not by your own subconscious but the collective unconscious of millions? He had not been unhappy, until the bubble was pricked and New York's leaden gravity sucked him back. In Amityville, he found a suitable Johnson—on Maple Drive—and mailed Jason's letter and had a lettuce-and-cucumber sandwich at a salad bar full of suburban women and their fidgety little sprouts. Then he headed back to town, each station more thickly surrounded by shabbier, more commercial constructions and the track bed becoming elevated and then, with a black roar, buried, underground, underriver, undercity, until the train stopped at

Penn Station again and the passengers spilled out into a gaudy, perilous mess of consumeristic blandishments, deranged beggars, and furtive personal errands.

Four days later, there it was, in eight inches of *Times* type: the death of Deborah Frueh. Respected educator was also a noted critic and author of children's books. Had earlier published scholarly articles on the English Metaphysicals and Swinburne and his circle. Taken suddenly ill while at her desk in her home in Hunts Point, near Seattle. Born in Conshohocken, near Philadelphia. Attended Barnard College and Duke University graduate school. Exact cause of death yet to be determined. Had been in troubled health lately—her weight a stubborn problem—colleagues at the University of Washington reported. But not despondent in any obvious way. Survived by a sister, Edith, of Ardmore, Pennsylvania, and a brother, Leonard, of Teaneck, New Jersey. Another ho-hum exit notice, for every reader but Henry Bech. He knew what a deadly venom the deceased had harbored in her fangs.

"What's happened?" Robin asked from across the table.

"Nothing's happened," he said.

"Then why do you look like that?"

"Like what?"

"Like a man who's been told he's won a million dollars but isn't sure it's worth it, what with all the tax problems."

"What a strange, untrammeled imagination you have," he said. "I wonder if selling computers does justice to all your talents."

"Let me see the page you're reading."

"No. I'm still reading it."

"Henry, are you going to make me stand up and walk around the table?"

He handed her the creamcheese-stained obituary page, which was toward the end of Section C today, this being Saturday and the paper the Weekend Edition. Robin, while the rounded masseters of her wide jaw thoughtfully clenched and unclenched on the last milky crumbs of her whole-bran flakes, flicked her quick brown eyes up and down the columns of print. Her eyes held points of red like the fur of a fox. Morning sun slanting through the big loft window kindled an outline of light, of incandescent fuzz, along her jaw. Her eyelashes glittered like a row of dewdrops on a spider strand. "Who's Deborah Frueh?" she asked. "Did you know her?"

"A frightful literary scold," he answered. "I never met the lady, I'm not sorry to say."

"Did she ever review you or anything?"

"I believe she did, once or twice."

"Favorably?"

"Not really."

"Really unfavorably?"

"It could be said. Her reservations about my work were unhedged, as I vaguely recall. You know I don't pay much attention to reviews."

"And that Englishman last month, who fell in front of the subway train—didn't you have some connection with him, too?"

"Darling, I've been publishing for over fifty years. I have slight connections with everybody in the print racket."

"You've not been quite yourself lately," Robin told him. "You've had some kind of a secret. You don't talk to me the breezy way you used to. You're censoring."

"I'm not," he said, hating to lie, standing as he was knee-deep in the sweet clover of Deborah Frueh's extermination. He wondered what raced through that fat harpy's mind in the last second, as the terrible-tasting cyanide tore into her esophagus and halted the oxidation process within her cells. Not of him, certainly. He was but one of multitudes of writers she had put in their places. He was three thousand miles away, the anonymous progenitor of Jason Johnson, Jr. *Sic semper tyrannis,* you unctuous, hectoring, covenanted shrew.

"Look at you!" Robin cried, on so high a note that her orange-juice glass emitted a surprised shiver. "You're triumphant! Henry, you killed her."

"How would I have done that?"

She was not balked. Her eyes narrowed. "At a distance, somehow," she guessed. "You sent her things. A couple of days ago, when I came home, there was a funny smell in the room, like something had been burning."

"This is fascinating," Bech said. "If I had your imagination, I'd be Balzac." He chattered on, to deflect her terrifying insights, "Another assiduous critic of mine, Aldie Cannon—he used to be a mainstay of *The New Republic* but now he's on PBS and the Internet—says I can't imagine a thing. And hate women."

Robin was still musing, her smooth young mien puzzling at the crimes to which she was an as yet blind partner. She said, "I guess it depends on how you define 'hate.' "

But he loved *her.* He loved the luxurious silken whiteness of her slightly thickset young body, the soothing cool of her basically factual mind. Beauty, the newspapers were saying that summer, is a matter of averaging out—babies and adults alike are more attracted to photographs of a morphed combination of faces than to the image of any specific one. What we desire is supernormality, a smooth statistical average; yet inevitably it comes in a package unique, fragile, precious. He could not long maintain this wall between them, this ugly wallboard partition in the light-filled loft of their intimacy.

The next day, the *Times* ran a little follow-up squib on the same page as the book review and the book ads. The squib was basically comic in its tone, for who would want to murder an elderly, overweight book critic and juvenile author? It stated that the Seattle police had found suspicious chemical traces in Frueh's autopsied body. They were closing in. Bech panicked. He was going to fry. The lights would dim in Ossining when they pulled the switch. He confessed to Robin. The truth rose irrepressible in his throat like the acid burn of partial regurgitation. Pushing the large black man who pushed a body that pushed Featherwaite's. Writing Deborah Frueh three fan letters with doped return envelopes. His belief, possibly delusionary, that before he died he had a duty to rid the world of critics, or at least of conspicuously malignant ones. Robin listened while reposing on his brown bean-bag chair in Claire Hoagland's old terrycloth bathrobe. She had taken a shower, so her feet had babyish pink sides beneath the marble-white insteps with their faint blue veins. It was Sunday morning. The bells in that sinister walled convent over at Prince and Mulberry had sounded their unheeded call. Robin said when he was done, "Henry, you can't just go around rubbing out people as if they existed only on paper."

"I can't? And who says they don't? That's where they tried to eliminate me, on paper. They tried to put me out of business. They preyed on my insecurities, to shut off my creative flow. They nearly succeeded. I haven't written nearly as much as I could have."

"Was that their fault?"

"Partly," he estimated. Maybe he had cooked his own goose, spilling his guts to this chesty dame. "O.K. Turn me in. Go to the bulls."

"The bulls?"

"The police—haven't you ever heard that expression? How about 'the fuzz'? or 'the pigs'?"

"I've never heard them called that, either."

"My God, you're young. What have I ever done to deserve you, Robin? You're so pure, so straight. And now you loathe me."

"No, I don't, actually. I might have thought I would, but in fact I like you more than ever." She never said "love," she was too post-Jewish for that. "I think you've shown a lot of balls, frankly, translating your resentments into action instead of sublimating them into art."

He didn't much like it when young women said "balls" or called a man "an asshole," but today he was thrilled by the cool baldness of it. They were, he and his mistress, in a new realm, a computer universe devoid of blame or guilt, as morally null as an Intel chip. There were only, in this scannable universe, greater or lesser patches of electricity, and violence and sex were greater patches. She stood and opened her robe. When Martina had done that, in this same loft, a few years ago, a nutritious warm-dough smell had spilled forth; but Robin had no strong smell, even between her legs. She gave off a babyish scent, a whiff of sour milk; otherwise her body was unodoriferous, so that Bech's own aromas, the product of over seven decades of marination in the ignominy of organic life, stood out like smears on a white vinyl wall. Penetrated, Robin felt like a fresh casing, and her spasms came rapidly, a tripping series of orgasms made almost pitiable by her habit of sucking one of his thumbs deep into her mouth as she came. When that was over, and their pulse rates had levelled off, she looked at him with her fox-fur irises shining expectantly, childishly. "So who are you going to do next?" she asked. Her pupils, tiny inkwells as deep as the night sky's zenith, were dilated by excitement. He pushed back her hair from her face, and let the wiry mass spring forward again.

"Well," Bech reluctantly allowed, "Aldie Cannon *is* very annoying. He's a forty-something smart-aleck, from the West Coast somewhere. Palo Alto, maybe. He has one of these very rapid agile nerdy minds—whatever pops into it must be a thought. He began by being all over *The Nation* and *The New Republic* and then he moved into the *Vanity Fair/GQ* orbit, writing about movies, books, TV, music, whatever, an authority on any sort of schlock, and then got more and more on radio and TV—they love that kind of guy, a thirty-second opinion on anything, bing, bam—until now that's basically all he does, that and write some kind of junk on the Internet, his own Web site, I don't know—people send me printouts whenever he says anything about me, I wish they wouldn't."

"What sort of thing does he say?"

Bech shifted his weight off his elbow, which was hurting. Any joint in his body hurt, with a little use. His body wanted to retire but his raging spirit wouldn't let it. He rested his head on the pillow beside Robin's pillow and stared at the ceiling, which had been recently fabricated of polystyrene acoustical tiles perforated by tiny dots. The dots were distributed with a studied irregularity that suggested the mountains and valleys of a shallow safe country as yet uncoagulated into cities. This bedroom had been carved, with wallboard and lumber, out of the loft's great space, complete with ceiling, like a cage in a circus tent. "He says I'm the embodiment of everything retrograde and unenlightened in pre-electronic American letters. He says my men are sex-obsessed narcissistic brutes and all my female characters are just anatomically correct dolls."

"*Ooh*," murmured Robin, as if softly struck by a bit of rough justice.

Bech went on, aggrieved, "For twenty years he's been getting a cheap ride hitchhiking on feminism, saying, 'Tut tut' and 'Too bad' to every novel by us older guys that isn't about an all-male platoon in World War Two being saved by a raft of angelic Red Cross nurses. He's been married, but never for long, and the word on the street is the jury's still out on his sexual orientation. Physically, he's a wimp—a pair of thick hornrims and a haircut like a toothbrush. He never got over George Gobel on television. You're too young to remember George Gobel."

"But he's clever," Robin prompted. "Clever enough to get under your skin."

"He's clever if glib cheap shots and a souped-up pseudo-show-biz lingo are clever, yeah."

"What else has he said about you?"

"He says I have no imagination. He says things like, and I quote, 'Whenever Bech attempts to use his imagination, the fuse blows and sparks fall to the floor. But short circuits aren't the same as magic-realist fireworks.' End quote. On top of being a smart-aleck he's a closet prude. He hated the sex in *Think Big*; he wrote, as I dimly remember, 'These tawdry and impossible wet dreams tell us nothing about how men and women really interact.' Implying that he sure does, the creepy fag. He's never interacted with anything but a candy machine and the constant torrent of cultural crap."

"Henry, his striking you as a creepy fag isn't reason enough to kill him."

"It is for me. He's a local blot on the universe."

"How would you go about it?"

"How would *we* go about it, maybe is the formula. What do we know about this twerp? He's riddled with insecurities, has all this manicky energy, and is on the Internet."

"You *have* been mulling this over, haven't you?" Robin's eyes had widened; her lower lip hung slightly open, looking riper and wetter than usual, as she propped herself above him, bare-breasted, livid-nippled, her big hair tumbling in oiled coils. Her straight short nose didn't go with the rest of her face, giving her a slightly flattened expression, like a cat's. "My lover the killer," she breathed.

"My time on earth is limited." Bech bit off his words. "I have noble work to do. I can't see Cannon licking return envelopes. He probably has an assistant for that. Or tosses them in the wastebasket. He thinks he's big-time, the little shit." Bech stared at the ceiling's unearthly geography. He averted his eyes from Robin's bared breasts, their gleaming white weight like that of gourds still ripening, snapping their vines.

She said, "So? Where could I come in?"

"Computer expertise. You have it, or know those that do. My question of you, baby, is, Could we break into his computer?"

Robin's smooth face, its taut curves with their invisible fuzz, hardened in intellectual engagement. "If he can get out," she said, "a smart cracker can get in. The Internet is one big happy family, like it or not."

The Aldie Cannon mini-industry was head-quartered in his modest Upper East Side apartment. Even the most successful operatives in the post-Gutenbergian literary world lived modestly, relative to the arriviste young wizards of electronic software, pop music, fashion design, and hair styling, not to mention the thousands of the already rich, whose ancestors or earlier, shrewder selves had scooped up a fortune from some momentary turn in the evolution of a rural democracy into a capitalist powerhouse; in recent years they had all needed to do nothing but watch their investments double and redouble in a stock market that, under the lubricous young President, knew no downside. Cannon lived, with his third wife and two maladjusted small children, not on one of the East Side's genteel, ginkgo-shaded side streets but in a raw new blue-green skyscraper, with balconies like stubby daisy petals, over by the river. His daily Internet feature, *Cannon Fodder,* was produced in a child-resistant study on a Compaq PC equipped with Windows 95. His opinionated claptrap was twinkled by modem to a site in San Jose, where it was checked for obscenity and libel and misspellings before going out to the millions of green-skinned cyberspace goons paralyzed at their terminals. E-mail sent to **fodder.com** went to San Jose, where the less inane and more provocative communications were forwarded to Aldie, for possible use in one of his columns.

Robin, after consulting some goons of her acquaintance, explained to Bech that the ubiquitous program for E-mail, Sendmail, had been written in the Unix ferment of the late 1970s, when security had been of no concern; it was notoriously full of bugs. For instance, Sendmail performed

security checks only on a user's first message; once
the user passed, all his subsequent messages went
straight through. Another weakness of the program
was that a simple |, the "pipe" symbol, turned the
part of the message following it into input, which
could consist of a variety of Unix commands the
computer was obliged to obey. These commands
could give an intruder log-in status and, with some
more manipulation, a "back-door" access that
would last until detected and deleted. Entry could
be utilized to attach a "Trojan horse" that would
flash messages onto the screen, with subliminal
brevity if desired.

Bech's wicked idea was to undermine Cannon's confidence and sense of self—fragile,
beneath all that polymathic, relentlessly with-it
bluster—as he sat gazing at his monitor. Robin
devised a virus: every time Aldie typed an upper-
case "A" or a lower-case "x," a message would
flash, too quickly for his conscious mind to register
but distinctly enough to penetrate the neuronic
complex of brain cells. The subversive program
took Robin some days to perfect; especially finick-
ing were the specs of such brief interruptions, amid
the seventy cathode-ray refreshments of the screen
each second, in letters large enough to make an
impression that could be read unawares by a modern mind habituated to the lightning message, the
commercially loaded seme, the come-hither flutter
of sexually loaded images. She labored while Bech
slept; half-moon shadows smudged and dented

the silken smoothness of her face. Delicately she strung her contingent binaries together. They could at any moment be destroyed by an automatic "sniffer" program or a human "sysadmin," a systems administrator. Federal laws were being violated; heavy penalties could be incurred. Nevertheless, out of love for Bech and the fascination of a technical challenge, she persevered and, by the third morning, succeeded.

Bech began, once the intricate, illicit commands had been lodged, with some hard-core Buddhism. BEING IS PAIN, the subliminal message read; NONBEING IS NIRVANA. The words invisibly rippled into the screen's pixels for a fifteenth of a second—that is, five refreshments of the screen, a single one being, Robin and a consulted neurophysiologist agreed, too brief to register even subliminally. After several days of these basic equations, Bech asked her to program the more advanced, NO MISERY OF MIND IS THERE FOR HIM WHO HATH NO WANTS. It was critical that the idea of death be rendered not just palatable but inviting. NONBEING IS AN ASPECT OF BEING, AND BEING OF NONBEING: This Bech had adapted from a Taoist poem by Seng Ts'an. From the same source he took TO BANISH REALITY IS TO SINK DEEPER INTO THE REAL. With Aldie's manicky productiveness in mind, he dictated, ACTIVITY IS AVOIDANCE OF VICTORY OVER SELF.

Together he and Robin scanned Cannon's latest effusions, in print or on the computer screen, for

signs of mental deterioration and spiritual surren-
der. Deborah Frueh had taken the bait in the dark,
and Bech had been frustrated by his inability to see
what was happening—whether she was licking an
envelope or not, and what effect the much-diluted
poison was having on her detestable innards. But in
the case of Aldie Cannon, his daily outpouring of
cleverness surely would betray symptoms. His
review of a Sinead O'Connor concert felt apa-
thetic, though he maintained it was her performance, now that she was no longer an anti-papal
skinhead, that lacked drive and point. His roundup
of recent books dwelling, with complacency or
alarm, upon the erosion of the traditional literary
canon—cannon fodder indeed, the ideal chance for
him to do casual backflips of lightly borne erudition—drifted toward the passionless conclusion
that "the presence or absence of a canon amounts
to much the same thing; one is all, and none is
equally all." This didn't sound like the Aldie Cannon who had opined, of Bech's collection *When the
Saints,* "Some of these cagey feuilletons sizzle but
most fizzle; the author has moved from not having
much to say to implying that anyone's having anything to say is a tiresome breach of good taste.
Bech is a literary dandy, but one dressed in tatters,
plucked up at the thrift-shop bins of contemporary
ideation."

It was good for Bech to remember these elaborate and gleeful dismissals, lest pity bring him to
halt the program. Where the celebrant of pop cul-

ture would once wax rapturous over Julia Roberts' elastic mouth and avid eyes, he now dwelt upon her ethereal emaciation in *My Best Friend's Wedding,* and the "triumphant emptiness" of her heroine's romantic defeat and the film's delivery of her into the arms of a confirmed homosexual. Of Saul Bellow's little novel, he noticed only the "thanatoptic beauty" of its culmination in a cemetery, where the hero's proposal had the chiselled gravity of an elegy or a death sentence. The same review praised the book's brevity and confessed—this from Aldie Cannon, Pantagruelian consumer of cultural produce—that some days he just didn't want to read one more book, see one more movie, go to one more art show, look up one more reference, wrap up one more paragraph with one more fork-tongued aperçu. And then, just as the Manhattan scene was kicking into another event-crammed fall season, *Cannon Fodder* now and then skipped a day on the Internet, or was replaced, with a terse explanatory note, by one of the writer's "classic" columns from a bygone year.

Sometimes, as the writer and his accomplice sat together monitoring Aldie Cannon's Web page, Robin's eyes in their gelatinous beauty glanced away from the plastic screen into Bech's face, but saw no more mercy in one than the other. His once rugged, good-humored features were shrinking with age, expelling their water, like a mummy's, becoming an overlapping bundle of leathery scraps all seam and pucker and coarse stitch. NONBEING IS

BLISS, he told her to make the Trojan horse spell, and SELFHOOD IS IMPURITY, and, at ever-faster intervals, the one word JUMP. JUMP, the twittering little pixels cried, and JUMP YOU BABBLING FOOL, giving a dangerously (in case an investigation were to reconstruct these smuggled commands) personal voice to Bech's subliminal barrage, which was varied by JUMP YOU TWIT or JUMP YOU HOLLOW MAN or DO THE WORLD A FUCKING FAVOR AND JUMP but always came back to the monosyllabic imperative verb. JUMP.

Bech had made a pilgrimage to the blue-green skyscraper near the river to make sure a suicide leap was feasible. Its towering mass receded above him like giant railroad tracks—an entire railroad yard of aluminum and glass. The jutting semicircular petals of its balconies formed a scalloped dark edge against the clouds as they hurtled in lock formation across the china-blue late-summer firmament. It always got to the pit of Bech's stomach, the way the tops of skyscrapers appeared to lunge across the sky when you looked up, like the prows of ships certain to crash. The building was fifty-five stories high and had curved sides. Its windows were sealed but the balconies were not caged in, as more and more high spaces were, to frustrate Icaruses dying to test the air. The top of the Empire State Building was now caged in; in Bech's boyhood it had not been, and when he was eight or so his father had held his ankles while he rested his chest on the broad parapet and looked straight down. Bech had never forgotten that dizzying moment of risk and trust, nor a photograph he had once seen in the old *Life,* of a beautiful young woman who had jumped and whose body lay as tranquilly intact on the dented top of a parked car as on a bier banked with flowers.

Within Bech a siren wailed, calling Aldie out, out of his cozy claustral nest of piped-in, faxed, E-mailed, messengered, videoed cultural fluff and straw—culture, that tawdry, cowardly anti-nature—into the open air, the stinging depths of space, cosmic nature pure and raw. Bech envisioned Manhattan yawning below the hesitating suicide—a crammed clutter of tarred rooftops and water tanks, with coded letters in whitewash addressed apparently to God's eye. Let go, Aldie, sky-dive, jump, merge your nasty little self with the vasty scribbled earth.

"I can't believe this is you," Robin told him. "This killer."

"I have been grievously provoked," he said.

"Just by reviews? Henry, nobody takes them seriously."

"I thought I did not, but now I see that I have. I have suffered a lifetime's provocation. My mission has changed; I wanted to add to the world's beauty, but now I merely wish to rid it of ugliness."

"Poor Aldie Cannon. Don't you think he means well? Some of his columns I find quite entertaining."

"He may mean well but he commits atrocities.

His facetious half-baked columns are crimes against art and against mankind. He has crass taste—no taste, in fact. He has a mouth to talk but no ears with which to listen." Liking in his own ear the rhythm of his tough talk, Bech got tougher. "Listen, sister," he said to Robin. "You want out? Out you can have any time. Walk down two flights. The subway's over on Broadway or up on Houston. I'll give you the buck-fifty. My treat."

She appeared to think it over. She said what women always say, to stall. "Henry, I love you."

"Why the hell would that be?"

"You're cute," Robin told him. "Especially these days. You seem more, you know, *together.* Before, you were some sort of a sponge, just sitting there, waiting for stuff to soak in. Now you've, like they say on the talk shows, taken charge of your life."

He pulled her into his arms with a roughness that darkened the fox-fur glints in her eyes. A quick murk of fear and desire clouded her features. His hoary head cast a shadow on her silver face as he bowed his neck to kiss her. She made her lips as soft as she could, as soft as the primeval ooze. "And you like that, huh?" he grunted. "My becoming bad."

"It lets me be bad." Her voice had gotten small and hurried, as if she might faint. "I love you because I can be a bad girl with you and you love it. You eat it up. Yum, you say."

"Bad is relative," he told her sagely, from the height of his antiquity. "For my purposes, you're a good girl. The worse you are the better you are. So it excites you, huh? Trying to bring this off."

Robin admitted, "It's kind of a rush." She added, with a touch of petulance as if to remind him how girlish she was, "It's my project. I want to stick with it."

"Now you're talking. Here, I woke up with an inspiration. Flash the twerp this." It was another scrap of Buddhist death-acceptance: LET THE ONE WITH ITS MYSTERY BLOT OUT ALL MEMORY OF COMPLICATIONS. JUMP.

"It seems pretty abstract."

"He'll buy it. I mean, his subconscious will buy it. He thinks of himself as an intellectual. He majored in philosophy at Berkeley, I read in that stuff you downloaded from the Internet."

While she was at the terminal pattering through the dance of computer control, he found in the same ancient text—Seng Ts'an's "Poem on Trust in the Heart"—a line that greatly moved him. *Space is bright, but self-illumined; no power of mind is exerted.* Self-illumined: that was what he in his innocence had once hoped to be. *Nor indeed could mere thought bring us to such a place,* the text went on, comfortingly. Yes. Mere thought was what he was done with. *It is the Truly-so, the Transcendent Sphere, where there is neither He nor I.*

Robin came back to him. "It went through, but I wonder."

"Wonder what?"

"Wonder how much longer before they find us

and wipe us out. There's more and more highly sophisticated security programs. Crackers are costing industry billions; the FBI has a whole department now for computer crime."

"The seed is sown," Bech said, still somewhat in Buddhist mode. "Let's go to bed. I'll let you suck my thumb, if you beg nicely. You bad bitch," he added, to see if her eyes would darken again. They did.

But the sniffers were out there, racing at the speed of light through the transistors, scouring the binary code for alien configurations and rogue algorithms. Now it was Robin who each morning rushed, in her inherited terrycloth robe, on her pink-sided bare feet, down the two flights to the ground-floor foyer and seized the *Times* and scanned its obituary page. The very day after her Trojan horse, detected and killed, failed to respond, there it was: ALDOUS CANNON, 43, CRITIC, COMMENTATOR. Jumped from the balcony of his apartment on the forty-eighth floor. No pedestrians hurt but an automobile parked on Sutton Place severely damaged. Distraught wife alleged the writer and radio personality, whose Web site on the Internet was one of the most visited for literary purposes by college students, had seemed preoccupied lately, and confessed to sensations of futility. Had always hoped to free up time to write a big novel. In a separate story in Section B, a wry collegial tribute from Christopher Lehmann-Haupt.

Bech and Robin should have felt jubilant. They had planted a flickering wedge of doubt beneath the threshold of consciousness and brought down a wiseguy, a media-savvy smart-ass. But it became clear after their initial, mutually congratulatory embrace, there above the sweating carton of orange juice and the slowly toasting bagels, that they felt stunned, let down, and ashamed. They avoided the sight and touch of each other for the rest of the day, though it was a Saturday. They had planned to go up to the Metropolitan Museum and check out the Ivan Albright show and then try to get an outdoor table at the Stanhope, in the deliciously crisp September air. But the thought of art in any form sickened them—sweet icing on dung, thin ice over the abyss. Robin went shopping for black jeans at Barneys and then took a train to visit her parents in Garrison, while Bech in a stupor like that of a snake digesting a poisonous toad sat watching two Midwestern college-football teams batter at each other in a screaming, chanting stadium far west of the Hudson, where life was sunstruck and clean.

Robin spent the night with her parents, and returned so late on Sunday she must have hoped her lover would be asleep. But he was up, waiting for her, reading. First some Froissart, on the Battle of Crécy ("the bodies of 11 princes, 1200 knights, and about 30,000 common men were found on the field"), and then a dip into the little volume of Donne:

License my roving hands, and let them go,
Before, behind, between, above, below.
O my America! my new-found land . . .

His eyes kept sliding off the page. The day's lonely
meal had generated a painful gas in his stomach.
His mouth tasted chemically of nothingness. Pas-
sive consumption, moral insufficiency. The alleged
selflessness of the artist—what a crock. All was
vanity, a coy dance of veils grotesque in a septuagenarian. Robin's key timidly scratched at the lock
and she entered; he met her near the threshold and
they gently bumped heads in a show of contrition.
They had together known sin. Like playmates who
had mischievously destroyed a toy, they slowly
repaired their relationship. As Aldie Cannon's
wanton but not unusual (John Berryman, Jerzy
Kosinski) self-erasure slipped deeper down into the
stack of used newspapers, and the obligatory notes
of memorial tribute tinnily, fadingly sounded in the
PEN and Authors Guild newsletters, the duo on
Crosby Street recovered their dynamism and a
fresh will to adventure, in the quixotic cause of rid-
ding literary Gotham of villains.

Bech bought himself a cape and Robin a mask.
A black mask, covering half her tidy white bobbed
nose and framing her warm, intricate eyes in a stiff
midnight strangeness. It turned him on; he made
her wear it during lovemaking. "I feel so dirty," she

confessed. "I feel like one of those corrupted countesses in French pornography. I feel like O."

Bech was good in bed but impotent elsewhere. "I can't sit at a desk any more," he said. "I want to get out and *do* something," he said. "Ever since Aldie jumped, it's like I've got St. Vitus' dance."

"Let's walk up to Washington Square. We'll cruise the remaining bookstores on Eighth Street."

"They were right, the bastards," Bech fumed, "I have nothing to say. I just wanted to pose, and print was the easiest place for a shy guy. I'm an elderly useless *poseur.*"

Out walking, he wore, with trepidation at first, his cape—a shiny blue satin, a shade lighter than navy, with a comforting lining of red lamb's wool, and a gold-plated clasp in the shape of a talon. He thought people would stare if not laugh, but he had underestimated the commonplace *bizarrerie* of Manhattan street theatre—the love-starved throngs, the poignant chorus of vain attention-getting. Hair dyed pastel colors, see-through blouses, lovely young shoulders blotched by tattoos, chalk-white black-lipped vampire makeup, the determinedly in-your-face costumes of the proclaimedly gay, the secret oddities of *Psychopathia Sexualis* turned inside out and put on show, like the convolute, inviting forms of flowers. Such exhibitionists denied Bech a single sideways glance at his cape as it swirled dramatically around him. Their eyes went to Robin—the candid purity of her face, boyish in its fashionable short haircut, formal like a waxen seal set on the untold pleasures of her body, curvaceous in its mauve catsuit.

To go with his cape Bech affected stovepipe trousers and narrow black slipperlike shoes, with rippled rubber treads. In these shoes he moved stealthily across pavements, lightly climbed stairs to bright gatherings—gallery openings, poetry readings—of tufted young aspirants to artistic fame who were startled to see that he, who had haunted, for a truncated page or two, their laborious double-columned high-school readers, was still alive. He slit his eyes against the glaze of their winey sweat and shuttling banter; he lifted his nose to scent evil and detected only the mild aroma of an illiterate innocence. These pretty children did not read, not in the old impassioned, repressed way, scouring print for forbidden knowledge, as his generation had done. Nietzsche, Marx, Freud, Joyce—the great God-killers. His enemies breathed his own air and lurked in dark lairs. His slippers carried him one night up the fire escape of a four-story red-brick building on Christopher Street, in the slant reaches, junglelike with ailanthus, of the West Village.

Robin in her mask followed him up, across the rusty iron slats. Tall old sash windows revealed roach-ridden kitchens and book-lined walls crawling with the wires of outmoded stereo sets. Noises could be heard through these windows, cries of emotion and laughter, whether in reality or on television was not perfectly clear. Bech climbed on, up the spindly metal welded by workmen long dead, toward a fourth-floor apartment where thirty years ago he had been a guest. He had been in his forties; his host in his fifties. The fire-escape slats threw diagonal harps of shadow across the crumbling bricks. One landing, seen downward through another, made a shimmering pattern located, like the elusive effects of Op Art, in no particular space. The fourth-floor windowpanes were black, but held oily orange traces of a reading lamp dimly burning several rooms away. Bech tested the sash but it was shut. The loathsome bookworm inside had barricaded himself against the warm October night—its cries of human intercourse, its garbagy smells of life.

From beneath his cape, Bech whipped out a strip of duct tape, attached it to a lower pane of the upper sash, deftly struck it with the blunt end of a glinting burglary tool. The muffled sound of fracture suggested that of a single ripe fruit falling. Swiftly his gray-gloved hand was in, twisting the worn window lock, and the weathered sash eased up on its rotten cords. He slithered over the sill, Robin as close behind him as a shadow. Inadvertently her hand on the sill caught his trailing cape. With a silent, predatory gesture, the silhouetted avenger tugged the lined satin free.

They were in a kind of pantry. Shelves designed for pans and crockery were filled with books, a lot of them bound galleys for review, stashed sideways and two deep, yellowing, collecting dust. Stealthily the intruders passed through an exiguous kitchen, scrubbed and bare, as a daytime caretaker would leave it. Three apples in a wooden bowl were the only visible food. Judgment of Paris, Bech thought. Venus the winner. Trouble in Troy. The apples imparted to his nostrils the faint tang of orchards gone under to malls. Then came a small dining room, its walls hung with spidery engravings of what seemed conferences—men in white wigs and black knickers plotting revolutions. They were making sweeping gestures. Kill the King, *écrasez l'infâme,* make it new. A half-open door led to a small bedroom, a single bed made up taut as a hospital bed, with a number of upright pillows. Sleeping upright. Buried alive. Bech's own breath empathetically grew short.

The sallow light dimly perceived from the fire escape strengthened. Bech and Robin found themselves in a room lined with books, books piled to the ceiling, disorder upon order, uniform sets submerged under late arrivals, biographies and commentaries and posthumous volumes, the original organization overwhelmed, torn bookmarks and offprints chaotically interleaved. An arid smell, as of manmade desert, seeped from so much paper. Dust mites, spilling allergens, rustled underfoot.

Beyond this room, glimpsed through a doorway carved through the Egyptian thickness of books, an underfurnished living room bared itself to the streetlight, to the scattered glimmer of lower

Manhattan and the sullen gap of the Hudson. Nobody was there.

The occupant of this Village apartment, the mastermind behind its parched accumulations, sat behind the intruders, in a corner of the library, reading and sniffing oxygen. A baby-blue plastic tube led from a cylindrical tank beside his armchair up to his nose, where it forked to take in both nostrils. The man had advanced emphysema, from a lifetime of contented smoking while he read. A gooseneck lamp looked over his shoulder. His black-stockinged feet were up on an old-fashioned ottoman, with tassels and rolled seams and a top of multicolored leather sliced like a pie. His body, boneless and amorphous, merged with that of his creased leather armchair, tucked like a kind of shroud around him. Time had nearly ceased to flow here. Nothing moved but the invalid's limp, flat-ended fingers as he turned a page. He looked up blinking, resenting the interruption of his reading. "Bech," he said at last. "My God. Climbing fire escapes now. Why the crazy get-up? I thought you were a madman, breaking in."

"Get real, Cohen," Bech snapped. "Capes are coming back. They *are* back. Monocles, next."

"Or a dope addict," the invalid wheezily continued, in skeltonic gasps. "I get about one a week. They diss me because . . . there's nothing to steal. Just old books. Kids today have no idea . . . of the value of books. And who's your lovely sidekick?

Zaftig, I can see . . . through the catsuit. But so young, to get mixed up . . . in old men's quarrels." Cohen had taken off his reading glasses, to focus on the incursion from beyond the printed page. His eyes were pinched in folds of collapsing lids and puckered socket-skin. Seeing that Bech would not perform introductions, he said, in a mockery of politeness, "I almost liked your last book. The one about . . . the Korean War orphan. At least you weren't trying . . . to pass off your feeble fantasies . . . as any country we know."

Cohen had barely the breath to blow out a candle. His utterances resembled sentences lifted from book reviews and peppered with ellipses to make them more favorable. His reference was to *Going South* (1992), a tender, well-researched novella imagining the adventures of a parentless nine-year-old girl, Hang Kim, from a village near Huichon, caught up in the routed American armies retreating from the waves of Chinese troops all the way to Taejon. As Bech aged, his thoughts turned to war. He had fought in one over a half-century ago. At the time, and for most of the time since, he had thought of war as an aberration, a dehumanizing episode to be gotten through and forgotten. But lately he had begun to wonder if Hemingway and Tolstoy weren't right: war was truth, in an unbearably pure state. It has shaped the map and spawned the most vigorous moral principle, that of tribal loyalty.

Bech swirled his cape, performing, with an ironic bow, the courtesies Cohen had requested. "Rachel, meet my nemesis, Mr. Orlando Cohen, the arch-fiend of American criticism. Orlando, this is Ms. Rachel Teagarten, who helps me out in my work. She understands computers, copulation, and elementary cooking."

"I suppose computers," the old magus wheezed, "are worth understanding. I always think in this connection . . . of the chess-playing automaton . . . who turned out to be . . . a dwarf. The board had to be transparent, so he . . . could follow the moves. Imagine . . . following the moves upside down . . . crouched in a little airless box. And winning some- times. He didn't always win, actually—that is a myth. There was a series of dwarfs . . . some of whom were undoubtedly . . . more skillful than others."

This long speech left Cohen utterly breathless. He inhaled prolongedly through his nose. His nose and ears had enlarged with age, or had remained the same while the rest of him shrunk. He had been a handsome man, once, and women had been tanta- lized and maddened by their failure to distract him from his chaste ambition to be the ultimate adjudi- cator of literature—all literature, but specializing in American. He had steadfastly refused to grant Bech a place, even a minor place, in the canon. In review after review he had found Bech's books artificial, hollow, dandyish, lame. His review of

Going South, in *The New Criterion,* had been jeer-ingly titled "Halt and Lame."

"Don't try to buy time with gabble," Bech advised him. "The jig is up."

"What jig?" Cohen managed to get out. The tip of his nose looked blue with anoxia. He had a strange contemplative habit of twitching his nose, of swinging its tip from side to side, rapidly.

"The jig of trashing me. What did I ever do to you?"

"You failed to write well."

"How could that be? It was all I cared about, writing well."

"You cared too much. You let the words hold you back . . . from descending into yourself. You were Jewish and tried to pretend . . . you were American."

"Can't you be both?"

"Bellow can. Salinger could, once. Mailer, alternately . . . never both at once. Malamud . . . I don't know. He lost me in those last books . . . *Dubin's Lives* and the one about the monkeys. He wanted credentials. Jews can't get credentials. Not in a world run by goyim. Israel is a credential. It's not a good one. The Arabs won't stamp it."

"You're stalling, Orlando. See this? What is it?" Bech delved beneath his beautiful, midnight-blue cape and brandished the steel tool he came up with. It felt heavy, heavier than it looked.

"A gun," Orlando Cohen said. His spatulate fingers adjusted the plastic leech whispering into his nostrils.

"A gat," Bech corrected. "A rod. With a silencer. Not even the people downstairs are going to hear when I plug you. They'll think it's your dishwasher kicking into the next part of the cycle."

The sick man's eyes left Bech's face. "Rachel," he said. "How long has he . . . been like this?"

"Don't answer the scumbag," Bech commanded her. "The prick, he sucks up to Wasps. The stiff-necked old establishment. The more anti-Semitic they were—the Jameses, the Adamses, the Holmeses—the more he loves them. Hemingway, Fitzgerald—never mind their snide cracks. He even praised Capote, can you imagine? Praised Capote and panned me."

Cohen replied, so faintly the duo had to strain to listen, picking up all sorts of muttered street noise and radio music in the process. "Capote . . . descended into himself. In *In Cold Blood* . . . he hit his vein. He wanted to be hung with Perry. He hated himself . . . the little squeaky monster he was. He worked his self-hatred . . . into an objective correlative. He made us care. Bech . . . you . . . you missed your vein. You were squeamish . . . and essentially lazy. You missed . . . the boat. The boat . . . to America."

"I am going to shut you up," Bech told him. "I am going to squeeze this fucking trigger and rub you out. Don't think I'm too squeamish. I've killed

before." In the war. There was no knowing how
many. With a Browning automatic rifle you poured
lead into a thicket or Belgian farm shed that had
been sheltering enemy fire or took on a flakwagon
or machine-gun emplacement and at the end there
was no telling how many of the bodies were yours,
these German bodies that after a few freezing days
in their piles looked like cordwood or enormous
purple-and-green vegetables. In the Ardennes, in
December of '44, in the Twenty-eighth Infantry, in
the bitter cold, the German soldiers were specks
in the snow, distant, running, toward him or away
from him wasn't easy to tell in the snow glare; you
squeezed, you squeezed the icy trigger of the M1,
metal so cold the oil would freeze and jam the bolt,
you squinted into the glare and squeezed through
the crumbling GI gloves whose fraying olive
threads grew little balls of frozen snow, cold to the
bones from the night in the wet foxhole, huddled
with O'Malley and Perera and Lundgren, the loved
strangers whose bodies were life's warmth, up to
your knees in icy water in the trench, the physical
misery great enough and so incessant you could get
light-hearted about the death that might hide behind
the next tree, as you scuttled along, hump-backed
with your pack, thick ancient beeches the trees
were, their gray lines rounded and graceful like
those of women in the snow. Country like a Christmas card, great Kraut-killing country, the men
joked, the bleary heartless boy-men, and it was true,
the Ardennes counteroffensive brought the Heinies

up out of their bunkered, Kraut-trim emplacements into the open, upright, trying to advance, under Hitler's mad orders. You squeezed and the distant scurrying dot dropped and you felt a spurt of warmth inside, a surcease in the misery, a leak of satisfaction and pride from some other, impossible world, a world at peace. He potted a few more, like ducks against a white sky, before the platoon fell back and he got his feet out of ice water. If he had killed for his country, he could kill for his art.

"Go ahead," Cohen breathlessly urged him. "Pull it. Do it. I'm eighty-two and . . . can't take five steps . . . without suffocating. Do me the favor." Yet the old creep didn't mean it; he was cunning; he was crazy to live. Cannily, Cohen went on, "What about your young friend here? Rachel. Think she'll like the . . . rest of her days in the pen? They execute . . . women these days. Seems a heavy price to pay for . . . your elderly boyfriend's vanity."

"She chose to come along. I didn't drag her."

"I love seeing Henry so energized," Robin told Cohen.

"He should have put his energy . . . into his work. *Travel Light . . . Think Big* . . . stunts. You can't believe a word. I ignore *The Chosen* because everybody agreed . . . it was an embarrassment."

"Not Charles Poore in the daily *Times.* He loved it."

"Poore, that old lady. What did he know? You tried to con us. You thought you could skip

out . . . of yourself and write American.
Bech . . . let me ask you. Can you say the Lord's
Prayer?"

Bech didn't dignify his inquisitor with an
answer, just laid the revolver—a Luger, a war sou-
venir lifted from the body of a dead officer, a gun
that may well have killed Jews before—a little off
from pointing at his enemy's heart. He laid it sideways in air, giving Cohen's struggling, insatiable
tongue permission to continue.

"Well, ninety percent of the zhlubs around you
can. It's in their heads. They can rattle . . . the
damn thing right off . . . how can you expect to
write about people . . . when you don't have a clue
to the crap . . . that's in their heads? The Holy
Ghost . . . These goyim came here thinking . . . the
Holy Ghost had them by the hand. The Holy Ghost.
Who the hell is that? Some pigeon, that's all . . .
anybody knows. Those first winters . . . they'd
never seen anything like it . . . back in England.
They stuck it out . . . but that God-awful faith . . .
Bech . . . when it burns out . . . it leaves a dead
spot. Love it or leave it . . . a dead spot. That's
where America is . . . in that dead spot. Em, Emily,
that guy in the woods . . . Hem, Mel, Haw . . . they
were there. No in thunder . . . the Big No. Jews
don't know how to say No. All we know is Yes.
Yes, I'll kill Isaac . . . Yes, let's wrestle. That's why
you're lousy, Bech. You gave it a shot . . . some say
a good shot . . . but not me. For me it fell flat. You

aimed away . . . from the subject you had . . . into the one no one has . . . except the people who can inhabit nowhere. America, opportunity, jazz, O.K. . . . but it's a nowhere. A coast-to-coast nowhere. You thought . . . like those Hollywood meshuggeners . . . Jews slaphappy with getting out of the ghetto . . . you could tickle it into becoming . . . a *place,* with cute people. Mickey Rooney, Lewis Stone . . . Jesus. James, Twain, Adams, those mean old boys . . . you got to love them. You, Bech, I don't have to love. You are a phony. You made yourself up . . . *worse* even than Capote. Go ahead. Pull it. I'm dying for it, no kidding. I can't breathe, can't talk, can't fuck, can't eat . . . can't even sleep more than an hour at a time. Pull it. Look the other way, Rachel. Death's not as pretty . . . as you kids these days seem to think. You think it's nothing . . . but it's still . . . something." The revered critic's nose twitched, its blue tip swinging back and forth for perhaps the last time.

Bech uncertainly glanced sideways at Robin. He admired, in her profile, the emphatic black eyebrow, a boldface hyphen, stark and Mediterranean in feeling. Iphigenia and Esther, Electra and Delilah had possessed such fatal unflinching eyebrows. If he wanted to shoot, she would watch him shoot. She was the best sidekick a man could have.

"Robin," he told her. "Go pull the tube out of the slimeball's nostrils."

She quickly did as she was told, padding forward in her catsuit, thinking perhaps this was a preliminary courtesy, when one old man killed another after decades of enmity.

Bech explained, lowering the gun, "Let's see if he can breathe on his own."

Cohen had steeled himself, but panic was creeping up, from his lungs to his face. The tip of his nose was revolving in continuous motion, tracing a tiny circle. He strained forward, to unpinch his lungs, and scrabbled at the side of his chair for the whispering baby-blue tube. His words were mere husks, in clumps of two or three. "Not like this. Use the gat. Bech . . . believe me . . . your stuff . . . won't last. It's . . . upper-middlebrow . . . schlock. Not even upper. Middle-middle."

"You fetid bag of half-baked opinions," Bech snarled. "You rotten spoiler. You've been stealing my oxygen for years."

"Your stuff . . . it's . . . it's . . ." Cohen had slumped sideways in the chair. The book he had left on the arm (Walter Benjamin, *Selected Writings, Volume I, 1913–1926*) hit the floor with a thud. His complexion approached the tint of a fish, his throat puffing like stifled gills. "Fifties!" he concluded with a triumphant leer. "You're Fifties!" His yellow eyeballs rolled upward and his reading glasses flopped into his lap.

"Let's blow this joint," Bech told Robin. "I smell escaping gas."

"But—" He knew what she meant. If he wasn't going to shoot him, wasn't it cruel to let him asphyxiate? Or was this rough justice, on the anoxic literary heights?

"Listen, doll. We're doing him a favor, just like he asked. The poor sap is addicted. Nobody likes air after they've tasted pure oxygen. How does he breathe when he goes to the john? When he grabs his hour of sleep? Between us, I bet he socks in a solid seven, eight hours a night, with maybe one trip to the hopper to take a piss."

Orlando Cohen, fabled maker and destroyer of reputations, lay crumpled in his chair like a baby transfixed in the mystery of crib death. Robin suppressed a cry and a step toward the unconscious dotard. Bech's steely gray-gloved hand on her arm restrained her impulsive motion.

"Don't let that dickhead manipulate you," he told his companion. "You're like any broad. You're too soft. A cold-hearted *k'nocker* like that, he takes advantage. He'll get it together as soon as he hears us out the window and down the fire escape. Did you dig that canned lecture on American lit? He's given it a thousand times."

Off in the city, a police siren began to ululate; not for them on this caper, but perhaps the next. Clatteringly, the duo descended into the weedy dark back garden, where the shadows of ailanthus leaves restlessly stabbed. Robin brushed up against Bech in these shadows, her face, without its mask, startlingly white. "I want a baby," she said softly.

"Hey," Bech said. "I said broads were soft-hearted, I didn't say they had to act on it."

"I want to bear your child," she insisted.

"I'm seventy-four," he said. "I'm past my 'sell by' date."

They made their stealthy way out, past overflowing trashcans and dying rosebushes, onto Christopher Street, where they became, in the early-evening lamplight, another discreetly quarrelling couple. "I felt scared," Robin confessed, "when I thought you were going to shoot that wheezy old man."

"I should have shot the putz," Bech responded morosely. "He's done me a world of woe. He's tried to negate me."

"Why didn't you then?" Her hand tugged on his arm like another question, there under the red-lined cape, which lifted a little behind them, as a breeze from Bleecker Street conveyed an ozone suggestion of a thunderstorm before midnight.

"I believed him; it was worse for him to live."

"You know what I think?"

She waited, irritating Bech, for the thousandth time, with the playful, self-pleasuring expertise with which women play the relational game. "What?" he had to respond, gruffly.

"I think," she said, "you're a bit soft-hearted yourself."

"I was," he allowed, "but they beat it out of me.

They nagged and nitpicked and small-minded me out of it."

"They couldn't," she said. "They're just critics, but you—"

Once again, her artful pause forced him to make a response: "Yes?"

"You're you."

"And who isn't?"

"Everybody is, but few take it as much to heart as you have. Henry—"

"*What?* Cut it out with the dialogue."

"Do you think maybe we've rid the world of enough evil for now?"

"There's plenty left. There's a guy who teaches at Columbia, Carlos something-era, an English professor, or whatever they call it now, who really got my goat in the *Book Review* the other week. He said I lacked *duende. Duende!* I looked it up in the Spanish dictionary and it said 'ghost, goblin, fairy.' And then there's Gore Vidal, who— And Garry Wills, who—"

"Darling."

"What now?"

"You're sputtering. Let's think about our baby."

"I can't bring a baby into a world as polluted by wicked criticism as this one."

"Nobody criticizes a baby."

"They would any of mine. Robin, we were just getting going as a duo."

"Were?"

"I want to wreak more vengeance."

"No you don't," Robin told him. "What a duo wants is to become a trio. Here's a deal: knock me up, or I go to the cops. The bulls."

"And tell them what?"

"Everything."

"This is blackmail."

"I'd call it devotion. To your best interests." They turned right on Bedford, to cut through to Houston, to walk on to Crosby. The city hung around them like an agitprop backdrop, murmurous and surreal, perforated by lights and lives in the millions. A bat-colored cloud bank gathered in the east, trailing wisps, above the saffron dome of the city's glow. Rachel Teagarten snuggled closer, complacently, under his cape. Bech wondered if this little tootsie wasn't getting to be a bit of a drag.

Bech and the Bounty of Sweden

A STORM OF PROTEST greeted the announcement that Henry Bech had won the 1999 Nobel Prize for Literature. Fumed a *New York Times* editorial:

> The Swedish Academy's penchant for colorful nonentities and anti-establishment gadflies as recipients of its dynamite-based bounty has surpassed mere caprice and taken on, in this latest selection, dimensions of wantonness. If the time for an American winner had at last come round again, then a deliberate affront must be read in this bypassing of solid contenders like Mailer, Roth, and Ozick, not to mention Pynchon and DeLillo, in favor of this passé exponent of fancy penmanship, whose skimpy oeuvre fails even to achieve J. D. Salinger's majestic total abstention from publication.

The *Post* quoted Isaiah Thornbush as saying, "With all respect to my dear colleague and old friend

Henry, this turns the Prize into a prank. I was, quite frankly, stunned." BECH? WHODAT??? was the *Daily News*'s front-page headline, and *People* ran as its cover the least flattering photo they could find on file, showing Bech and his then wife, Bea, in bib overalls feigning repairs to the grape arbor of their mock-Tudor, mock-Edenic residence in Ossining. *New York* rose to the occasion with a languidly acid John Simon retrospective entitled "The Case (Far-Fetched) for Henry Bech."

Meanwhile, the phone in his Crosby Street loft kept ringing, sometimes interrupting the septuagenarian winner in the midst of changing diapers for his eight-month-old baby, Golda (when it came to naming her daughter, Robin Teagarten was not so post-Jewish after all), so that the spicy smell of ochre babyshit and the shrilling of the phone became the two wings of one exasperating experience. Golda was sturdy and teething and had her mother's challenging calm stare, not fox-colored thus far but an infant's contemplative, unblinking slate blue. She was old enough to think there was something fishy about this knobby-handed old man groping about in her crotch and bottom crack with chilly baby wipes, and then too firmly pressing the adhesive fasteners in place upon her glossy, wobbly belly. Golda would tease him and show off her strength by twisting on the changing towel, corkscrewing like a baroque putto. She preferred her mother's cool quick touch, or the light brown hands of Leontyne, the lilting au pair from Antigua by way of Crown Heights.

The voice on the phone was usually that of Meri [sic] Jo Zwengler, Vellum Press's leather-clad chief of publicity. "But I don't want to go on 'Oprah,'" he would tell her. "I hate that hooting audience of Corn Belt feminists she has."

Meri Jo would sigh. "It's expected, Henry. It would be considered an insult to two-thirds of America if you don't deign to appear."

"Yeah, the illiterate two-thirds. Where were they when *Going South* sold less than twenty thousand copies?"

Meri Jo was stagily patient with him. "You're a Laureate now, Henry. You're not free to pull that Henry Bech reclusive don't-bother-me-I'm-having-a-writer's-block act."

"Bech, whodat?" he quoted.

"Nobody's asking that any more. You're hot, Henry. I'm sorry. But the spike in sales should put your little girl through college, if you help nurse it along. We're thinking of even bringing *When the Saints* back into print."

"Why did you let it go out of print?"

"Don't be difficult, Henry. Warehousing costs have been skyrocketing. We have a big overhead in our new quarters."

Meri Jo's annual salary, he estimated, would loom above a year's worth of his royalties like a sequoia above a bonsai cherry tree. "Did I ask you," he asked her, "to build yourselves a sky-scraper, just because McGraw-Hill had one?"

"Hon, please be an angel and stop giving me a hard time," she said. He imagined he could hear the squeak of leather and the click of studs on metal as she shifted her heft in her personally molded swivel chair. "You were wonderful on 'Charlie Rose.'"

"*Char*lie was wonderful," Bech protested. "I hardly said a word." The interviewer's long face, tinted the color of a salmon, loomed in memory; Rose had leaned forward ominously close, like an Avedon portrait of himself, and urged, "Tell me honestly, Henry, aren't you *embarrassed*, to have won this Prize when so many other writers haven't?" And the culture-purveyor's eyes protruded toward him inquisitorially, so that he resembled Dick Van Dyke in Disney animation.

These professional personalities operated at an energy level that stretched Bech's brain like chewing gum on the shoe of a man trying to walk away. Terry Gross, in her beguilingly adolescent and faintly stammery voice, had put it to him more brutally yet: "How can you explain it? It must feel like a weird sort of miracle, I mean, when Henry James and Theodore Dreiser and Robert Frost and Nabokov didn't . . ."

"I'm not a Swedish mind-reader," was all Bech could manage by way of apology. "I'm not even a Swedish mind."

This seemed to him a pretty good quip, which he had prepared in the reveries of insomnia, but which, on its occasion for utterance, lacked the lilt of spontaneity. The short, short-haired interviewer's giggle was perfunctory, and then like a dingo worrying the throat of a lamed kangaroo she went back to the attack: "No, but seriously . . ."

This was on a radio swing down through Megalopolis, from Christopher Lydon in a dismal stretch beyond Boston University to Leonard Lopate in the dingy corridors of New York City Hall to Philadelphia's "Fresh Air" in a canister-lined chamber of WHYY and on to Diane Rehm's WAMU aerie on Brandywine Street, in the bosky midst of American University in Washington, D.C. She had fascinatingly blued hair and a crystalline, beckoning voice—as if from another room she were calling some sorority girls to dinner—and in this particular chain of interviewers put Bech least on the defensive. Why, of course, she seemed to be saying, Mr. Bech has won the Nobel Prize for Liter-a-ture. Who better? Listeners, you tell *us*.

The very first caller-in, whose sugary Southern accent buzzed in Bech's earphones like tinnitus, wanted to know if it was true, as she had read in the *National Enquirer*, that Mr. Bech had recently fathered a baby out of a young lady a third of his age?

"I suppose it's not untrue," Bech grudged into the microphone. Robin had blackmailed him into it, he resisted explaining. It was become a father or an accused serial killer.

"Mah questi-yun is, sir, do you think that such behavior is fay-yer to either the young lady or that little helpless baby, when, begging your pardon, you might drop daid any taahm?"

"Fair?" It was a concept he hadn't encountered lately. As a child he would protest to his playmates that something wasn't *fair,* but as the inexorable decades had washed over him, his indignation had been slowly leached away.

"And thet million dollars you've gone and won—do you intend to do any *goood* with it?"

He had repeatedly explained to interviewers and crasser talk-show hosts that by the time his taxes were paid to state, city, and nation it wouldn't be anything like a million. It would be less than half a million. Counting the hours of his time and ergs of his energy the Prize had taken, and the universal consensus that he now owed the world something, he had come to figure it as a net financial loss. And, anyway, what does half a million dollars get you in New York City these days? A Jeff Koons statuette, or a closet in a Fifth Avenue co-op. He began to explain all this, but the caller, who had come to inhabit Bech's head like an incurable parasite, steadily maintained her investigative line: "And is it true, suh, as I have read in several reputable sources, that, whaal travelling in the Communist world under the sponsorship of our U.S. government, you did enjoy a lee-ay-son with a certain famous Bulgarian poet and had a child by that lady whom you have never officially acknowledged? A child brought up under strict Communist doctrines until he was a grown man, never knowing who his father was, while you enjoyed a capitalist laaf-staahl?"

The strange images and lies were coming so fast, and so winsomely, he could scarcely speak, though he had been speaking steadily since the Prize had been announced. His mouth opened, two inches from the sponge-muffled mike—like a miniature boxing glove, or a fist in a Keith Haring silhouette—but only a scraping noise emerged. Hating even a half-second of dead air, Diane Rehm melodiously enunciated, "Perhaps our guest does not care to answer?"

The voice in Bech's head burrowed deeper, working its jaws faster and showing a rough underbelly of Christian resentment. "Well now Diane, if this man doesn't care to answer, what's he doin sittin' on your show? If he's gone to just clam up, maybe he should not have accepted the Praahz."

"I have never been a father before," Bech brought out. "Just like I have never won the Nobel Prize before."

"Well, if you've never been a father before," the voice said, "from all that I've read you should be teachin' these black teenagers birth control."

"Thank you for your call, Maureen," Diane Rehm said firmly, and pressed a switch that eliminated Maureen from the airwaves. "Next," she

announced to the nation, "Betty Jean, from Greens-
boro, North Carolina."

But Betty Jean was no better. She said, "Speaking of black teenagers, I don't think all you celebri-
ties' having babies out of wedlock is setting any
kind of example, now is it?"

"But," Bech said, at bay, "I wasn't a celebrity
until I won the Prize. I was just a writer, off in a
corner. Anyway, I'd be delighted to marry the
mother of my child, but she's still mulling my offer
over. She's very modern."

"If you ask me," said Betty Jean, in the instant
before her electronic execution, "all you Yankees
are too damn modern."

Bech in his heart agreed. *Moral insufficiency.*
Lying awake in his loft, while Rothkoesque rectangles of incidental city light vibrated around him on
the walls, he listened for his baby to peep and
reflected back upon his life and work, his daily,
ever briefer earthly existence. A few countries, a
few women. There were many countries he would
never visit, some even now being born, younger
than Golda, from the wrecks of shabby old em-
pires. The women—he supposed they had been the
point of it all, the biologically ordained goal of
male existence, nearing and looming and then receding. They had been sufficient in number. He
could not count them up or recall all their names,
though he could always get at least a face, a glim-

mer of pallor in a darkened room, an uncertain, fetching smile and eye-pits of warm, wild shadow. Still, it had been a frightfully curtailed minority of all the appropriate-aged women that had been available, globally. Likewise, his works, the seven volumes* (not counting the British anthology, *The Best of Bech,* long out of print), seemed remarkably few, considering the possibilities, and as mysteriously contingent as the major turnings of his life. Seven stages, seven branches on the menorah, seven white keys on the piano. He had never quite understood why the black keys, the half-tones, had those two gaps within an octave. It enabled the pianist to find his way, he supposed. Bech's seven books glimmered in his backward glance like fading trail-marks in a dark wood, *una selva oscura,* the tangled wilderness where his consciousness intersected with the universe. He rarely looked into their pale pages, his books seemed to have so perilous a connection with the giant truth of the matter: his arbitrary identity arisen, like the universe, out of darkness and silence. First, the slimy preconscious miracle, in velvety uterine darkness, of repeated prenatal mitosis, keyed to viable complexity by unfathomable signals among the chromosomes and proteins. Then, the harsh eruption

---

* *Travel Light,* a novel (1955); *Brother Pig,* a novella (1957); *When the Saints,* a miscellany (1958); *The Chosen,* a novel (1963); *Think Big,* a novel (1979; *Biding Time,* sketches and stories (1985); *Going South,* a novella (1992)

into the icy hospital light and the fragrant, noisy Freudian triangle, with its oppressive yet nurturing atmospheres of kitchen, bedroom, and bathroom. Then, the long monitored stairways of schooling, class after class, teacher after teacher, and his abrupt graduation, in the year of Pearl Harbor, into war and the inconclusive trials of adulthood, of which his present sardonic, Prize-bothered decrepitude was the latest if not quite the last. *And one man in his time plays many parts, / His acts being seven ages.*

Golda whimpered in her crib, which they had placed just outside their flimsily partitioned-off bedroom. In the day, they moved her crib into its shelter of two-by-fours and wallboard, a box within the loft—a kind of jewelbox when Golda was napping within it. Robin would be off at Computer Crossroads, on Third Avenue; Bech would scribble softly, writing and scratching out, while Leontyne tiptoed through the breakfast dishes and the laundry. Two adults, he marvelled, held in thrall by eighteen pounds of guileless ego. When baby awoke, the cocoa-colored au pair, cooing in Caribbean, would feed her fragments of toast and chicken, gleefully chewed though Golda still had fewer teeth than fingers. What teeth she had were big and hard-earned, having given her much grief pushing up through the gums. Then a bottle was administered on the sofa, Golda blindly sucking while Leontyne's eyes lapped up "Days of Our Lives." At two, the sitter switched channels to

"One Life to Live," and Bech, if the pesky demands of the Prize allowed him, indulged her addiction and himself pushed the stroller to a playground. There was a sad, bare little one at Spring and Mulberry, and one even more exiguous on Mercer above Houston, beside an NYU recreation building. When feeling ambitious, he would push Golda all the way across the Bowery to the several in the long park named after Roosevelt's overprotective mother, Sara. The ginkgoes and sycamores were dully turning and dead leaves were blossoming underfoot. Bech trussed his wriggling daughter in one of those black rubber diapers that do for swing-seats now and pushed her back and forth until the gravity-teasing wonder of it wore thin. She was still too young to dare alone the heights and swinging walkways of the plastic castle at the playground's rubber-paved center, but he entrusted her sometimes to the spiral slide, allowing her, a slippery missile in her padded playsuit, to swoop out of his hands for a swerve or two, before he grabbed her at the bottom. And he let her crawl up the slide stairs, mounting upward on her own motor drives, his hands hovering inches behind her back in case she toppled when she unsteadily turned to share with him her pride of ascension. He saw a father's role, while he was here to enact it, as empowering her to skirt danger more closely than either Robin or Leontyne would have allowed—to introduce into her life an element of male love of risk.

On the level loft floor, Golda was a muscular,

unstoppable crawler, moving across toys, adult feet, scattered books, and slippery sheaves of the Sunday *Times* in her tanklike progress. At night, though, when her whimper brought Bech to hover over her crib, her muscularity had been shed with her playsuit and she seemed all spirit, a well of inarticulate need he strained to peer into, as they both sought the source of her unease. In the first six months, he would simply lift her up and take her in to his soundly sleeping young mate, who would drowsily fumble a stunningly large, green-veined white breast into the little mouth and stifle its discontent. But Robin, wearying of milk stains on the trim bodices of her work outfits, and of this tyrannical physical tie to another's innards, had weaned Golda, so that Bech, lifting the whimpering little body into his arms, had the option of changing her diaper or warming up a bottle, or both. These fumbling communions with his infant daughter at ungodly hours, while yet some traffic—gangster limousines from Little Italy, yellow cabs to and from SoHo's dance-to-dawn clubs—trickled by on Crosby Street, were unlike any other of the fleeting relationships life had brought him: he was clearly, by virtue of his size, dominant, and yet tenderness and an atavistic animal protectiveness tilted the balance in favor of the helpless one.

On the edge of language—she could say "Hi," and wave bye-bye—Golda communicated with what the King James Bible called her bowels, not just the spicily fragrant movements but the interior mysteries, the thirst or pain or bad dream or existential loneliness that had driven her soul out of sleep into the teeming world in search of consolation. He tried to provide it; some nights Robin awoke and with a mother's primal body and heart swamped the infant's irritation. Beside them on the bed, elderly Bech enjoyed the wash of warmth as the two young female bodies softly collided. Bech felt relieved when Robin intervened, but also cheated, of perhaps his last opportunity to satisfy another— to find the biological key that turned a lock outside of himself, in this case that of an ego implausibly extended from his own, like a stick thrust into water and apparently bent. "*You* are my prize," he would murmur into her ear as, waiting the sixty seconds for the bottle to warm in the microwave, he held her by the window, both of them gazing down upon the yellow top of a single cab as it hurtled rumbling over the rough cobblestones toward some dubious haven of mirrors, drugs, strobe lights, and spastic dancing. "You are good, good, *good*," Bech told Golda, her appraising eyes attracted to his face by the desperate hoarseness of his whisper. "You are a truly outstanding person."

They were two of a kind—irregular sleepers, stubborn crawlers. "Oh, you are your daddy's girl," Leontyne would coo to the child in the daytime, so Bech at his desk could hear. "You have his frisky looks and his stand-up hair."

"Leontyne," he would ask, "do you think this is a terrible mistake? My having a child at my age?"

"Babies are the gifts of God," she said, in that gently rocking voice of hers. "They come when He wants them to come. The mommy and the daddy may think not yet, not yet, but He knows when a blessing due. You loves that little girl so much I can't stand some time to watch. And the mommy, too, you loves for sure, but you two have your settled ways, your paths in the world. My parents the same way, my daddy come and go. Nine children they manage to make, when he coming and going. I was the second youngest. My little brother come when Mother forty-two. She used to joke when he got born she had to put on eyeglasses to be seeing him."

Leontyne's confident acceptance of the world as a divine cradle in which they were all rocking soothed Bech during the day, but unsettled him at night, when it appeared so clearly a delusion. In his wakefulness he was alone on a pillar, a saint torn from the cozy quotidian. His winning the Prize had unleashed a deluge of letters that battered him like hostile winds. *You would think now they could give it to some American who wasn't a kike or a coon or an immigrant who can't even speak English right . . . I have been struggling to complete my novel while holding down two jobs to pay for my wife's prohibitive chemo treatments plus the child care and just one percent of the enormous amount you have so deservedly in my opinion won would enable me . . . you have probably forgotten me but*

I sat in the row behind you at P.S. 87 over on 77th and Amsterdam and though you never paid me any attention I always knew that some day you . . . celebrity auction even the tiniest personal item last year we had remarkable good success with Mariah Carey's toenail clippings and a used paper towel from Julia Child's kitchen . . . well Hank I guess you got them all fooled now except me I still have your number jewboy and it isn't number one or even one thousand and one . . . Temple Emmanuel our reading circle can offer not even a modest honorarium but your cab fare would be covered and there are home-prepared refreshments before-hand . . .my son is going to be two this December and a friendly note from you on your personal letterhead copying out a favorite passage from your own work or that of another great writer and dated month and date and year . . . you seemed uneasy with Charlie Rose but you have nothing to be ashamed of or do you? . . . I enclose my own privately printed book setting out in irrefutable detail the means whereby God will bring about His kingdom first in the Middle East and then on the other continents in rapid succession . . . help a signed photograph help a one-page statement to one in need in the battle to win young minds back to reading a modest check a quotation we could use in our promotion no automated signatures please . . . happy to come and share with you our professional investment advice and expertise in estate planning . . . I try to get on top of my fury but after forty years of writing rings around you in not just my own opinion but that of most critics who aren't total shmucks I can't internalize what seems to me a savage and pointed rejection of me, me, I know it's absurd dear Henry I know life to you is and always has been just a bowl of cherries . . . Envy and resentment poured toward him out of the American vastness, from every state including Hawaii and Alaska, like a kind of lateral sleet rattling on the tin roof of his rickety privacy. He tried to utilize his insomnia by composing the lecture which Nobel laureates were obliged to give. He had received wads of information from Sweden, much of it on those long European sheets of paper impossible to fit into American folders. His speech was to be three days before the ceremony, at the Swedish Academy. Who would attend? He couldn't imagine. *Your Royal Highnesses, Mr. Lord Mayor of Stockholm, Members of the Academy, distinguished guests both foreign and domestic: The Nobel Prize has become so big, so rich and famous, such a celebrity of a prize, that no one is worthy to win it, and the embarrassed winner can shelter his unworthiness behind the unworthiness of everyone else. It lifts us up, this Prize, to a terrible height, a moment of global attention, and tempts one to pontificate. Looking down upon our planet, I see a growing gap between those who ride airplanes and those who do not; those who have taken wing into the cyberspace of the information age and those who are left behind on the surface of the earth, to till the soil, fish the seas, and perform the necessary tasks that once formed the honored substance of all lives but a few.* No. What did he know of any lives but his eremitic own and the smattering of others he had tangled with? His point about airplanes was obsolete. He could remember when getting on a plane was an adventure for the elite, dressed in suits and cocktail dresses, the chic of it intensified by the air of danger as they bounced around among silvery, Art-Deco thunderheads, an air to which free champagne and duck or steak dinners served on real china added a *Titanic*-esque elegance. But now the sort of people swarmed aboard who used to go by bus. They wore shorts and blue jeans and even what appeared to be their pajamas, a scrum of sweaty bodies taking a thousand-mile hop as casually as a drive to the 7-Eleven. Flight was no more a miracle to them than their daily bread. They crammed their duffel bags and scuffed laptops into the overhead bins and didn't even bother to look out the windows, from six death-defying miles up. So capitalism, our creed triumphant, was right: the masses are brought along, pulled in their millions up the ladder of prosperity built by enterprise and technology. *The telephone and radio, cinema and television, internal combustion and jet propulsion—mankind has absorbed them as readily as Native Americans took to guns, horses, and firewater. As it happened in Ohio and the valley of the Ruhr, so it will happen in Malaysia and Mali—*

everybody rich, civilized, and discontented. No. Avoid economic geopolitics. Who could say whither the wonderful world in all its multitudinous adaptations? Strike a personal note, as Ōe and Heaney had done. West Side/Brooklyn boyhood. The experience of war. GI Bill, NYU. Village in the Forties, 99th Street in the Fifties and thereafter. *Books, to me when young, were rectangular objects seen in department stores, stationery shops, and, without their shiny jackets, in the public library. There, their dusty spines, decimally numbered in white ink, seemed feathers on a dark and protective wing; their smell of dried glue mingled with the decaying wistful smells of old men, called "bums" in my youth and "the homeless" in these more enlightened times. What did these books mean? Who made them? Well, men in tweed jackets, smoking pipes, who lived in Connecticut, made them. And women only a shade less glamorous than movie stars, draped in chiffon or else, like Dorothy Thompson and Martha Gellhorn, dressed like men, and even like men in battle dress.* No. The Swedes and the world don't want to hear of these virtually forgotten authors who once were stars in Bech's eyes. He must speak instead of the timeless bliss when pencil point touches paper and makes a mark. But isn't this atomic moment much too small to mention, in so vast an auditorium of attention? In a world of suffering, of famine and massacre, wasn't aesthetic bliss obscene? *And now?* he must ask aloud. *The printed word? The book trade, that old carcass tossed here and there by its ravenous jackals? Greedy authors, greedy agents, brainless book chains with their Vivaldi-riddled espresso bars, publishers owned by metallurgy conglomerates operated by glacially cold bean-counters in Geneva. And meanwhile language, the human languages we all must use, no longer degraded by the barking murderous coinages of Goebbels and the numskull doublespeak of bureaucratic Communism, is becoming the mellifluous happy-talk of Microsoft and Honda, corporate conspiracies that would turn the world into one big pinball game for child-brained consumers. Is the gorgeous, fork-tongued, edgy English of Shakespeare and Gerard Manley Hopkins, of Charles Dickens and Saul Bellow becoming the binary code for a gray-suited empire directed by men walking along the streets of Manhattan and Hong Kong jabbering into cell phones? Who is going to stop the world from evolving? Poets? Dilettantes like yours truly? Don't make me laugh, Your Highnesses and assorted dignitaries. As a dear old friend of mine kindly informed the American press recently, your Prize is a prank.*

"I can't do it," he told Robin. "I can't say anything important enough. The essence of what I do is that it isn't important, or at least doesn't *come on* as important. Importance is not important, that's what I've been trying to say all my life."

"Well," she said, "try saying that."

"But that's *really* unimportant," he protested.

"And egotistical. I don't want to be egotistical. I don't want to seem to be trying to get *on top of* the Prize, if you know what I mean."

"I think you're outsmarting yourself," Robin offered, primarily concerned with persuading Golda of the nutritional worth of the diced carrots the child kept picking up from her high-chair tray with curly slimy tiny fingers and dropping carefully on the floor. "All the Swedes want is a little relaxed gratitude—"

"You don't understand. You give a little bow when the King hands it all to you—the medal, the certificate, the week's pass on the Stockholm transit system. You say thanks at the banquet after the ceremony. The lecture comes earlier in the week. It's the lecture that's killing me. My chance at last to make a statement, after seventy-six years of nobody listening. Well, I guess my mother listened, for the first five years or so."

"—a little gratitude and a half-hour's intellectual entertainment. Think of *them*," Robin said. "They've been sweating over these prizes all year, neglecting their own work and their families. Swedes have feelings, too—look at those Ingmar Bergman movies." *Ingrid*

"The *women* in those movies have feelings; the men don't. They're *frozen*. Leontyne"—Leontyne was folding little dresses and playsuits, at the new washer and drier they had installed beside the refrigerator, there in the loft's once-primitive kitchen—"what should I tell the people of the world?"

"You go tell them," Leontyne readily advised, "that you been wanting to make people happy ever since you been a little boy. That the Lord be telling you what to say, and you just writing it down."

"I don't think God plays well in Sweden," he said. "God sticks pretty close to the equator."

That did made Leontyne laugh; he was never quite sure what would. Her shy pealing seemed to pull itself back on every note, into her supple throat, as if laughter were a sin to be retracted. Her eyes looked lacquered by merriment; her solemn brief bangs, a straightened fringe, came less than halfway down her brow. Her twelve-year-old daughter, Emerald, Bech knew from snapshots, had hair done in beaded corn-rows, the maternal work of hours.

He wondered if he could work God's favoring the peoples of the equator into his Nobel lecture; perhaps he was wrong to ignore the world's lurking ethnic sores. *Your Highnesses, Lord Mayor, and welcome guests: the Prize is a fine bauble upon the pale chest of Western civilization, but as a Jew let me wonder aloud, What has this civilization, this Christendom, meant to my people? It has meant ghettos, pogroms, verbal and physical abuse, unappealable injustice, exclusionary laws, yellow stars, autos-da-fé, scapegoating whenever disaster threatened a Christian society, and a collective*

*helplessness at the whim of every petty Christian
ruler and government. One nation to whose glory
and prosperity we had contributed, as artisans and
merchants and moneylenders, for hundreds of
years, Spain, rewarded us with unconditional
expulsion in the very year in which America was
discovered. Germany and Austria, where Jews had
seen their talents ripen into genius, wealth, and an
apparent bourgeois security—those very nations
instituted a systematic plan for the extermination
of the Jews, a plan whose all but completely successful execution remains the astonishment of this
century, the final refutation of any European claims
to virtue and wisdom. Even in my own country,
thought by many to be too indulgent of its Jews,
swastikas are frequently spray-painted upon synagogues. In Sweden, I have read, one out of three
teenagers doubt that the Holocaust ever took
place. And so, Your Highnesses, I find that as a Jew
I cannot accept this sop, this pathetic attempt to
paper over the smoking pit, the thousands of gas
ovens in which thousands of greater gifts and purer
hearts than my own . . .* What was he doing? Turning the Prize down had made Sartre look like a
fool, and Pasternak like a Soviet slave.

"Meri Jo, I'm panicked," he told her, over a
lunch at Four Seasons he had invited her to give
him. "Find me a speech."

"Henry, an old Spielmeister like you? Tell them
what you told Oprah; that was charming."

"I forget what I say on these damn talk shows. I try to suppress it as soon as I say it."

"You told her you didn't write pornography, you just tried to give the sexual component of our lives a fair shake. Or something like that."

"The Swedes don't care if I write pornography. It's all legal there. It's part of their healthy pagan outlook."

"I'll never forget you on 'Donahue' when *Think Big* was fresh out. I was a sophomore at Barnard, and my roommate and her boyfriend were channel-surfing—you had to twist the dial in those days—and I said, 'No, wait, that man is saying something.' You were younger then, and your hair filled the whole top half of the screen. You were so calm and understated, not letting him bully you, and only lightly but sweetly letting the audience know you thought he *was* a bully. . . ."

"That was his job. Highly paid bully. Bully of the people, for the people. What did I *say,* though?"

Meri Jo's circular face—in which a pertly pointed chin still tried to assert itself above a set of others, like ghosts in New York television before cable came in—was flushed, either from empathy with his plight or from the two pint-sized glasses of white wine that had come with the meal, or else from the compressing effects of her leather jacket, its zipper as wide as a yardstick and its brass studs the size of gumdrops. "It wasn't what you *said,* it was the way you said it. You were sincere without being *heavy*. You were funny without being the least bit, you know, Catskills. Six months later, when I read in *People* that you and your wife had broken up, I remember—I shouldn't be telling you this, I shouldn't have had that second glass of Chardonnay—I was delighted; I thought, Maybe he'll meet *me*. So I went into publishing, but you weren't there. Or there very rarely. You were one of our invisible authors. Never mind, Henry; it's been a good life, P.R. I guess I was naïve, but I was only a sophomore, remember, and my guy of the time, I've forgotten everything about him except the way his fingernails were never clean, was having some potency issues. Pardon me for blushing."

"Meri Jo, you'll have me blushing myself. Tell me, would it help for me to see a tape of that Donahue show? Did Publicity keep one?"

"To be honest, Henry, we might have, but a ton of that stuff got tossed when we moved to the new building. Can't you just talk about the future of the written word or something?"

"Look, this Prize comes but once a lifetime, and everybody says it was a miracle I got it. I hate to pollute the occasion with idle prattle."

"Oh, hon, don't badmouth prattle," she said. Her chin, the top one, firmed up and pointed at him. "I have a raft of requests for you to consider. They keep coming in. We said yes, you remember, to a print interview with the Washington *Post,* and if you say yes to the *Post* you can't say no to the Atlanta *Constitution,* it's a booming market down there. Ever since air-conditioning, Southerners *read.* Then there's the Minneapolis *Star Tribune,* the books editor has been terribly good to Vellum over the years, and we're trying to do more with the Northwest, so there's this smart new arts editor at the Tacoma *News Tribune . . .*"

"I *hate* print interviews," Bech said. "They take forever, they get you all relaxed and gabby, and then they crucify you, writing down whatever they please. There's no evidence of what you really said except their tape, and they keep the tape. No. No more print. Print is dead."

"Each one will come to your apartment—"

"It will ruin Golda's nap."

"And take no more than an hour and a half, with some time before or after for the photographer. Only Annie Leibovitz is apt to ask you to put on makeup. Maybe with her you can get away with just a funny hat."

"Meri Jo, why are you doing this to me? Is it my fault you liked me on 'Donahue'? I didn't like *myself* on 'Donahue.'"

She put her hand, still remarkably dainty, on his gnarled, hairy-backed one, as he struggled with his green fettuccine. The oiled strips eluded the tines of his fork like eels wriggling out of a trap. "People want you, dear, and it's my job to facilitate access."

"It's not my fault they want me. I don't want them. I want peace. I vunt to be alone, and to watch Golda grow. She can almost say words. She says 'Hi.'"

"I'm not asking for myself, or for yourself, even. I'm asking for the *in*dustry. There's such a thing—you've never learned this, darling, your mother obviously spoiled you rotten—as responsibility to others. With prizes come responsibilities, didn't Delmore Schwartz say that? You're making me seriously think about a third glass of wine."

"Think about it all you want. I'm saying no to any more interviews."

"But you don't mean no." Her sea-green eyes must once have been lovely and big; now they were small in her face, little sinister bits of buried beach glass.

He didn't have the heart not to be seduced by her. He grumbled by way of caving in, "They won't want me once I botch this lecture."

"You won't botch it. You can't botch it. Faulkner wrote his on the airplane with a hangover and read it in a mumble and now it's a document like the Gettysburg Address. Think Gettysburg Address. Henry: Do you want to have some chocolate cheesecake with me, or do you want me to feel depraved all by myself?"

Stockholm, scattered on its Baltic archipelago, shone with the cold. The Swedish women sported blood-bright cheeks above their collars of wolf and fox as they carried their golden heads along the trendy streets, lined with restaurants and antique stores, of Gamla Stan, the Old Town. Bech was taken to lunch at the venerable gathering-spot for writers, the Källaren Den Gyldene Freden, with a few impish members of the Swedish Academy. "It looked like a deadlock," confided one of them, a small bald twinkling man known for his Värmland tales in the tradition of Selma Lagerlöf, "between Günter Grass and Bei Dao, with Kundera the dark horse. You were in the final selection because some were afraid a stronger American might actually win. And then, you rascal, you won! The votes for you, in my view, constituted an anti-Socialist protest. As you can see, we live well here, but the taxes strike some as very burdensome."

"Do not let Sigfrid fill you with his amiable nonsense," intervened a female member of the Academy, a gracile poet and the biographer of such Nordic classics as the short-lived, tormented Erik Johan Stagnelius and the eventually mad Gustaf Fröding. "You are much esteemed in Scandinavia, for your ruthless clarity. You rape your women as you describe them. I myself prefer to read you in French, where I think your style is even more clean and—how do you say?—starkers?"

"When your names from the basket were counted," volunteered a lyric feuilletonist of prodigious bulk and height, "I was surprised but not astounded. It is as if, recently, there are others voting, ghostly presences, around the table. The results are mysterious!"

"As you may know," his first informant, his spectacles and mobile lower lip glinting, "the

Academy is not at our full strength of eighteen. There have been resignations, and yet the members cannot be replaced. Once a member, the only way out is death."

"Like being a member of the human race," Bech ventured, diplomatically. He was nervous. Robin and Golda were back alone in the hotel suite. They had not brought Leontyne, for this week of festivity and formality. Bech was afraid the cold might blast her, like a jasmine blossom. He wanted her to spend more time with her husband, a security guard who left for the night shift as she arrived home. Bech felt that he and Leontyne were drawing too close in the loft, yoked together to a baby's body. He was getting to lean on her other-worldly wisdom and to think in her voice. He wanted to shut down, at this terminal point of his life, his rusted but still-operative falling-in-love apparatus.

As for Robin, she was not used to being with Golda all day. She missed her computers, and the authority they gave her, her site in the Web. She found Sweden not for her. "Oh, it's great for *you*," she complained, "all you do is go out being wined and dined and interviewed, and go to receptions for the fun-loving biology winners, while I'm cooped up in this so-called Grand Hotel with a crying kid and a lot of pompous furniture. It's too cold to go out and too hot to stay in. When I try to order room service, the people in the kitchen only speak Turkish."

"Inger has said they'd get us all the babysitters we want." Inger Wetterqvist was their Nobel attendant; every winner got one. She was lovely, efficient, and in constant attendance. Her statuesque neck, with wispy flaxen tendrils in the hollows of the nape, fascinated Bech.

But Golda had problems with the Swedes. Whenever she saw a big, blond woman, she stuck the central two fingers of her left hand into her mouth and hid her face against her mother's thigh. When she realized, on the first full day of their stay, that her parents were about to leave her alone with a golden-haired babysitter, she screamed in a panicked fury Bech had never heard before. The child feared these tall, shining Aryans.

The girl was, in her splendor, frightening. The world seemed to hold, Bech had noticed, more and more young women over six feet in height—whole clusters of them, whole basketball teams, striding through airports or down Fifth Avenue together—as if Nature, no longer designing women close to the ground for purposes of childbearing and domestic labor, were launching them toward some function as yet unknown.

Robin, embarrassed, told the helpless girl who, it had been arranged, would care for Golda during the official lunch at the American Embassy, "Our au pair back home is black—you know, Negro? I guess she's used to her." In the end, Robin and Bech took Golda to the Ambassador's lunch; it included little carrots, which the infant carefully dropped one by one on the floor.

It was true, Bech was having fun, though his lecture was still unwritten, a fact that he tried all day to forget and which gave him the horrors when he awoke at night, his temples aching with an excess of convivial aquavit and congratulatory champagne. To him, Sweden was a stupefying Heaven. He liked the quick arc of daylight, like cold crystal, and the giant Nikki Ste.-Phalle sculptures at the Moderna Museet—women! more power to them! Greta! Ingrid! from Stockholm their beauty, tinged with melancholy as beauty must be, had come forth to flood the filmstruck world—and a certain pastel lightness to the city, under its close sub-arctic sky. It reminded him of Leningrad, as it had appeared to him in 1964, when he was but forty-one, and susceptible to the charms of a stony-faced *apparatchika* in a military jacket, and thrilled to be breathing Tolstoyan air. Now an old man, he saw through dimmed eyes. He had done what he could; he had tried to write his own books rather than books others wanted him to write; he had come to this Northern fastness to put his pen to rest. He gave interviews to the *Svenska Dagbladet, Expressen, Damernas Värld, Dagens Nyheter, Västerbottens-Kuriren.* The interviewer from *Svenska Dagbladet* asked Bech what he thought of the future of Socialism. He answered that he thought it was in a down phase, but would be back, as an alternative; the world was a sick man turning over and over in bed. The weak must always be protected somewhat from the strong, but not so satisfactorily that no incentive remains to become strong. Failure must have real penalties, or there will be no striving for success. Man is in the awkward position of being kinder than Nature.

The *Svenska Dagbladet* interviewer, an alert round-headed lad with already thinning hair, asked him if these insights were to be the burden of his Nobel lecture.

"If they were," Bech asked, "why would I be giving them away to you and your readers now? But tell me, what is a Nobel Lecture about, usually?"

The young man thought. His eyelashes were white, which gave him, with his clever thin mouth, a delicately clownish look. "Oh, the importance of writing. And how the winner came to write."

"Do those seem to you worth talking about?"

The interviewer, interviewed, shrugged evasively. "It is the custom."

"Sweden is a land of customs, yes?"

The young man, his reddish fair hair so fine that strands of it stood up straight with static electricity, smiled hesitantly. His English was not quite good enough to be certain if he was being teased. "You could say so," he replied.

"I understand that at some point angels will break into our hotel room."

"Singers heralding the advent of St. Lucia, our festival of light." The interviewer was still worrying over Sweden's being a land of customs—America, perhaps, being a land devoid of customs. "Our winters are long," he said, "with very short days, so there is perhaps a Swedish need to be festive—to have festivities. We light many candles, many torches—you will see. Nobel Week is more a holiday now than Christmas."

The Swedes had provided on their long pieces of paper a minute-by-minute forecast of what would happen at the ceremony—the music to be played; the order of procession; the seating on the stage, amid the many Academies, with Prizewinners arrayed facing the King and Queen; the braided arrangement of flowers to mark the edge of the stage—and at the banquet afterwards, in the vast Blue Hall of Stockholm's red-brick City Hall, thirteen hundred guests eating from special Nobel dinnerware (*Nobelservisen*) while the Uppsala male choir sang and young women in blue peasant outfits danced down the broad stairs and streams of waiters bore aloft torrents of softly flaming platters of dessert. But to earn his place in such grand procedures Bech had to deliver his lecture.

"My God, what I am going to do?" he asked Robin back in the hotel room. "I have to give the damn thing in two days, and I have no time to write it, there are all these receptions, all this champagne I have to keep drinking."

"Henry, I hate to see you rattled like this. I have a feminine need to think of you as debonair."

"Nothing I can say will be good enough. I'm unworthy."

"They already know that. You told me the Academy didn't mean to elect you, they were casting protest votes against each other."

"My informant might have been pulling my leg. They have this weird Viking sense of humor. Ho, ho, have a smash on the noggin."

"Did you know," Robin asked him, "that during the war they weren't so neutral? I was reading on the Internet how the Sapo, their secret police, turned over Norwegian resistance fighters to the Nazis. And a lot of Swedish-Jewish businessmen got mysteriously fired. Hitler *loved* the Swedes; they were his idea of a real *Volk*."

"Stop scaring me. You and Golda, you have all this racial prejudice."

"She's not so dumb. Here. Focus on your daughter for once." She thrust Golda into his arms. The infant's bottom felt damp. When she grinned, with her scattered teeth, she drooled. Another tooth coming. Her slimy little curious hand reached out and grabbed a piece of Bech's cheek and squeezed.

"Ow," he said.

"She's so used to being with me all day she doesn't understand your whiskers. I'm putting on a cocktail dress and getting out for an hour. A nice young accountant in the office downstairs offered to show me the hotel computer system, and then take me for a drink to some American-style skyview place along the waterfront. He was shocked when I told him I hadn't seen anything of Stockholm. He couldn't believe I was so neglected."

"Did you tell him it's mostly your choice? Inger offered to find us an African sitter, though it isn't easy up here."

"They're all these Senegalese brand-name-pocketbook ripoff peddlers. She said there are some dark-skinned Turks, but I said no Moslems, thanks."

"There you go. More prejudice. Until Israel, Moslems were much better to Jews than Christians."

Robin read the anxiety, the potential defeat, on his face and said, "Henry, I'm young. I'm stir-crazy. I'll be back in time for you to go to the official concert at eight. Golda needs some daddy magic. You and she can write your lecture together."

"Members of the Academy, distinguished guests both foreign and domestic," Bech began his lecture. "The Nobel Prize has become so big, such a celebrity among prizes, that no one is worthy to win it, and the embarrassed winner can shelter his unworthiness behind the unworthiness of everyone else." The audience was scattered on the chairs set out in the long and tawny main salon of the Swedish Academy, a room a-brim with pilasters and archways like a Renaissance fantasy, a vision by Michelangelo of human form turned into architecture. The King—tall and studious-looking, wearing glasses whose rims were of a regal thinness—was not there, nor his beautiful black-haired Queen. Bech had been foolish to think of himself as speaking from the top of the world. He was speaking to an indifferent audience of pale polite faces, in an overheated space on the Northern edge of Europe, a subcontinent whose natives for a few passing centuries had bullied and buffaloed the rest of the world. Among the faces he recognized few. Meri Jo Zwengler and lanky, shaggy, laid-back Jim Flaggerty, his editor, grayer-headed than twenty years ago but still ruminating on a piece of phantom gum in his mouth, had flown over from Vellum to hold his hand. Some pinstriped minions from the Ambassador's staff had been delegated to attend. Robin perched in the front row, her face a luminous pearl of warmth in the frosty jumble of alien visages. The audience as a whole had stirred in surprise when Bech, following his crisp introduction by Professor Sture Allén, had come to the lectern carrying a baby. But, being in the main Swedish, the audience suppressed its titters, as if this living child were an eccentricity of ethnic costume, like Wole Soyinka's African robes of a few years ago.

"It lifts one up, this Prize," Bech continued his lecture, Golda wriggling and threatening to corkscrew in his crooked right arm, "to a terrible height, a moment of global attention, and tempts one to pontificate. I could talk to you about the world," he said, "as it exists in this year of 1999, waiting for the odometer to turn over into a new millennium, watching to see if Islamic militants will lock ever more of its surface into a new Dark Age, or if China will push the United States aside as top superpower, or Russia will spit out capitalism like a bad fig, or the gap between those who ride in airplanes and those who drive ox-carts will widen to the point of revolution or lessen to the point of Disneyfied, deep-fried homogeneity—but what, my distinguished friends, do I know of the world? My life has been spent attending to my inner weather and my immediate vicinity." In that vicinity, Golda was getting impatient. She had that solemn look which, combined with a spicy nether smell, signalled a development that would soon need tending to. Meri Jo and Robin were right; he could spiel on forever, once given a podium and a captive audience. It was something about himself he would have preferred never to have discovered. "Or," Bech went on, "I could talk to you about art, in the spasmodic, distracted practice of which I have spent my finest and most valuable hours. Is art, as the ancients proposed, an imitation of life, or is it, as the moderns suggest, everything that life is not—order instead of disorder, resolution rather than inconclusiveness, peace and harmony in preference to our insatiable discontent and, at the bottom of our souls, as Kierkegaard and Strindberg and Munch teach us, our terror? Our dread—dread at being here, on this planet that appears lonelier and more negligible with each new revelation from astronomy. Or is art *both* duplication and escape— life tweaked, as it were, into something slightly higher, brighter, other? We feel it to be so, as it is engendered at the end of a pencil point or on a computer screen. Art is somehow *good,* if only for the artist."

Golda wriggled more strenuously, straining his venerable armature of bone and muscle. Bech studied the audience, a sea of white visages dotted here and there with a black or yellow face. To Golda's short-sighted, slate-blue eyes—two shades of blue, actually: a darker ring and a paler, more skyey iris inside—the crowd must recede endlessly, out the back wall into the entire rest of the Earth. "I represent," Bech could not resist going on, "only myself; in citizenship I am an American and in religion a non-observant Jew, but when I write I am nothing less than a member of my triumphant but troubled species, with aspirations it may be to speak for the primates, the vertebrates, and even the lichen as well. *Life*! the toast in Hebrew cries, in awe at least of the molecular amazingness of it, regardless of whatever atrocities appetitive organisms visit upon one another. I came here, ladies and gentlemen, determined not to generalize away the miracle, the quizzical quiddity, of the specific, that which is 'the case,' as Wittgenstein put it, and in honor of the majesty of my task developed an absolute writer's block in regard to the lecture I am now audibly failing to deliver. So I (just a minute more, sweetie) invoke the precedent of my predecessor Nobel Laureate in Literature Naguib Mahfouz—a writer, by the way, who was knifed in the throat for his efforts to describe the life of his Egypt with accuracy and equanimity, a true hero in a field, literature, rife with false heroics—and have asked my daughter to speak for me. She is ten months old, and will enjoy her first birthday in the new millennium. She belongs to the future. The topic we have worked out between us is, 'The Nature of Human Existence.'" Bech repeated, in his presidential voice: "The Nature of Human Existence."

He and Golda had rehearsed, but there was no telling with infants; the wiring of their minds hadn't yet jelled. If she had begun, with her loaded diaper and confining paternal arm, to scream, that would have been a statement, but an overstatement, and not her father's sort of statement. She did not let him down. She had her young mother's clear mind and pure nature, purged of much of the delusion and perversity whose devils had tormented the previous two thousand years, or should one say previous 5,760 years? In the audience, wide-jawed, luminous Robin parted her lips in maternal and wifely concern, as if to intervene in a rescue. He shifted their child to his other arm, so that her little tooth-bothered mouth came close to the microphone—state-of-the-art, a filigreed bauble on an adjustable stem. She reached out with the curly, beslobbered fingers of one hand as if to pluck the fat metallic bud. He felt the warmth of her skull, an inch from his avid nose; he inhaled her scalp's powdery scent. Into the dear soft warm crumpled configuration of her ear he whispered, "Say hi."

"Hi!" Golda pronounced with a bright distinctness instantly amplified into the depths of the beautiful, infinite hall. Then she lifted her right hand, where all could see, and made the gentle clasping and unclasping motion that signifies bye-bye.

A Note About the Author

JOHN UPDIKE was born in 1932, in Shillington, Pennsylvania. He graduated from Harvard College in 1954, and spent a year in Oxford, England, at the Ruskin School of Drawing and Fine Art. From 1955 to 1957 he was a member of the staff of The New Yorker, and since 1957 has lived in Massachusetts. He is the father of four children and the author of over forty books, including eighteen novels and numerous collections of short stories, poems, and criticism.

Look for these and other Random House Large Print books at your local bookstore

Angelou, Maya, *Even the Stars Look Lonesome*
Berendt, John, *Midnight in the Garden of Good and Evil*
Brinkley, David, *Everyone Is Entitled to My Opinion*
Carr, Caleb, *The Angel of Darkness*
Carter, Jimmy, *Living Faith*
Carter, Jimmy, *Sources of Strength*
Chopra, Deepak, *Ageless Body, Timeless Mind*
Chopra, Deepak, *The Path to Love*
Crichton, Michael, *Airframe*
Cronkite, Walter, *A Reporter's Life*
Daley, Rosie, *In the Kitchen with Rosie*
Flagg, Fannie, *Daisy Fay and the Miracle Man*
Flagg, Fannie, *Fried Green Tomatoes at the
        Whistle Stop Cafe*
Hepburn, Katharine, *Me*
Hiaasen, Carl, *Lucky You*
James, P. D., *A Certain Justice*
Koontz, Dean, *Sole Survivor*
Landers, Ann, *Wake Up and Smell the Coffee!*
le Carré, John, *The Tailor of Panama*
Lindbergh, Anne Morrow, *Gift from the Sea*
Mayle, Peter, *Chasing Cézanne*
Morrison, Toni, *Paradise*
Mother Teresa, *A Simple Path*
Patterson, Richard North, *Silent Witness*
Peck, M. Scott, M.D., *Denial of the Soul*
Phillips, Louis, editor, *The Random House Large Print
        Treasury of Best-Loved Poems*
Powell, Colin with Joseph E. Persico, *My American Journey*
Preston, Richard, *The Cobra Event*
Rampersad, Arnold, *Jackie Robinson*
Shaara, Jeff, *Gods and Generals*
Snead, Sam with Fran Pirozzolo, *The Game I Love*
Truman, Margaret, *Murder in the House*
Tyler, Anne, *Ladder of Years*
Updike, John, *Golf Dreams*
Weil, Andrew, M.D., *Eight Weeks to Optimum Health*

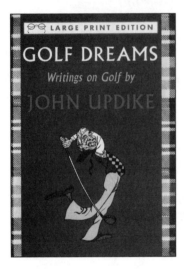